DRAGGED
DOWN
DEEP

For Mom.

"The winds and the waves are always on
the side of the ablest navigators."

*- Edward Gibbon, English essayist, historian,
and politician. 1737-1794*

Thank you for being that able navigator.

Special shout out to all things lurking in the deep, physically and mentally.

"There are more things in heaven and earth,
Horatio, Than are dreamt of in your philosophy."

– Hamlet (1.5.167–8), Hamlet to Horatio

DRAGGED DOWN DEEP

Michael Okon

CHAPTER 1

ARIZONA HIGH DESERT

THEY SAY THE early bird gets the worm, and that was the only explanation for Logan Osbourne to be hanging by his bloody fingernails from a six-story cliff in the middle of nowhere.

He shifted uncomfortably, his leather jacket creaking, the sun rising over a ridge so that the intense rays burned through his clothing.

His boots were not made for climbing, but they were well worn and flexible enough to allow him to find a sturdy toehold on the rock wall. He wasn't dressed for scaling rocks, didn't have a shred of that kind of equipment. He had never thought to bring it along. The steady grumblings of the guide he'd hired drowned out the sweet morning bird calls.

"I told you that you could get a better look from that

ridge over there," complained Kangee Singing Voice, whose first name translated to "Raven" in his native Sioux. He wore an eagle feather in his jet-black hair probably as a nod to his ancestors who once roamed these hills. Logan smiled indulgently at him knowing the guide considered it part of the show and was a good photo op for the tourists. Though the man was safely ensconced on an outcropping of rocks ten feet below Logan, his agitation was apparent by the nervous movements of his hands. Logan saw him gesture with one finger to a smaller plateau on the other side of the basin. "Didn't you get good enough pictures from across the valley?" The guide's brows were lowered with consternation. "I mean, you have a zoom lens." Kangee raised his voice, as if Logan couldn't hear him. "This land is sacred, man, I could get in a lot of trouble for this."

"I know....I know...." Logan said soothingly. He was not really listening to Kangee's litany. He wished Elliot Sheppard, his colleague and best friend were with him instead, but noooo, he drew out the word in his head. Elliot had decided to run home to do a food tasting for his wedding. Once Logan's eyes spied the nest from the other side of the canyon, he had to get closer. It was as if a giant magnet was pulling him up that cliff.

This was a once-in-a-lifetime experience, possibly the scientific find of the century. Food was food, Logan had told Elliot. Why someone would waste time eating something that ended up as sewage, Logan shook his head at the thought. He frequently had to be reminded to eat. It was not important to him. He found it distracting, to say the least. It drove his aunt crazy every time visited her.

The guide's grating voice interrupted his musings. "You don't belong here. You're no Sherpa, and this isn't Mt. Everest," Kangee whined.

Logan let go of one hand, letting himself sway from the cliff. He hung on with one muscular arm, as though hanging from a jutting boulder was something he did every day.

"Dude," Kangee wailed. "I don't want your death to be on my insurance."

Logan eyed the guide's ratty clothing. "Seriously, you're insured for this?"

"I told you I was a professional." Kangee's voice was indignant, which brought a smile to Logan's lips. It was hard looking pissed off while clinging to a rock wall sixty feet in the air. "For Christ sakes, move onto the ledge."

Logan accommodated him by placing his feet firmly on an overhang. "Better?" he asked. For him, it was a great feeling. Logan closed his eyes, enjoying the sun warming his face. A light breeze ruffled his hair. He sighed with contentment. The relief was short-lived, the guide's glare hijacking the moment.

Logan casually leaned over to look at the other man's face. Kangee was beet red with rivulets of sweat pouring down his round cheeks.

"No, today you're the Sherpa." Logan pointed to him. He reached up, exploring the next protuberance of rock with his fingers, looking to gain purchase and haul his body upwards, then added, "Hardly Mt. Everest. This is barely a hill."

Logan considered telling him about his trek in the mountains of Turkey or the time he actually did climb Mt. Everest in Nepal, then decided against sharing the information.

Kangee wasn't interested in much beyond the promised two hundred-dollar bills folded neatly in Logan's back pocket.

Logan's foot slipped, sending loose debris below. Kangee ducked dramatically, making Logan roll his eyes. Logan paused, letting the tiny avalanche cease while he scanned the vast canyon. Its beauty was breathtaking. It looked like a fiery cauldron with orange and red rocks. The stone was flecked with mica so bright, it made him squint. Looking down, he watched a crooked creek wind its way through the rocky canyon floor sparkling like a silver ribbon. Stacked giant boulders dotted the landscape in shades from sand to rust.

He searched the horizon, noting that the cliffs' flattened surfaces made them resemble tabletops, the corners rounded from years of running water. The sun was a dazzling yellow ball burning his eyes. There was not a cloud in the sky.

"Hold on, for Pete's sake!" Kangee yelled, dodging a second minor avalanche. "All you said you wanted were some pictures! I'm going to get thrown off the reservation!" He began a stream of complaints Logan had listened to for the last forty-five minutes escalating as they climbed higher. "You've gotten plenty of shots already. You never said anything about going up the mountain."

Logan looked at the unrelenting sunlight, wishing he'd worn a hat. His dark hair was plastered to his head from the shimmering waves of heat. He should have left his jacket back at the car, along with Kangee, he thought ruefully.

It wasn't even nine in the morning, and it was stifling. His newly inked tattoo itched, the bandage chafed by the strap of the canvas bag he had over his shoulder.

Elliot said he had been too hasty with the tattoo; Logan

wasn't even sure he got the colors right. But the shop was there, the tequila was flowing at a steady rate, and he barely felt a thing.

The inked skin bothered him less than Kangee's complaints. "Well, I've come too far to go back at this point. You can return to the jeep, Kangee. I can see where I need to go and don't need your help anymore."

Logan glanced down at the rental. The black four-by-four looked like a dung beetle against the desert floor.

He knew it wasn't much further to his destination. The nest was above him, just over the next outcropping of rocks. Though it was well hidden, a colorful shell stood out in the desert landscape, and when he spied it from the other side of the canyon, he took off racing up the side of the cliff like King Kong climbing the Empire State Building, Kangee whimpering like a baby behind him.

He estimated the distance to the next ledge where the thorny nest rested, the smooth shell of a giant egg within reach. His heart hammered with excitement. He could see the top of the speckled blue surface of the humongous egg resting there. Maybe he should have included a tattooed egg on his shoulder as well. It was gorgeous, the color as bright as the Arizona sky above him. Looking at the vibrant shell, Logan knew seeing it through a camera lens couldn't do it justice.

It was so close, Logan's fingers itched with anticipation of touching the smooth surface of the shell. He had hoped to get a glimpse of the legendary creature, a few pictures with the camera the university had loaned him. Logan knew photos would not be enough. He never dreamed he'd be able to see an actual live specimen. Living, breathing proof of the mythical Thunderbird was within his reach.

"I'm not going to hurt it," he said more to himself than Kangee, his tone soothing. "I just want to examine it."

He flexed his sore hands, gritty from the sand embedded in them. He had done it, finally done it, and when he returned to the campus, close up pictures of the egg in hand, plus some sort of DNA sample, not only would he get the elusive grant money but also the promised chair to start up a new department in Cryptozoology. His team would be the first to be acknowledged, accredited, and recognized for the course of study in this new field of science. It was long overdue in his opinion, not that anybody cared what he thought. More importantly, he'd beaten Aimee to the finish line. She would have stolen the egg.

A grin spread across his tanned face, his teeth gleaming from the stubble of his beard. He wished he had a cigar to celebrate. Maybe tonight, when he Skyped to inform Elliot of their discovery. He would include Elliot, they were partners, after all. Partners in crime, he added with a laugh. They'd done some serious rule breaking together over the years just to get in the vicinity of a cryptid.

They'd been researching the legendary bird for a long time. Sacred to many of the indigenous tribes of North America, it was called the Thunderbird because of its powerful wings, which were said to have created thunder for the world.

This past year, both Logan and Elliot had interviewed Native Americans such as Kangee from Vancouver to Mexico, cataloging their folklore, searching for a common thread. Whether it was Lakota, Ojibwa, or Sioux, Logan was convinced the great bird could be found outside the realms of their mythology. Sightings were rare, they learned, but they existed, becoming more commonplace recently. It was as if there were an explosion of people seeing the mythical creatures.

The two known photographs were grainy and looked doctored, but still the stories persisted. There had even been a half-baked special on one of the cable networks. It was a laughable production and did more to relegate his field to fiction than any of the pictures that popped up in the National Enquirer.

The trail had started months ago with the tale of the capture of a huge creature in Mexico, its wingspan the length of a barn. Someone had called his mentor, Professor Haversham reporting the information. The professor validated the data, giving the leads to Logan and Elliot with the intent to bring in reliable proof. Elliot respectfully bowed out of this trip, but Logan wouldn't let anything interfere with his pursuit of evidence.

The mythical bird was reportedly hidden in the jungles of the Yucatan, but the political climate and drug wars made traveling there both dangerous and nearly impossible.

Logan took off for a few weeks. School was out, and he traveled there on a hunch, a pocketful of pesos and two leads to meet Guillermo Sanchez. All care of Professor Haversham.

Six hours on one plane, four on another. Twenty minutes later he negotiated a fare for a three-hour ride with a driver who spent the entire time practicing his English, babbling about his recent trip to Cincinnati.

"You sure you want to go there?" he asked when Logan rattled off the address. "It's not safe, not a good place for Americans. I can take-"

"No, it's all good. I have a meeting."

"I'm not sure *I* want to go there."

Logan didn't even look up. "There's an extra twenty in it for you."

"Forty." the cabbie demanded.

Logan nodded once. "Okay. Let's go."

"Really?" The cab driver's eyebrow rose over his sunglasses. "With whom?"

"Who what?" Logan asked without looking up. He was reading his notes.

"Who are you meeting?"

Logan said nothing for a minute then asked, "You taking me there or do I have to find another cab?"

"I got it, man. It's your money." He pulled out abruptly from the parking space preventing Logan from getting out of the car. They drove for a bit, the silence allowing Logan to close his eyes. It wasn't long before the cabbie resumed his small talk. Logan suppressed a sigh, as the inquisitive driver circled back to the topic.

"Why are you here, man?" the cabbie asked. "What kind of meeting?"

Logan gazed out the window without a response. He stopped sharing what he did for a living to avoid the inevitable eye-rolling and snide comments. Most people didn't understand, their responses varying from condescension to contempt.

The driver placed his sunglasses on the top of his head, his dark eyes watchful. "You a narc or something?"

Logan shook his head with a smile. "I'm a tourist. I like to immerse myself in the local culture."

The driver's lips thinned, his eyes darting to the mirror as if to study him.

For the rest of the trip, the vehicle was thick with sullen silence.

Logan started with the first lead, taking them to an address in a small village that appeared deserted. The driver pulled over, twisting so his arm draped over the back seat. "Look everybody is gone, this is not a good sign."

"Maybe they're taking their siestas." Logan's voice was bored.

"You think this is funny? Told you it's no good, man. I don't want no trouble. That will be fifty dollars more. Not pesos."

"There's not going to be any problems." Logan held up his hand, a folded twenty in his palm.

"I'll take my money now." The driver reached out for the cash.

Logan snatched his hand away. "When I get back. Don't forget, we have another stop."

The driver shook his head. "You're crazy."

Logan leaned over the front seat and pointed to the address. He looked down at the numbers on his crumpled paper. "That's it. That's the place."

"Look, the first sign of trouble, I'm out of here. With or without you."

"Suit yourself." Logan slid across the seat to exit the cab when a green weathered door of the colonial style building swung open, revealing a man with a gun slung over his shoulder, his hard face staring at them.

Logan sighed. *This was not a good sign.* Still, it wasn't the first time he'd faced a hostile situation. Once he explained, paid them the necessary bribes, he was confident he could get the information he needed. It wasn't as if he were there for anything but science. He opened the door placing one foot on the pavement.

"Trouble!" the driver shouted. "Hold on." The cabbie punched the gas and took off, jerking Logan into the smelly back seat, the door swinging shut.

"What the- Why are you leaving?" Logan yelled back. "He wasn't pointing the gun at us."

"Yet! I told you the first sign of trouble we're outta here." The cabbie tore down the street, his forehead sweating. "Town belongs to the Ramira Clan. They are bad dudes. Nobody gonna talk to you. I ain't gonna end up in a ditch. You're not paying me enough. You looking to score drugs, or something?"

"No! Not at all."

"I can get you-"

"I said, I'm not interested," Logan interrupted.

The cabbie shrugged, then said, "You have two stops. Gimme the next address."

"Go back. I won't be long." Logan tried to reason with him. "I've done this before. It's no problem."

The driver never slowed the car. "Then pay me what you promised. I'm leaving you here. I'm not staying," he grumbled turning face-forward blabbering in a mixture of languages.

Logan spoke to him clearly in Spanish. "I'm doing nothing illegal. You don't have to be scared."

The driver responded with a spate of curses, then followed with, "I got a wife and three kids. I don't need no cops, you get it, man?"

"I'm not doing-"

"It's not you. It's them. They don't ask questions. What are you looking for?"

Logan weighed the value of sharing the information. He learned to be careful of talking about his job. Fighting the impatience building in his chest, he said, "Look, I'll pay you double what we agreed."

He heard the driver say, "You're nuts man. It ain't worth it. You can see, ain't nothin' there but criminals." Logan saw him staring at him through the rear-view mirror. I don't think you're a tourist." The driver waited for an answer, then mumbled, "Tourists don't come here."

Logan sat back. He watched the taxi driver's face, fear imprinted on his features.

Twisting, he glanced back at the narrow streets, his trained eyes looking for clues. The guy was right Logan had to admit; there didn't appear to be anything big enough to store a bird of that size.

He shrugged, then rummaged through his knapsack for his notebook. Opening it, he found the sticky note attached to the inside flap of his leather planner. "Alright, then take me to the next stop." He rattled off another address in a little-known town further south.

"If you looking for drugs, I can-"

"I said, I'm not buying drugs."

The driver made a left, getting onto the main road.

They rode in silence for a while.

"Who is Ramira?" Logan asked.

"Better you don't know," the cabbie said, his gaze sharp. "Ramira controls everything in this area. If you don't want drugs, what kind of business do you have with them?"

"I'm looking for something."

The cabbie laughed. "What you do, you know, do for work?"

Logan scratched his sweaty neck. "I'm a teacher... a researcher."

"In a school?" the driver asked.

"I work in a college," Logan said. "For a professor."

"If you're researching for something, you ain't gonna find it here. Ramira don't like questions. Don't like... attention."

Logan digested the information. Maybe it was a dead end. He'd traveled deep into territories where warlords controlled everything. Oddities were scarce in those situations. Things that Logan sought brought potential attention and he'd learned one thing concerning cryptozoology, most people wanted no part of these discoveries. This made his investigations difficult. If the area was crime-ridden, people didn't want the notoriety it brought. The flip side, he'd learned, was most villages hid the truth as well, fearing the sensationalism that was usually followed by ridicule and finally, the debunking. It was a tough business he'd chosen, but he never regretted his choice.

Logan sat back with another shrug. Much as he wanted to stop, he wasn't suicidal. Well, not much, in his opinion.

The second address was located fifty miles north of Guatemala, a village in the middle of nowhere. Logan got out, his legs stiff from the long ride. His khaki shirt clung to his back; the wrinkled sleeves rolled up revealing his tanned arms. "Stay here."

"No way, man. I'm going there." The cabbie pointed to a sleepy taqueria. "I'm hungry." He waited, then added, "I said, I'm hungry. I need some money to eat."

Logan dug into his pocket and handed him a few crushed bills.

"You want something, too?" he asked.

Logan shook his head. "Nah, not hungry."

"Okay, but I'm not gonna stop at another place."

"It's alright." Logan waved him off and walked into the one-story building.

It was a repair shop, an old '48 Ford pickup on the single lift. Light filtered in through a glassless window. The air was thick with the smell of grease and oil. Mariachi music played on a tinny transistor radio that was probably older than Logan. A wooden counter had an antique register, the drawer open, a fly buzzing over its empty interior.

"I'm looking for Guillermo Sanchez," Logan said in Spanish.

The sound of footsteps on the wooden floor, made Logan spin to find a heavyset man walking toward him, a rag in his beefy hands.

"What do you want with Guillermo?" he asked.

"That's between me and Guillermo," Logan said. "Do you know where I can find him?"

"He left yesterday." He walked behind the warped wood

of the counter, slamming the register closed. The bell chimed breaking the silence of the shop.

"Can you tell me where he went?"

"Why should I?" the mechanic eyed him suspiciously. He placed both hands on the counter, the rag bunched in his fist.

Logan saw the distrust in the mechanics eyes. He relaxed his stance, allowing the man to size him up. He let the mechanic hold his gaze but kept his face neutral. Waiting for the right moment, he said, "I heard he has something I want… something I've been searching for."

The mechanic laughed. "Yeah, you and everybody else."

Logan's back straightened, his face alert. "Someone else was here?"

The man nodded.

"A woman? A woman with dark hair?"

The mechanic didn't answer. He wiped the dirty counter as if he were a barkeep. "There are many women with dark hair around here. What are you searching for, señor?" he asked.

"I think you know," Logan responded.

The mechanic's face remained expressionless. He pulled a stool over and sat down. When he spoke, his voice was soft. "A chimera. A legend. A story."

Logan realized the man was waiting for his reaction. He could be anywhere in the world, whether he was in the mountains of Russia or the Sahara Desert, it was all the same. A slip in his emotions and he would lose the opportunity for information. The sources were weary of ridicule, disbelief, or exploitation.

As if Logan read his mind, the man said, "You want to come here and make fun of us. Take everything and give nothing back."

Logan kept his face impassive. "No," he added urgently moving forward. "No, I-"

The man waved his hand in dismissal, his mouth turned down in disgust. "You don't respect anything, you people."

"Are you Guillermo?" Logan asked. "Did you tell the woman... did you take her to see it?"

"I told you, Guillermo is not here." He rose to his feet as if to signal the conversation was over.

"I have money." Logan regretted his outburst as soon as the words left his mouth. *Rookie error*, he admonished himself. He was close, he could feel it. He blocked the man's path. "I'm not here to hurt it."

"Sure. You just want to see the *ave diablo*?"

"It's not a devil bird," Logan responded. "This is about the truth."

"So, you want to study it, dissect it, kill it?" The man's face was intense with hatred.

Logan backed away horrified. "No. I mean, study it, yes, kill it, never! The bird is sacred. It's a precious part of your culture. People should know the truth. Know of its existence. We have to protect it."

The man paused, his narrowed eyes sizing Logan up. "Why should I trust you?"

"Because Aimee Dupres will try to find it, first."

"The woman with the dark hair."

Logan nodded curtly; his throat tight. "You want me to be the one to discover it."

The man didn't answer. The silence built up around them like a thick blanket.

"I need to locate it first." He paused and thought for a while how to express his thoughts. "We have different motives."

"What is her motive?"

Instead of responding, Logan asked, "Did you trust her? The woman who was here first?"

The mechanic raised his eyebrows, then laughed a bit. "She will not like the place we sent her. It is what you call a wild, what do you call it? A wild duck chase?"

"Goose chase," Logan corrected, suppressing a grin. "She'll deserve it. We're different."

"Perhaps I'll send you on a wild goose chase as well, eh?"

"That's not the bird I want to see." Logan smiled. "I am a scientist. A cryptozoologist. I want to prove it exists, validate the legends."

"How do I know you are telling the truth?" the man demanded.

Logan paused knowing that every word that came out of his mouth could bring him closer to finding the bird. "I am an animal behaviorist. I'm getting my postdoc degree, and I work for Professor Arthur Haversham, the most renowned animal behaviorist in the world. We are trying to legitimize cryptids. We want to prove that the mythology is not a fable, but a genuine part of your culture because we respect your people. I have dedicated my life to finding these creatures and proving they are not figments of imagination. They are real, they exist."

The mechanic sized him up and added, "You are not like the others, I think."

"Not at all. If the bird is real?" Logan started, waiting to see if the man would confirm the information. "If the Thunderbird indeed exists it will prove the legends of the native people are based in truths. It can be revered and protected for the miracle that it is."

"Guillermo is not here," the mechanic said after a lull in the conversation.

Logan felt himself deflate. Closing his eyes, a sigh escaped him.

The mechanic studied him for a long time. He went behind his counter and grabbed a pad, then scribbled an address on a piece of paper.

"For real?" Logan asked, hope blooming.

The man nodded. "I don't know if it's still there. It may have been taken to a safer

spot. The woman-"

"She's relentless." Logan pulled out a wad of bills.

The mechanic shook his head. "No, señor. We don't care about your money. We care about the Thunderbird."

Logan gazed at the wide expanse of the volcanic highlands; their surface covered with lush greenery. Sweat trickled down his back in the un-air-conditioned cab. The driver shifted impatiently. "I thought you said that was your last stop," he whined.

Logan dug into his pants and pulled out some cash. "Fifty dollars more," he told him. "American."

"Two hundred, American," the driver answered. "It's very far."

Logan closed his fist around the money, ready to stuff it back into his pocket. He had been reckless, spending Haversham's money as if it was endless. But he couldn't stop, he was so close.

"Okay, okay. It's gotta be at least a hundred more, then?" The driver tried to snatch the cash.

Logan yanked his hand away.

"Come on. You gotta give me some of it now."

"How long?" Logan asked.

The driver pulled at his lower lip. "I don't know. It's very far. Another hour, maybe more? Depending on traffic. Just give me the money now."

Logan looked out at the dusty streets. "Seriously?" he laughed.

"Okay, okay. I'll take you straight there, no funny business. Forty-five minutes."

Logan shook his head. "Take me and I'll give you the money there."

The driver smiled. "*Vamonos.*"

If Logan thought the other village was remote, this was a village that time forgot.

The air was weighted with humidity, the road a narrow, twisting path surrounded by dense foliage. There was not a building for miles. The car slowed, and they arrived in a small town that consisted of a rutted main street with four tumbled-down buildings clustered together.

Logan got out; his muscles cramped from sitting. The

driver dropped him at a cantina, an adobe building with one crude window. "I don't know how long I'll be."

The driver pointed to a flowering tree. "I'll be in the shade over there."

Logan walked into the saloon, dust motes sprinkling the stagnant air like fairy dust.

In the corner sat a man so wrinkled, he looked like a walnut. Wearing a stained white suit, he was hunched over a ceramic bowl, dipping a tortilla into a stew that made his lips smack with appreciation.

"I'm looking for Guillermo," Logan stated.

The old man looked up, shook his head and went back to eating his meal.

"Guillermo?" Logan inquired again. "The mechanic sent me."

"Eat first," the man said after a long pause. He jerked his head toward a doorway, shouting for somebody named Teresa.

A woman shuffled out of the back, her face as seamed and brown as the parched earth outside. Her hands resembled the claws of a vulture. Logan considered them as she placed a plate of food before him. The aroma of ancho chilies wafted up. Logan's stomach gurgled. He couldn't remember the last time he'd eaten.

The old woman laughed, her dark eyes merry. She made quick movements of her hands toward her mouth in the universal mime of eating. Logan nodded with a smile, took the proffered spoon. He was suddenly ravenous and tired at once and knew he had to eat to survive. Logan tucked into his bowl of stew, spooning chunks of pork into his mouth.

Logan finished his meal, sitting back in his chair replete. He suppressed the questions bubbling inside of him, excitement warring with the knowledge that he was close and didn't want to alienate the old man.

Guillermo pushed his plate away, burping noisily. "You are here for the Thunderbird?"

"Si?"

Logan nodded wordlessly.

"Many people ask about the Thunderbird." He leaned forward as if to confide a secret. "Nobody believes us. After all, we are just simple people." He made a rude noise.

"I believe you," Logan said, watching the man for a reaction.

"It has been a secret for many years. It's dangerous to be the holder of this secret." The old man sat back, picking at his teeth with a dirty fingernail. He took a folded map from a pocket, then waved it in his hand. "Information is not free, and you do not look like a wealthy man." He placed the map on the tabletop under his empty plate.

Logan watched the man's face and replied, "Sometimes it's not about money."

Guillermo laughed and said, "I think you are very smart. Si. You are right, it's not about money. But how do I know I can... trust you?"

"How do I know you are telling the truth?" Logan said.

The man laughed, his yellowed teeth like a collection of pebbles in a riverbed. He pulled out a long green feather from the deep recesses of his suit jacket. The color was as bright as the emerald trees on his uncle's Christmas tree farm, and just as lush. Logan reached for it, but the man snatched it away, shaking his head. "I don't think so." He let it drift down onto the table between them.

It was like nothing Logan had ever seen before, the shaft was long and thin, broken in the middle, so when Guillermo straightened it, it stretched to over twelve inches. The vanes gave it an oval shape, the barbs iridescent in the fading light. The color natural. This was not fake.

The man grinned, his face full of pride.

Logan eyed him warily. He had bought many false leads over the years. He knew he was close, and it didn't matter how much this man wanted. He would pay anything for the chance to see the bird. He was on his own and had thrown Haversham's money around like water in order to get here. He had used it all. He would have to dip into his own savings. He couldn't call Haversham for more funds, not again.

The elderly man spit in the corner with disgust. "Others want it, señor. I have heard a woman is searching for it."

Aimee, he thought, his heart pounding loudly in his ears. He had to get to it before her. "Can I have the feather? I will pay you for it."

"Why pay for the feather, when I can give you the entire bird."

"You would do that?"

The man nodded. "For the right price, I can give you its direction. Nothing more. The rest is up to you."

"Why?"

Guillermo sat up straighter and Logan could see the integrity and pride in the man's eyes. "It's about the greater good. You need to get there before that woman, Aimee… Aimee Dupree. Sí?" He nodded.

"She's been here?" Logan asked.

The man rolled crumbs of tortillas on the table into a ball. "Not yet. But I have heard of her. She has a certain reputation."

Logan felt his face flush. The skin tightened on his scalp. "She can be charming." He knew that for sure, had gotten lost in her charm. Logan paused hesitating with his next comment. "She has deep pockets. She will pay you more money."

"For what, so she can capture it? Destroy it? Put it in the circus?"

Logan blurted. "That would be a travesty."

The sharp cackle of a startled bird broke the quiet. A flock of green and red long-tailed resplendent quetzals exploded from a tree and took off above them. They watched the birds, the national birds of Guatemala, in shared appreciation. "A little too north. They're usually found further south."

"We love our birds. All our wildlife." Guillermo's eyes pinned him with hard intensity. He sighed gustily. "It is a problem, senor. You need proof yet we don't want the bird taken."

Logan kept his voice as steady as he could. "I would protect it with my life."

"You see, sometimes money is not the issue," Guillermo said.

"Then why all the charade about demands for money," Logan asked.

Guillermo held up a hand. "We have everything we need here. The Thunderbird must be kept safe. With no natural predators, it has flourished, and it is a matter of time before it's discovered and destroyed. We have to keep it hidden in places where it can have its freedom."

Logan nodded. "I understand. But if she gets to it first, everything you fear will happen."

Guillermo waited a beat before replying, "And if you find it?"

"I can educate the public and keep the Thunderbird protected in its natural surroundings."

"You cannot capture the bird."

"I would never take it. We just want proof."

"Can you promise that?"

"I must get there before her, Aimee. How much time do I have before she catches up?"

The man laughed. "Oh, several days. She will not find her way from the jungle for some time."

Logan tilted his head and asked, "What happens when she does get there?"

"Then it's on to its next hiding spot, as we have done these past thousand years."

"What can you tell me about the Thunderbird?"

Logan recorded every priceless story from the man's vast store of tales. They talked well past midnight. Teresa ushered him into a room with a rusty iron cot that squeaked noisily when he flopped on it. Logan smiled, thinking of the bed he'd shared with Aimee in Haifa last summer. It had been equally loud. His smile faded; his heart constricted. The Aimee he knew then was not the woman she was today. He rolled over, forcing her from his thoughts. Aimee would turn up, she always did. He had to get there first. He let the stories the man told wash over him, satisfied he would beat her to the specimen.

Yes, they had seen a Thunderbird. Yes, it was big as a barn. The colors… Logan couldn't believe the sketches in vivid detail the older man had shared. This bird was sacred. It had been taken away in secrecy by Guillermo. North, to its breeding ground. To safety. Logan had just enough cash to get back to the states, Guillermo refused to take anything.

Logan had the map and a destination. That end of the trip was Arizona.

Another couple of plane trips, all heading back to the States.

He called Elliot to wire him additional money and Logan's pockets were flush again. He'd pay him back once school started in the fall.

Logan pulled into the small town of Sierra Mesa, Arizona late Sunday night in his rented Jeep, disappointed the tiny museum was closed on Mondays. He cooled his heels at the tattoo shop next door, tatting up his shoulder with his impending discovery. Painful, but worth it, he eyed the colorful image, flexing his lean muscles to see it move. Between the cost, and the risk of infection, Elliot would have called him an idiot and told him to wait until he was back home for such extravagant body art.

Elliot had booked Logan into a small hostel near his destination. It was close to a college town, and he felt at home there among the visiting student population. The hamlet was filled with quaint restaurants and small artsy shops boasting Native crafts in turquoise and silver.

Using the internet at a cafe, he found a local guide in

an advertisement. They met at the museum early Monday morning. The guide shook his head when Logan revealed where he wanted to go. "That's sacred land. You're not allowed there."

He got up, abruptly leaving the building. Logan followed him out.

"I just want some pictures of the scenery," Logan called.

The guide put on his hat. "No!" he shouted, racing down the steps of the building.

"Fine. I'll go it alone," Logan said more to himself than anyone else.

Another man was leaning against the adobe structure. He peeled himself away from the wall, coming up silently behind Logan.

"I'll take you," he said simply. He was as tall as Logan, with the sun-darkened skin of his ancestors. "My name is Kangee Little Song."

"You don't even know where I'm going," Logan told him.

"I know where you're going, and I know what you want to see."

Logan nodded, "Yes, I want to take some pictures of the mountains."

Kangee smiled slyly. "You don't want to see mountains."

Logan said softly, "That's right."

"I can take you." He tilted his head while he looked furtively around. "I got the supplies." He pulled a nylon backpack from the ground. "See? It's like I've been waiting for you. I have water, a first aid kit, a flare gun. I'm a pro."

The guide was confident, cool, as if he'd done this a million times. Logan was thrilled.

"Pictures only, right?"

Logan nodded. "Pictures only," he confirmed, holding up the Canon camera he had on loan from Haversham.

The guided laughed. "The camera in your cell phone would be enough. That's what most of you people use." He paused for a long minute. "It's going to cost you."

"Yeah, yeah, sure. No problem."

Logan was going after the find of the century. Money was the least important thing to him.

That particular moment had finally brought him to this spot, dangling precariously off a cliff with his guide.

Kangee's incessant complaints didn't rate high on his list, either, as they hung off suspended against the rock wall. He looked down to see the guide's glossy head below him. They had started the climb hours ago. He could feel his heart beating like a kettledrum as his feet brought him closer to the summit.

Heaving himself upward, Logan hooked his boot on the next outcropping, sliding onto the narrow ledge. He lay flat, hugging the warm rock. He placed his cheek against the stone, suppressing his excitement. His eyes smarted, and he admitted wryly it was from relief mixed with joy.

Logan could swear he heard angels singing. It was right in front of him, bigger than any kind of egg he'd ever seen, the colors vivid, exotic. Having more of a cornflower hue with tiny speckled green spots, the egg lay on its side.

Attached to the nest were bright red strands of something light and soft that waved like streamers, as if celebrating the impending birth.

Man, Logan thought, *Elliot would die if he saw this.*

He had to get moving. He knew they didn't have much time. He rolled onto the balls of his feet and crouched down, his arms wide.

Logan reached out, his mouth open in awe, his pulse pumping like a piston, as his fingers wrapped around the fine crimson strand caught in the mess of broken branches. It was a feather, the merest wisp, delicate and intense in contrast to the pale pallet of the desert. Logan separated a couple of plumes. He reached into his pocket for a small plastic envelope used for specimens. He stuffed a feather in, then secured it.

"What are you doing up there?" Kangee yelled. "Sunbathing?" His voice was worried. His guide wasn't so cool now. Logan smiled. Kangee held up the expensive camera. "Here, take this. Take some pictures, and let's go already."

The guide swung the camera in an upward arc for Logan to catch.

"Don't drop the camera," Logan warned, his eyes only on the oversized egg. "You know what? Just hold the camera for now. I don't need it yet." He wanted to examine it, revel in the moment.

Kangee climbed upward, his face coming level with the ledge where Logan now crouched.

"Where are you going? You can't touch that!" Kangee whispered.

Logan ignored him. Reaching out, he gingerly picked up the egg, marveling at its solid weight. His palm caressed the warm surface.

Here was solid proof. There would be no question of

the validity of its existence. "I've got it," he called out to the guide over his shoulder. "Hand me the camera now."

He crawled around looking for broken pieces of specimens to take back to the lab.

"Got what? You're taking it? Are you crazy? You never said anything about taking eggs!" Kangee was screaming now. He looked wildly around and slipped down a few feet. "I'm getting out of here. You're on your own, Kemosabe."

"Yeah, I hear you, buddy. Everybody for miles around can hear you. I'm not taking anything," Logan said under his breath, totally absorbed with his find. He looked down to see Kangee sliding down the cliff as if his butt were on fire, the nylon bag with their supplies slapping his back as he went.

Logan pulled the canvas bag he had strapped to his body, resting it on the ledge. He jerked with a start when the egg suddenly bucked in his hands. Hugging it to his chest, he felt the vibrations inside the hard shell. He would protect it with his life. A slow smile spread across his face. This was more than he could have possibly hoped for. He needed to take some pictures, but Kangee had the camera.

"Are you coming?" Kangee shouted breathlessly from a few feet below him. "Dude, I'm outta here."

Logan looked down the steep incline, seeing the top of Kangee's head. "You're not going to believe this," he called down. "I think it's about to hatch. Come back up. Toss me the camera, now." He held out his hand, knowing the guide would have to move back up.

"It's too far." Kangee's back was covered in sweat, his

shirt dark with it. "You got a ton of pictures on the other side of the canyon with the telephoto lens."

Yeah. But this won't be fuzzy or grainy. This would be up close, Logan thought to himself.

"Don't take the egg, man," Kangee called up. "They're gonna flay me alive." He continued his descent.

"I told you I'm not taking it. Just bring me the camera. Hurry!"

The steady *tap, tap, tap* under Logan's finger reminded him of his discovery. He felt a vague sense of unease. He didn't belong here, but it was an unbelievable opportunity. Not only proof, but the possibility of photographing a live hatching.

So much rested on this happening. The image of his father's face flashed in his mind. He wished he could share this discovery with his late father.

Logan heard the mother bird before he saw her when a keening wail filled his ears. Kangee's scream of terror came a second later. He glanced down toward Kangee's shout. Logan stood, speechlessly staring at the beautiful creature.

The guide's dark eyes were bulging from their sockets. "Put the egg back! She's going to kill us!"

Logan was buffeted by a windstorm created by the mother's black leathery wings. Outraged shrieks shattered the air. The foul odor of its body filled his nostrils. The smell of death clung to the bird's dry, weather-beaten wings. "Don't worry, Mama," he said softly. "I was only admiring your baby."

Shiny, iridescent green feathers covered its chest, a crest of the odd red feathers curled coquettishly around its small turquoise head, strangely incongruous with its reptilian features. The creature was the size of a small plane, with long, calloused limbs that sported twelve-inch sharp claws.

As if programmed to respond to its mother, the egg wobbled in his hands, the insistent tapping becoming furious. The mother shrieked like a banshee.

Logan reacted without thinking, turning to scale down the cliff, realizing he was still holding the egg close to his chest. It weighed about the same as the fifty-pound kettlebell he worked out with in the gym. It felt solid, not fragile as he'd thought it would.

He called to Kangee to stop, but he didn't answer. His back to the rock wall, the guide was standing on a small ledge, his face covered, the camera dangling from his hands.

Logan assessed the rock shelf where Kangee stood shaking with fear. The entire face of the cliff was filled with ledges and outcroppings for them to hide. The shelf that Kangee stood on jutted out, almost enclosing him. "Squeeze into the crevice. I'll distract it," Logan called.

"Put the egg down!" Kangee wailed.

"It's okay. I think it's going to hatch. Wait!" Logan wanted nothing more than to watch the event.

Kangee ignored him, scrambling from his perch, frantic to escape. Logan could hear his panicked breaths coming in short pants. If he didn't do something fast, the guide would hyperventilate.

Logan crouched to put the egg down, Kangee's cry of alarm making him twist. He could feel a powerful wind gusting, making his skin ripple. He wanted to get some closeups, pictures to record the moment but his hands were occupied with the egg. He tried to find his cell phone, but it was out of his reach in his opposite pocket. The excitement overpowered any fear he might have felt.

The mother bird hovered just above Logan, her sharp talons lashing out, her beak poised. She caught his jacket and pulled him. His feet lifted away from the surface of the rocks. He fumbled, losing his footing, but held tightly to the bucking egg in his arms.

He heard the leather of his jacket rip. Logan gripped the ledge with one hand, his fingers leaving their imprint for all posterity in the soft sandstone as he pulled himself back onto a narrow piece of rock below the nesting place. He glanced backward. She was so close to him; he looked her straight in the eye. She moved nearer, trying to wipe him from the cliff face with her flexible wing, her beady orange eyes narrowed with hostility, until she saw her egg poking from the top of his arms.

He could swear she looked from him to her egg. The timbre of her calls changed from anger to distress. She fluttered in a frenzy, her movements stirring up a sandstorm of grit that blinded him. His eyes watered, and Logan sighed with resignation.

This was not going the way he wanted. The Thunderbird cawed loudly, then circled away, hovering out of his line of sight, watching him carefully.

He spared another look at his guide, satisfied that Kangee was well on his way to the ground.

At least he had the pictures he had taken from across the ridge of the nest, he thought, eyeing the camera flapping from its strap on the guide's back as he raced down the mountain. Maybe he could get Kangee to snap a few shots once he was on the ground.

"Whatever you do, don't drop the…" Logan called when he heard Kangee screaming as if he was being tortured. He watched the camera slip off the guide's shoulder to his elbow and finally down his arm. It hung suspended for a minute, then fell in a graceful arc to the ground.

It came apart as it bounced off the jagged rocks, landing at the bottom in a million little pieces.

"… camera," Logan finished with a curse.

Hanging onto the rocks he pushed himself up another level to return the egg to its home. The head poked through the crack; its feathers plastered to its bald head. Logan lost his breath with wonder.

Without thinking, he reached for his jacket pocket awkwardly trying to get his cell again, losing his balance for a minute, then grabbed the rock wall. *Pictures, he needed pictures.* The camera was gone, he had to get something, at least one shot!

He still had a feather as solid proof, that is, if he didn't fall off the cliff and smash into a bloody mess next to the camera.

Their bag of supplies followed the camera landing in a puff of dust.

He could hear the guide yelling like a maniac as he descended. Logan looked from Kangee's form to the monster hanging in the breeze, observing him. She was going to eat them alive.

With a heavy heart, he recognized this was turning into an epic failure. He needed to get this precious bundle to its spot and try to escape, with no record of the event. He watched the mother floating anxiously nearby.

Pushing upwards with one hand, the other wrapped protectively around the egg, Logan was unmindful of the fact that his new charge chose that moment to poke its razor beak through a small crack in the surface of the egg.

The half-hatched chick seized Logan's index finger, slicing it to the bone. He endured the pain with a long-suffering groan. "Another time, hatchling," he told it, knowing he had to return it before either he or the guide was turned into dinner.

He placed the egg carefully onto the ledge, giving it a gentle nudge so it rolled to rest against its nest. He left a bloody mark on the egg's surface. His hand throbbed, the blood welling in a ruby-colored gash.

Logan slid on his belly to the edge. He maneuvered so that he leaned on his flat stomach, then overbalanced himself enough to plummet downward a few feet, his chin and flank abraded by the rock face as his hands and knees stopped his descent and gripped the soft stone.

His palms were scraped raw, staining bloody handprints on the cliff surface.

The bird shrieked loudly. The sound bounced off the canyon walls, making Logan wince.

"Kangee!" he yelled. "Take a picture with your phone!"

The bird dipped, swinging toward the guide, who took off like an Olympic runner toward the car. Kangee was out in the open with no cover. The creature pursued him like a fighter bomber, her claws clenched into fists.

Logan knew he had to distract it, so he screamed loudly,

the sound echoing like a gunshot in the valley. With a loud cry, she wheeled around, looking for all the world like a kite on a string, her gaze zeroing in on Logan, who was exposed on the rocks like a termite.

She came right at him and slammed into his body crushing him against the rocks. She attached herself to the wall, enveloping him like a giant moth.

He could feel their hearts beating together, the hot breath of hell on the back of his sweating neck. The wings pushed at him as if trying to scrape him off the rock face. Dust rained down where the bird's talons dug into the surface stone. She gave an ear-splitting shriek of frustration, then ejected from the cliff.

She flew upwards, circling like a vulture, waiting for him to fall.

Logan slipped, his feet going out from underneath him. He landed hard on his butt on a short outcropping. He saw Kangee was nothing more than a dot on the horizon, halfway to the town where they'd started from.

The bird crowed triumphantly. It rose high in an arc, then danced on the breeze, facing off from the other side of the canyon. The wind rippled along the wings, making them look like fabric.

Logan used the opportunity to rocket down the side of the cliff. His torn fingers gripped the fissures, nails breaking off. His toes dug in, catching himself from falling to the canyon floor. His abused knees were a mess, the skin along with the material of his pants worn away.

Logan twisted his head around to get a look at the magnificent creature flapping angrily, stirring up a hurricane. He watched the red crest of feathers on the top of her reptilian head wave at him.

He fumbled again for his cell phone from his pocket, his numb fingers unable to grab a hold of it.

Logan felt tears smart his eyes at this lost opportunity.

The sound of the bird's flapping distracted him from giving his loss any more thought. The wings reminded him of the sails of a ship catching wind. His regrets vanished and the cell phone was forgotten as she charged forward, coming at him in a frontal attack, her claws catching the hole of his jacket, ripping it another few inches, dislodging him once more so he slid further down, the rock burning his face.

The creature wheeled away, coasting around the canyon, her loud cries surrounding him. With a screech, she swooped down triumphant, once again queen of her domain.

Logan wasted no time scrambling, or perhaps plummeting, he later remembered, down to the base of the cliff.

Kangee's supply bag lay on the remains of his camera. He reached for it but missed, the returning predator making him dodge for a deep valley between two boulders.

He squeezed in the tight ravine. The bird landed above him and pecked through the tall rocks, trying unsuccessfully to get him.

He was trapped. He debated if he could wait her out. He eased the phone from his chest pocket, taking a series of pictures as well as some video, his fingers stiff and achy. It wouldn't be *National Geographic* material but at least he would have some element of proof.

Logan looked at his watch. Twelve hours to nightfall, he

counted. His blood froze as a new call rent the air from the opposite direction.

Hot damn, here comes Papa, he thought wildly. He filmed his attacker, but it moved with a speed that was hard to follow.

He glanced up at the beast filling the sky over him, wondering just how big the mother bird's mate was going to be. Her reptilian head looked up quickly, searching for help.

The hatching mewed from the nest.

"Hey!" he shouted; his voice raw. "Junior's calling!" The mother bird watched him, its beady eyes sharp with hostility.

The newly hatched chick gave another weak cry, drawing the mother's attention. She abandoned her pursuit to fly upward in a giant circle.

She was magnificent. Logan waited what he thought was ten heartbeats, then rushed from the rocks, reaching out to grab the supply bag, then made a dash for the car.

He took off sprinting, his heart beating wildly, the bag swinging from his wrist. Dodging boulders, he wouldn't look up but concentrated on the objective of escaping alive. He could hear the beat of wings behind him from the other bird.

Sweat poured from his scalp onto his abraded face, the stinging pain blinding him. He jumped over a small stream, becoming airborne like a basketball player, but felt the hot wind of the monster's flight fanning his back.

Logan spared a quick glance, his lips tightening. This one was twice the size of the other, its beak thicker, the eyes angrier. *Uh-oh, Daddy's home.* Logan leaped over a cluster of rocks that would have set his high school track coach into a spasm of ecstasy.

The car appeared around the bend, below him in a small dip. He picked up speed, his boots flying over the ground.

Logan knew he was close. One leap and he was golden. He backed up, gauging the distance, his breathing harsh in his own ears. Gathering speed to make the dive for the vehicle, he raced toward the end of the small plateau.

Digging his feet in, Logan sprang forward, jumping to the safety of the car. He leaped high into the air, the bag flying ahead of him, dragging him with its weight. He braced himself for a fall that never came.

The Thunderbird grabbed his jacket in his beak and soared high. Logan watched unbelievingly as the ground grew further away. He gathered the nylon bag to his chest, his fingers digging frantically inside. *Where was it?* He searched, his hands clumsy.

The canyon filled with the creature's screams as he got a bird's-eye view of the entire area.

His palm closed around the butt of a flare gun. Twisting sideways, away from the bird's face, he pulled the trigger. The pistol erupted in an explosion of bright red light.

The monster's eyes rolled with fear. It stopped dead in midair, hung suspended for a nanosecond, then dropped altitude at an alarming pace.

They were falling toward the ground. Logan braced himself for impact.

The bird opened its mouth with a loud call. Logan felt the air rush past him as the Thunderbird dropped him.

He picked up speed falling toward earth. Closing his eyes, he awaited the crash.

Logan heard the cries grow more distant as the bird moved upward, guiding his small family to disappear into the horizon.

Logan plummeted down and landed sideways on a bed of stiff grass, the breath rushing out of him. With numb fingers, he pulled out his cell phone, snapping unfocused pictures of the pale down on the belly of the fleeing Thunderbirds.

A face floated into his line of view, framed by a curtain of dark curls.

"You're a mess, Logan."

"Aimee," he whispered, regret tinging his voice.

He felt her hands run down his limbs, hissing when she patted his tattoo.

"You'll live." She plucked his cell phone from his numb hand, shaking her head. "I need this." She bent down to caress his aching cheek. "You make everything so hard."

He opened his mouth to reply, his sight wavering, the piercing sun blotting out her face. She disappeared and he wasn't sure if he dreamed her.

He lay there wondering why he was three times a fool to want to do this. He rolled flat. The world receded for a moment, and he was back with his father in a boat twenty years ago.

Oh yeah, he thought vaguely. *That's why.*

CHAPTER 2

THE HAMPTON BAYS - TWENTY YEARS EARLIER

THE BOAT WAS little more than a skiff.

"Dad, I don't like this," Logan whispered fiercely. "Dad!" he repeated, his breath coming in short gasps. Frost formed around his mouth when he spoke. He shivered from the cold.

George Osbourne ignored his son. *Nothing new there,* Logan thought, his mouth turned down. His father was leaning far over the side of the boat, nose nearly touching the water. He looked like he was going to fall in.

Logan pulled his father by the belt, tugging until the reluctant man turned impatiently, slapping his hand away.

"Stop." His father's voice was a harsh whisper. "You'll scare it away."

"This is nuts, Dad. I want to go home!"

"Are you kidding? I thought you'd want to see this." His father lurched around, sending the boat rocking precariously.

They both crouched, holding onto the sides of the skiff with both hands. Logan looked longingly through the thick mist at the indistinct outline of the shore. It was chilly. The cold air penetrated his jacket, making his skin pebble with goose bumps. His nose ran, and he swiped it with his sleeve, the coarse material irritating his skin.

Most nine-year-olds would be in bed at this hour, he wanted to shout at his father.

His father had that look again. His blue eyes were distant, murky as the ceiling of clouds obscuring the night sky. Logan glanced up, longing to see the constellation of Orion. Its presence was the only stable thing in his life that fall.

The sound of a loud splash filled the small inlet.

His father stiffened and twisted in his seat. "There. Did you hear that, Logan? She's here."

"You don't even know if *she's* a she," Logan protested.

Forget about that, Logan thought. He was sure his father had finally gone over the deep end, as everybody else was saying lately.

"Oh, she's female alright." His father's eyes brightened for an instant. "I know it." George grabbed his notebook and scribbled away like a lunatic.

Logan bit his lip. "Can we please go home now?" He did his best to sound pitiful, shivering for added effect. "I'm cold, Dad."

It didn't matter. His father was deep in thought. Logan doubted he'd even heard.

He didn't want to be here with his father, not anymore.

It was stupid. Logan wouldn't tell anybody about these nightly excursions that ended just before the sun rose in the sky. He knew to keep his mouth shut even though he'd had detention twice that week for falling asleep in class. It was enough his father was known as a weirdo in his community. He didn't need to be labeled as an incompetent parent. Unstable as his homelife was, Logan was afraid someone would yank him out and put him in some facility.

Logan rested his head in the palm of his hand. He didn't want anyone to know what was going on in his home. He stared at his father's hunched back, his eyes softening. He loved him, felt more like a parent than a child. His father had been a good man once. Devoted if slightly absent-minded, he seemed to have receded into a shell after Logan's mom left. Logan still hoped his father would return to his former self. They had managed somewhat after she took off. It wasn't great, but they fell into a rhythm of sorts.

They had the small apartment on the Lower East Side despite losing his mother's erratic salary as an artist. They could have kept it too if his father hadn't melted down. Logan knew it was a good thing the Hampton cottage had been bought and paid for years ago, or else they would have lost that too when his father quit his teaching post at NYU. Logan's whole life derailed as his father unraveled.

Logan stifled a sigh. He hated pity.

"I can hear you sighing." His father's voice was nasty.

Logan straightened, trying to look alert. He pasted a smile on his face, but his eyes stung a bit. His father's tone hurt.

Lately he'd been unreasonably angry most of the time;

that was if he even bothered to remember Logan was around. Logan stacked his father's supplies in a corner of the boat. Keeping his hands busy made the situation feel more normal.

His dad had changed in the last few weeks. He had less patience, as if he were running out of time or something.

"Sly said-"

His father spun so fast; Logan grabbed the rocking skiff thinking it was about to capsize. "I don't want to hear what Sly says! Sly is a scuba diver. I am a scientist!"

Sly is my friend, Logan wanted to reply. *He listens to me.*

Logan loved the attention he got from owner of the local scuba shop. Anything he asked Sly was answered with patience, as if Logan was the most important kid in the world. Sly could talk about anything, and Logan truly enjoyed him. There was a time when his parents were close with Sly as well, but all that had ended when his mother left. George cut them off from everybody.

"I thought you'd understand. This is important, vital. Our findings have the potential to change the world," his father grumbled.

"Homework's important stuff too," Logan said.

"Stuff." His father's voice mocked him. His father was a college professor. He loved education. "You compare this to school, to something as pedestrian as homework!" Spit collected in the corners of his father's mouth. "Grow up, Logan!"

Fury roiled in Logan's thin chest. *Grow up? He should grow up?* Maybe his father should take responsibility instead of dragging him all over the world looking for...

"You grow up! There's no such thing as mermaids! This is crazy!" Logan exploded.

Logan was half out of his seat, his hands clenched into fists. Breathing heavily, he peered through the soupy air, looking for his father. All he saw was the back of his gray-haired head.

George was curled over, his wrinkled shirt untucked from his baggy pants. He was on his knees, shining a light into the opaque water of Tilowanney Swamp, just inside one of the inlets of the Hampton Bays.

Logan looked at his father's scrawny arms. He was thin to the point of emaciation, looked older than his fifty or so years. Logan often had to remind him to eat. They survived on a steady diet of bologna sandwiches or canned soup. The only real dinners Logan consumed were at his friends' Penny and Rory's house when their mother invited him.

Logan and his father had been sitting on the water for several hours the third night in a row. His teacher was asking questions lately, suggesting Logan speak to someone.

"Speak about what?" Logan asked the teacher the day before yesterday. "Everything's fine," he told Mrs. Allus nervously, as he stood in front of her desk.

He had watched Mrs. Allus consider his face. She had sharp little eyes that calculated his every move. He wondered what she saw when she looked at him, his face flushing with shame when his stomach grumbled noisily, Logan studied his worn sneakers and pulled at his too-short sleeves to cover his bony wrists. Did she notice an underfed boy with a quick and intelligent mind in a shirt that should have been given to Goodwill? Did she see his pants were too short for his skinny ankles?

He was a straight-A student who managed on little or no sleep, whose grades lately had found themselves slipping into new territory. Failure was unfamiliar, and it was uncomfortable for him. He admitted his sinking grades bothered him. He had never gotten those before. Dark circles ringed his eyes. He had no appetite. Logan felt caught like one of his father's specimens under a microscope.

It was like being trapped in a bad dream. He thought about calling his Uncle Jack, his father's brother, and sharing what was going on. Last Christmas, he'd caught Aunt Minnie watching him intently. She'd sent him home with plastic containers filled with food. Life could be so easy living with them. He looked at his father again with a resignation, knowing another desertion would kill him.

The water lapped around them, bringing Logan back to reality. He studied the floor of the boat, wanting to stay mad, but he couldn't. He loved his dad. He missed the fun man his father used to be. While George's interests never moved to football like his Uncle Jack, his father's boundless curiosity had created opportunities for Logan and his mom to travel the world searching for oddities in nature to examine.

He missed the old days, when it was the three of them on the shores of Hawaii or climbing mountains in Tibet, not sitting in a rusty bucket of a boat with a disgraced college professor consumed with finding the impossible.

Logan jiggled his leg impatiently, making the boat shake. George hissed at him to be still.

He worried his bottom lip thinking about the homework waiting on his desk to be finished. There was a state report on Nevada due and he had a test coming up, but his father didn't care.

George operated on a different plane, a strange reality, that was beginning to scare Logan. His father's world was being replaced by mythical creatures and the pursuit of proving their existence. He went from believing in improbable accidents of nature to the stuff of imagination.

It was dead quiet. The water was still as glass. Logan glanced around, his eyes stinging. He dashed a hand over them, willing the tears not to fall.

It wasn't fair. Nothing in life was fair. Just eight months ago, he was living with two parents in their apartment in Manhattan. After the desertion, his father disconnected himself from life. It became Logan's job to protect his fragile parent. *He had to*. What else could he do, let them lock him up? How could his mother take off like that? His heart heavy, he wondered why she left and where she could have possibly gone.

Logan cleared his throat to make a sound, as if to remind his father he was in the boat. Frustrated, he fought the urge to shout, *I'm still here!*

Logan closed his eyes wearily, remembering his well-ordered life before Mom bugged out, before his father's job abandonment forced the permanent move out to the vacation cottage.

His father's life had been disrupted, ripped apart. Logan knew he couldn't understand his mother's rejection. His father spent days alone in his bedroom, and when he had reentered the world, he'd ripped Logan's apart. The move East took Logan from everybody he knew to the end of the earth, in the middle of nowhere.

Well, the end of the island, actually, and not exactly away from everybody, Logan admitted. He did have Penny and Rory, the local kids who lived around the block.

Again, Logan wrestled with the idea of contacting his uncle. Fear froze him. If his life had been interrupted before, once they got wind of his father's behavior, who knew where things would fall? *Nope*, Logan thought, *I have to take care of this myself.*

An owl hooted from the shadows of the towering trees that rimmed the shoreline. He could hear its great wings flapping. The wind picked up, making the small boat rock on the waves. The water rippled around them. The surface became pocked with whitecaps as if it were being disturbed.

Something changed in the air, making Logan feel jittery. He put his palm on the handle of the motor.

"Dad let's go home. Nothing's here."

Logan watched a shadowy form swim near the boat, and the hairs on the back of his neck stood up. A small dorsal fin peaked above the water. Judging from its size, he knew this had to be a youngster, a little over six feet. A full-grown nurse shark could grow as long as fourteen feet. He didn't feel like meeting the mother.

"Shark!" he said urgently as he glanced around, seeing clusters of dark shapes surrounding them. "There's a ton of nurse sharks swimming here." He moved around restlessly. "Dad, I don't like this."

"I saw her." George persisted; his face alight with hope. "I was here yesterday, and she broke the water."

George pushed his glasses up the bridge of his nose. His large blue eyes looked at his son. Logan knew his father didn't see him. The glasses slid down again, the plastic on the earpiece worn away from his father's habit of chewing the end of the arm.

Logan looked at his hopeful expression and fought the urge to laugh.

If anyone was the epitome of a nutty professor, it was his father. Wiry gray hair sprung out in uneven tufts around the oval of his putty-shaped face. His father had been handsome once, Logan knew. He had seen the pictures, but time and his mother's desertion had taken a toll on the older man.

George opened and closed his mouth like the fish he had spent a lifetime studying. He was an ichthyologist, the best marine biologist in the country, but his latest crusade, Logan now realized, was what had destroyed his career. His father went from being a respected icon in the field, to a silly buffoon chasing unicorns.

Logan searched the shoreline for home, longing to row back. He missed the rustic one-story building with an intensity that brought tears to his eyes. "Let's go home, please," he pleaded.

His father didn't hear him.

In the old days, that house had been filled with light and love. His mother painted. His father walked the sandy shores picking up shells and telling him what they were called. Logan knew the house now was dank, musty, and unused. His mother's paint tubes were cracked and dry.

The lights were never on; the heat barely worked. It didn't matter. It was home, and he wanted to curl up on his bed and imagine nothing had changed.

If only things could get better. Logan had seen a letter from his father's boss last week. He was an old friend. There could be an opening in the fall if George would go back to his traditional subjects.

The letter was tucked in a secret draw in the desk in his father's bedroom. It was not going to happen. Logan sniffed, letting a tear drop onto the floor of the boat.

Barely a month ago, it had intensified beyond the sightings. His father stated that he had made contact. Last week, he came home drenched from a dive into the sound, babbling. He was barely coherent. He walked from room to room, mumbling, pulling out books, painstakingly drawing illustrations in that dog-eared diary of his, the damp papers curling as he pulled at them nervously. He spent hours tucking notes in the rolltop desk he used.

George planned to write a paper about his discovery, publish it in a reputable science journal, and wait for them to apologize and beg him to come back. It would be big, make all the papers. The professors who laughed at him would eat crow. He would get the prestigious Linnaeus Discovery Prize in science at the very least, he assured his son.

Logan knew that this last episode put the final nail in the coffin. There would be no going back. No way his father could regain the respect of his peers. He was out of his mind, off his rocker, *nuts*. He belonged in Cedar Haven; the creepy asylum located on an isolated island across the sound.

Logan looked pityingly at his father, who was stirring

the water with his thin fingertips. The full moon broke through the fog, making everything look as though it had been dipped in silver. His father's face was painted blue by the light.

"You had to have been asleep, Dad. You told me you fell asleep in the boat that day. You dreamed about it."

"I should have taken you with me," George said, his voice full of resentment.

"I was in school," Logan explained to him as if his father were the child. "I have to go to school, remember. Besides, Mom would want me to go to school."

His father's eyes blazed. "Then she should have stayed," he snarled. George waved his hands dismissively, his mouth tense and angry looking. Logan recognized the signs. He was getting moody again. It was a mistake to bring up his mother.

His father ignored him now, staring at the water, his eyelids half-closed. The older man was exhausted too, Logan knew.

"Please." Logan felt tears leak out from his eyes. He was tired. He cried for want of sleep. Exhaustion pulled at him, making his head feel heavy. He fought the urge to lie down in the bottom of the boat and drift off.

Logan wiped his face. His chest filled with an emotion he didn't recognize. He paused, trying to identify it.

He was sad, overwhelmingly sad.

The boat creaked, creating a hypnotic rhythm with the steady lap of the waves. Logan drifted as he listened to the watery concert. They lapsed into silence for a minute, and he heard his father's soft voice.

"Do you hear her, Logan?" he asked. "She's whispering to us. Listen."

"It's just the wind, Dad." Logan closed his eyes, hopeful that he'd hear something else, anything to prove his father hadn't gone batshit crazy as everybody was saying.

"She's asking, 'Does King Alexander still live? Does he rule the world?'"

Logan strained his ears, but only whisper of the waves answered his father's hoarse voice.

"It's his sister Thessalonike," his father continued.

"I know, Dad." Logan bent over to look over the bow next to his father. "But we are in Long Island, not Greece, and nobody is going to answer. Those people lived like two thousand years ago."

"He lives and reigns and conquers the world." George stood, crowing the required answer into the night. The boat wobbled.

Logan implored, "Sit down. You'll overturn the skiff."

His father straightened his arms, stretching upward as if he were praying to the heavens.

Logan shook his head. His father was too far gone.

Mermaids, he thought contemptuously. He had been brought up on mermaid myths his entire life. They had searched for them from the Cornish coasts to the waters of Hawaii while on vacation from school. His father had dragged his mother and Logan to obscure villages, where he spoke to the locals while Logan played in the white sands of foreign beaches.

Could this be the reason mom left? Logan sat up, the thought striking him.

It was all his father talked about. He refused to do anything but study the legends. Mermaids might have consumed his father, but he knew the difference between reality and fantasy, or at least Logan thought he did back then.

George stopped talking. He turned to observe Logan, a sleepy look on his face. He held up his small notebook. "Don't despair, son. She'll show up. I drew her. Look. I wasn't dozing when I did this."

He held up the rectangular notebook that was always in his back pocket. He had a three-inch whittled-down pencil that he kept stored in the tight round spirals. There was a crude drawing of a lithe creature, as if a child had created it.

It was more streamlined than most of the illustrated mermaids Logan had seen around the world. She had masses of long hair strategically covering parts of her body. He wasn't sure if his father had drawn that for modesty, as if by obscuring that part of her made her more real.

He felt his skin go hot; his face reddened as anger filled him. *This is what you believe?!* he wanted to shout. He struggled for a minute, then blurted angrily, "This is what you sacrificed Mom and me for!"

Logan wanted to pull back the words as soon as he spoke them. His chest tightened when he observed his father's wounded face. He closed his mouth, mildly ashamed he'd spoken to his father like that.

He loved him. He loved his father despite their distance right now. He wanted to rise and hug him, but his body was frozen. They stared at each other in silence, the only sound was the restless sea slapping the sides of the boat.

Logan watched his father's visage crumple into soft,

wounded folds. The young boy couldn't help the words that came next but regretted them for the rest of his life. "At least she escaped."

"We love doing this together, little buddy." His father spoke softly. "Just you and me. Mom didn't like the research. Never wanted to be part of the team." His voice rose. He seemed to catch himself, then continued in a whisper. "We'll be famous. The father and son who had the find of a lifetime. Let's see what my colleagues have to say about this when we show them proof."

Logan looked at his father. His eyes silvered with tears. George was ranting about his grandiose plans again. Logan's bottom lip quivered a bit.

"Look, Logan," George said. "You've heard the rumors."

Logan was tired. He looked at the shore, knowing there was a bed waiting for him. He just wanted to go home.

Logan cried out, "That's just tourist crap. It's all crap. You created the stories about the Mermaid of Minatuck because you want to believe it. You are making everybody angry. They don't want us in town anymore. Even my teacher told me to tell you to stop."

"But it's the truth!" His father said slowly.

"Only in your head," Logan replied. "Everybody is saying you are crazy. Nobody will invite me to their house anymore."

George shook his head as he shoved his notebook back into his pants pocket. He wasn't listening. "You have to understand, son. There have been sightings for hundreds of years all over the world. Why not here?"

"Yeah, like Bessie, the Loch Ness Monster."

"Nessie."

"Whatever. It's all fake." The boat lurched as if smacked, sending it into a spin. "Whoa. Okay. We're done here." Logan scrambled to the seat and grabbed the oars, which were there in case the engine failed. One slipped through his hands, landing with a slap in the water. "It's too dark. You can't see anything anyway."

Even the heavens conspired against him as the clouds parted revealing a bright full moon and an endless curtain of stars. Logan rolled his eyes.

His father leapt up, rocking the boat. Water splashed over the sides, soaking Logan's sneakers. George pushed his wire-rimmed glasses on top of his silver-haired head and nearly bent in half to look into the black depths. "I see something. Wait! It's her, Logan." He crouched on his knees. "We've done it. It's her." He was singing his words happily.

"Stop that!" Logan's voice cracked.

The boat rocked again. George reached his hand in up to his elbow. He went deeper, the water hitting his shoulder.

Logan wasn't sure if the older man was reaching out so much as being pulled in. Logan jumped, his face blanching when his father screamed with excitement. "I've got her! I've got her hand!"

"Stop!" Logan called out, picking up both oars again. "You are going to fall in!" Sometimes he didn't know who was the father and who was the child. "I'm tired of taking care of you. I don't want to do this anymore. You're crazy!"

His father pulled his arm from the water. A spray of cold liquid fanned above his head like a downpour. George faced the star-filled sky, ecstatic, his eyes alight with triumph.

Logan wondered if he glowed from the light of the moon or something else.

Logan's jaw dropped as a green-skinned form leapt from the water, its slender arms raised above its head.

Logan had the impression of leathery skin dusted with silvery iridescence and long black hair that wrapped around its waist like a snake.

The creature dove back into the water, soundlessly.

Both George and Logan looked over the edge of the boat to see the beast just under the surface, its yellow eyes gleaming in the night.

"I told you!" George shouted. "I knew it!"

Logan's eyes locked with the creature's and to his shock, it blinked.

The creature circled them, then disappeared for a minute.

"What is that thing?" Logan whispered hoarsely.

"I don't know." George pulled at his lip. "A GeorgePiscatus or SyreinLogan. What do you want to call her?" he asked, his face lit with excitement. "Get the camera ready, Logan. She seems friendly. And I think she's coming back."

Logan reached for the camera.

"Come to Papa," George cooed.

The dark head broke the calm surface of the water.

Logan sucked in a breath. It wasn't a siren of the deep. It was ugly, with thick fish lips and two holes for a nose. The eyes weren't warm and friendly. They were cold and calculating.

Logan could hear the wheeze of gills rippling along its slender neck. Her eyes were close together and gleamed gold, the pupils large, huge, almost filling the entire eye socket.

Logan stared at the goggled-eyed, feral face. It hissed,

its round mouth opened baring rows of sharp teeth, the lips stretched tightly against them.

Long fingers with sharp claws reached out and grabbed his father by the neck, pulling him forward. Logan gasped, scrambling to hold his father's legs.

"No!" he screamed, trying to balance in the rocking boat.

Green muscled arms, dripping with fronds, lashed out, catching Logan on the side of his head. He fell forward as his father's body was yanked from the vessel. Logan clawed at the creature, grabbing a slimy foot with six webbed toes.

The creature's limb slipped from his fingers, kicking him squarely in the jaw. He lashed out and grasped the creature's foot, the long talons on the toes puncturing his skin. He released it, his palm throbbing.

Dizzily, Logan got on all fours. The boat rocked violently, its edge smacking his chin, making the world tilt on its axis. Just before his eyes rolled back in his head, he wondered hazily what kind of mermaid had toes.

CHAPTER 3

LOGAN DROPPED HIS satchel on the bed. He looked longingly at the clean linens his Aunt Minnie had put on the pillows. HIs aunt would kill him if he lay down in his dirty clothes.

He sighed, his eyes gritty from lack of sleep, then gazed out the window.

Logan stretched, a shivery one that made his bones crack. His shoulder still ached from the fall from the cliff. He rubbed it absently.

A long-distance trucker picked him up when he was walking along the highway and dropped him at a local urgent care. He spent a few hours x-rayed and stitched up, and when asked about his injuries Logan explained he was hurt off-roading on the surrounding dunes. He booked the first plane home to New York in the morning.

His eyes were drawn to the lush meadow framing the property. It was surrounded by a thicket of trees as if he were in an emerald glade.

The sun shimmered on the rolling green lawn in front of the farmhouse. It was muggy, the air oppressive with the promise to be a scorcher.

Uncle Jack would be returning from the fields soon, Logan knew. It was late morning. Traffic on the 95 was backed up all the way from the bridge, and it had taken forever to get upstate from the airport.

His car was parked on the same bald spot on the lawn he'd used when he lived there. It was filthy, covered in dust from its month-long stay in LaGuardia Airport. He squinted as he leaned out the bedroom window, his hands resting on the sill. *Clean me* was written across the hardtop of the jeep. He wondered briefly how someone had managed to mark the car's roof.

The sun illuminated dust motes floating in the room making the space look slightly enchanted. Logan could stare at it for hours marveling how different the same phenomena looked in places around the world. Tilting his head, he let his imagination wander, *forest gnome or fairy*, he laughed to himself. Since he'd chosen his field of occupation and started his investigations, he allowed himself these strange flights of fancy. Not that he shared it with anyone else. After what happened to his father, he wouldn't make that mistake. No slips of the tongue until there was corroborative proof. He was never going to make the same mistake his father did. Logan allowed his body to relax into mindless exhaustion.

He stifled the urge to throw himself on the mattress. The

old threadbare patchwork quilt folded neatly at the foot of the bed caught his eye. Much as he wanted to lose himself to a nice long nap, he sat down, his bandaged hand resting on the comfort of the old material. His exposed fingers snagged on a loose thread, reminding him of his earlier injury. He sucked in his breath at the pain.

The quilt was a relic of his earlier life, one of the only things he had left from his mother. Logan knew she had made it for him the summer before his fifth birthday. He remembered the day clearly. He had arrived home with his father, sunburned and exhausted after a long day in the skiff to find his mom in the living room, squares of fabric spread across the floor. Tufts of white bunting lay like discarded clouds on the faded carpet.

The old pedal Singer sewing machine pumped away, his mother's foot rising and falling with each stitch as she attached mythical creatures to the coverlet.

Carly Simon's mournful voice blared from the stereo set. His mother's eyes were closed. She was singing loudly and slightly off key, but he didn't mind. She looked happy, and that made his boyish self grin. She had a long braid that swung as she moved, and he knew she would finish by standing and waltzing around the room with her sewing creation, her ruffled peasant skirt swaying in time to the music.

Logan stared at the ancient material; the fabric so worn the cotton packing lay shriveled underneath. He touched it reverently, naive images of mermaids and serpents, great hulking snow monsters, and dragons making him sentimental.

He knew Aunt Minnie couldn't bring herself to get rid

of the quilt. A smile tugged at his lips. He loved his aunt with all his heart. He appreciated her sentimentality in the largely male domain they called home. He knew his uncle would have dumped the quilt years ago as rubbish.

He heard the clang of pots being pulled from their cabinets, the smells of a home-cooked meal wafting up the staircase. Meat sizzled on the cast-iron pan. There was the efficient sound of something being chopped in preparation for cooking.

Hmmm, bacon frying. His stomach gurgled. Bacon butchered and cured right here on the farm with his grandfather's recipe.

He patted his flat stomach. It was a long time since he'd sat at a table with linens and real dishes. His mouth watered. Would there be time for his aunt to make biscuits? He wouldn't mind eating anything she cooked. He knew he would savor the experience of being taken care of as he ate.

He hoped home fries would make an appearance. He didn't remember the last time.… His eyes slid shut, and he moved sideways, his face crushed in the smell of the starched sheets. *Aunt Minnie won't mind, will she?* was his last coherent thought.

The scrape on his cheek pained him but not enough to make him move. His arm had gone numb. It was lying cramped underneath his chest. For a minute, he looked around in confusion. *Was he still in Arizona?* His body aches reminded him of his tangle with the Thunderbird.

The sound of his aunt humming happily penetrated his doze, and the memories of the last few days came rushing back. He grunted in pain as he pushed himself off the bed.

His new cell phone lay on the night table, he bought it as soon as he landed in New York. He had a vague memory of Aimee taking his phone, but that was impossible. She was supposedly trekking around the jungle in Mexico and nowhere near Arizona at the time. He probably lost it when the giant bird dropped him. But that didn't explain the loss of all his pictures.

He frowned, picking it up. Every photo he'd taken had been erased from the cloud. Not that it mattered much. He knew the bulk of them were the same fuzzy quality of the material used in those sleazy newspapers that reported alien sightings.

Logan squinted at the bedside clock. Fifteen minutes. He'd slept fifteen minutes and no dreams.

Always a good thing, no dreams.

He knew his aunt was waiting to hear from him, and he owed her that, at least until Uncle Jack came home.

He stretched, every muscle protesting, then went into the bathroom in the hallway he had shared with his cousin Nathan many years ago.

Nathan used to sleep across the hall in a bedroom that faced the rows of trees the farm produced. Nathan hated the farm, enlisting in the army as soon as he could, disappointing Uncle Jack. Neither Logan nor Nathan ended up working the soil. The lure of finding and proving the existence of mythical creatures pulled Logan away, and a roadside bomb in Afghanistan took Nathan out of the picture, ending his uncle's dream of keeping the farm in the family.

Logan rubbed the dark stubble on the firm chin his

aunt liked to call determined, sucking in his breath when he pulled the barely healed skin.

Stripping off his tee, he leaned on the sink facing the mirror, his eyes resting on his newest tat, a Thunderbird, the raptor beak curling around the curve of his shoulder. After washing his hands, he placed his palm on his skin, feeling the heat of healing. It was scabbing, but the colors were beautiful. He turned sideways, comparing his new art with his other arm. He had a partial tattoo sleeve arm starting on his forearm and ending just above his shoulder. The memorial tattoo he'd made for Nathan covered his shoulder blade. It was his first, celebrating his cousin's life and honoring his sacrifice. He went back to his room and pulled the antibacterial soap from his backpack. With great care, he washed his new acquisition, then patted it dry.

The other tattoos commemorated every project he'd worked on these past five years. With each new adventure, he got an inked image reminding him of his discoveries. He had been in some dicey situations. It was not the fun and exciting expedition he first imagined. Logan loved every minute, reveling in the danger. Each creature decorating his body had a corresponding scar to match the experience. He looked at the spot over his heart thinking he once considered an image of Aimee inked there. She left her mark when she broke it. He thought about all of his wounds, both inside and outside. They were a part of him and had contributed to developing the person he was today. Looking down at his palm, he stared at the puncture wounds he received that fateful night he lost his father. He called them his war wounds. They toughened him, taught him to keep his beliefs private, his thoughts and opinions to himself unless he understood his audience.

The Steller's sea cow that he helped catch off the coast of China was immortalized on his bicep. The huge, blubbery creature was thought to be extinct. It wasn't an elegant creature. With its humped back and thick middle, it looked more like an overgrown manatee. He admired the gray coloring. The artist had managed to shade the tattoo, so it caught the wrinkles of its thick skin. Logan knew most would find it unattractive, but to him it was a thing of beauty.

He moved his arm, the sea cow undulating with his rippling muscles. He watched it, drifting mindlessly for a moment, and he was back on the *Silver Sea*, the scientific ship where he'd spent one break during college searching for that mythical creature.

He'd met Aimee that summer. She was the love of his life. The expedition caught the sea cow. They found it together and he was filled with the notion of the two of them searching for the unexplainable together. She moved in with him, and they traveled the world as a team, Elliot joining their duo after they graduated. She was brilliant. Her scientist mind was matched with an adventurous heart.

Aimee was fearless in her pursuit of creatures. Everything changed when she took a job in the private sector. One day, she was gone, moving back to Europe, no explanation. Last he'd heard, she was making her way up the corporate ladder, at some big think tank. She was head of acquisitions. Every so often, he'd find himself watching her Ted talk, where she walked across a stage, her long-legged stride in high heels, her slim arms folded as she talked excitedly about finding new creatures. She was charming, with a winsome smile, and direct gaze.

Logan shook his head. He knew the corporation had steered clear of them. He couldn't understand how they got to her, or even when. Haversham spoke about their race to discover new species, sensationalizing them with documentaries that manipulated audiences with their dog and pony shows.

Logan didn't care about money, for that matter neither did Elliot. He was sure Aimee was of the same mind. She certainly didn't seem to care when they lived on their limited budget in the basement apartment in Farmingdale, Long Island.

He admitted they needed more to live. Both he and Aimee worked as teachers under Professor Haversham during the school year. Summer was reserved for research and exploration. They hit all the hot spots together, searching for chupacabras in South America, mermaids in the middle east, dragons in China.

They had all the tools he needed from the university. What more could she have wanted? He had to admit now, Aimee had access to much better toys. Still, with a little duct tape and whatever he could find, Logan always managed to get the job done. And, he smiled, it was so much fun. For a minute he missed her. Taking a deep breath, he tucked the painful memory away, deciding he didn't want a reminder of her. While he may have suffered scrapes and bruises from each of his adventures, they brought him joy. Aimee's desertion brought him pain and the last thing he wanted was to become a wallowing sap like his father.

He leaned over, looking at his reflection, thinking of Aimee's long hair and full lips. She would have taken the egg. Stolen it from its mother, all on film for the pleasure and joy of great ratings and a happy audience. This was about science not sensationalism.

He raised his arm to look at the soft underside. The half-finished mermaid taunted him. He squinted at the incomplete face. *Why couldn't he finish it?*

The mermaid's green-tinted back was facing him, her dark hair swirling around her covering cleavage and ending just after her incompleted hips. He considered the curve of her cheeks, then looked at the lower portion. He should have really gotten her bottom half done, but he couldn't seem to find the right tail.

Logan thought back to that terrible night, all he remembered were dull flashes. He shook his head. Sometimes memories hurt too much to explore.

A chill made him go back to the bedroom to reach for a fresh shirt from his closet. He held it up to his nose, inhaling the scent of sunshine, then slid it over his body art.

He plugged in his laptop, then hung his leather jacket on a hook behind the whitewashed door. He paused, touching the jagged hole torn during his latest adventure, when his aunt called from the bottom of the stairs. He threw the jacket onto the bed.

"In a minute," he responded.

That rip and the feather were the only proof Logan had managed to obtain, his camera a victim of circumstances, smashed to smithereens. The images he captured on his cell phone were mysteriously gone forever.

He retrieved his specimen envelope from the hidden pocket in his jacket, marveling at the crimson strand inside. He held the delicate feather, blowing gently, watching it wave in the gentle breeze he created. He snipped off the bottom of the feather and sent it out in an envelope addressed to Professor Arthur Haversham for DNA research. Dr. Haversham would run the necessary tests. If not him, then his assistant Vadim would do it.

His journal lay on the bed. He placed the top half of the feather in the crease of the book and closed it with a satisfied whack. *That's for me*, he thought. *My proof.*

Both Logan and his guide had escaped with nothing more than a few abrasions. His hip ached from his fall and his chin was still raw. The scrape on his side wrapped around his whole abdomen.

He shrugged. Everything was a victim of his passion, his job, cryptozoology. He didn't have a reputation in the field yet, but he was close, he thought wryly.

He had almost done it this time. If only Elliot had been there with him, they might have succeeded.

He looked at his hand, a long row of black stitches from just outside his palm to the end of his index finger.

Logan cupped his hands in the shape of the egg he had held for barely a minute. It was heavy, more heft than he'd expected. He still beat himself up about his loss. He had the specimen in his grasp, for Chrissakes. The real deal.

The egg had actually rolled in his hands, propelled by the life inside of it. The tiny crack, the impending birth, had made time stop and his breath seize in his chest. He touched the scrape on his chin where the rough rock wall had burned his face.

The egg—if only he had managed to bring back a piece of shell from the egg.

"Logan," his aunt called, "I have your eggs ready. They're getting cold."

Eggs again. Logan laughed.

He descended the steps, planted a kiss on Aunt Minnie's cheek, then slid into his chair at the kitchen table.

Uncle Jack came in, dusty with pollen from working in the field. He smelled of the evergreens he tended, brushing off the dried leaves caught in his iron-gray mane.

His uncle sported a ponytail left over from his commune days, when he and Aunt Minnie danced in strawberry fields to Joni Mitchell's music. Thinking of it made Logan homesick for his mother. They had introduced his parents to each other.

The older man hooked a chair with his foot and sat down heavily.

"Hot out there." He slapped his nephew on the shoulder. Logan winced. He was still sore from his tumble down the rocky incline. "When did you get in?"

"He just got here. He hasn't eaten yet." Aunt Minnie placed two piled plates before them. There was a column of toasted bread in the center. "Eat bread." She grabbed two slices and put them on his plate.

Everything about his aunt was spare, from her reedlike figure to her economical movements. Aunt Minnie wasted nothing, whether it was food, money, or words. "I don't want to hear that carnivore diet stuff. You look half-starved."

Logan ducked his head, tucking into the pile of fried potatoes on his plate. They were as delicious as they smelled. This was the only place he ever felt hunger. Hunger made him feel vulnerable. His aunt had a way of making him feel cherished.

He caught his aunt's gaze on the fresh wound on his chin hiding under the stubble. "Don't they feed you on those trips?"

Logan swallowed a mouthful of milk, feeling like a kid. "There was no *they* on this one."

Uncle Jack looked up, his eyes observant. "I thought you were funded by the university. Hey, I took out the canvas top. I could help you put it on the jeep if you'd like."

Logan nodded in agreement. "That was the trip to Mexico. This was Arizona. The money stopped when I couldn't find anything in the Yucatan."

"So, why'd you go to Arizona?" his uncle asked. He was mopping up his eggs with a bit of sourdough bread.

Logan shrugged.

"He had a lead," Aunt Minnie supplied helpfully.

"Waste of time. Damn waste of time. Sent you to that college…"

"University, and he got a scholarship. Didn't cost you a dime, Jack." His aunt was at the sink scraping the frying pan. "Don't go crying about the cost. He worked all eight years of his education."

"Waste of time and money," Uncle Jack repeated with conviction.

"It wasn't *your* time or money," Aunt Minnie huffed.

Logan put down the fork, the eggs tasteless in his

mouth. He hadn't been home five minutes and Uncle Jack was starting. He didn't want to work on the farm. He never did. It was a bitter disappointment to his uncle that neither one of the boys was interested.

"I appreciate everything you've done for me, Uncle Jack. You gave me a home when…"

"You stop that. You're my brother's only son. What'd you expect? Be put in an orphanage?" said Uncle Jack.

"I'm hardly an orphan," Logan said under his breath. "Well, maybe I am at this point."

"Don't look at me. I haven't heard from your mom in over… eight years," Aunt Minnie said. "Not a shred of responsibility, that one. Always going off on her crusades." She waved her hand, and droplets of water flew off to dot the curtains. "She used to check in and let us know she was alive." His aunt became thoughtful. She shivered. "Ooh, I felt like someone just danced on my grave." She looked at Logan, her brow furrowed. "She always asked about you."

His uncle made a rude noise, and Logan knew Aunt Minnie was trying to make sure his feelings were intact.

"Some people aren't supposed to be mothers, Aunt Min," said Logan. "You've been more of a mother to me than she ever was."

His aunt walked by to ruffle his thick, dark hair. "You need a haircut," she told him gruffly. "Nobody takes care of you. You still seeing that girl, the one from out of the country? Amy?"

He shook his head. "No, her name is pronounced *Ah-mee*. Not for some time." Logan looked down, feeling that sensation in the middle of his chest. He pressed his palm there as if to ease the pain. *No, not pain…* a twinge, the same one when he thought about either of his parents.

"You eat too fast." Aunt Minnie was eyeing him critically.

"It's nothing." Logan shook his head.

"Drink another glass of milk," his aunt ordered, her eyebrow raised.

"Aunt Minnie," Logan said. "I'm almost thirty years old. Enough." Logan pushed the plate away and sat back, signaling he was finished.

He loved his aunt and uncle. Despite Uncle Jack's ribbing, he knew he had their unconditional support in anything he did. He had expected to work on the farm. He'd majored in agricultural studies at first. But Logan discovered he wasn't into working Uncle Jack's crops of conifers. They were farmed exclusively as Christmas trees. He thought it wasteful, so his uncle toyed with bringing in llamas or even camels for milk. People with allergies could tolerate camel milk.

Logan changed his major to animal behavioral sciences with the intent that he'd return after college to be there with Uncle Jack, especially when Nathan left. Somehow Logan never did come back home. There were always places he had to go, exciting stories about strange creatures needing to be explored. *There was Aimee*. He was looking for something that seemed just out of his reach… like his father.

Logan still harbored some anger about his father. It seemed as if it were part of his DNA, a feeling that he was left out.

For years he had refused to talk about the incident that ended his father's life. It seemed almost dreamlike, and for a while, Logan wasn't sure what part of his father's death was real or a product of his imagination.

He ended up pushing it to the deepest corners of his mind, where it became a faded memory. He knew not to mention it, especially when they marginalized his story. Worse than anything else were subtle threats he associated with that period of his life.

He remembered waking in the community hospital after his father had disappeared into the water. He told them about a creature, recounted every detail seared into his memory. Their response was to give him pills.

Post-Traumatic Stress, the doctors diagnosed.

The shock of seeing his father kill himself, they wrote on his reports.

The accident remained hazy at best; the images blurred by what he was told had happened. They confused his nine-year-old mind. Made him feel unsure, as if he was mixing what he read in books or saw in the movies. *He knew what he saw!* He saw a fearsome creature snatch his father from the boat.

It was a suicide, the Hamptons police chief insisted. Chief Kain had rescued him from the skiff, brought him to the local hospital, then set Logan straight. "Your father was a sad man. Sad about his wife, his job," the officer told him, his hand heavy on Logan's sore shoulder.

Logan looked down at his bandaged hand. *Then how did I get this?*

Your father did it, with fishhooks.

No, no, no, it was a mermaid! A creature that yanked him from the boat.

Doc Leeds, the town physician was there to treat him. He had known the doctor his whole life, he had stitched the spot over his eyebrow after a fall and put a cast on his arm the following summer. Both he and the police chief repeated over and over that there was no creature; it was a figment of his mind, created to deal with the trauma of his father's tragic death. Doc Leeds's voice was soothing and pleasant, the chief growled like an angry animal. They kept at him day and night. Logan firmed his lips defiantly. He knew what he saw, and the more he argued, the more they did things to him.

Logan didn't like to remember those times. He spent weeks in the hospital. He was isolated and drugged. The time passed in a sluggish haze. He wondered where his aunt and uncle were. He asked for them repeatedly and was told they were on the way. He wanted his mother. His memories were spotty.

Logan recollected waking to see Chief Kain standing at the foot of his bed. The officer walked close to him, leaning over. He gripped Logan's chin with such force it would leave a bruise. The skin near his contusions pulled, bringing tears to his eyes. He struggled, picking up shadows, dark suited men. Why were they in his room?

"You will stop this crazy talk, boy, or we are going to put you in a place where you'll never see anyone again."

"But I saw…"

Kain squeezed, pinching his jaw. "Nothin'. You saw nothin' but that crazy father of yours jumping overboard."

"That thing took him. If he jumped, you'd have his body."

"The sharks got him. Ain't nothing but bones now."

He shoved Logan's head sideways until the boy was look-ing out the window. The hospital faced the harbor, and in the distance the hulking outline of Cedar Haven blurred the horizon.

"See that? It's the nuthouse, and there's a bed there with your name on it. We shoulda put your father in there when he started all this stuff. I swear, Logan Osbourne, if you go in there, you'll never get out."

"Red, that's enough," Doctor Leeds said.

Logan blinked, bringing the brick building across the bay into focus. Cedar Haven was an old asylum built during the nineteenth century on a small island in the middle of the sound. People spoke about the place in hushed whis-pers, saying it was put there so you couldn't hear the inmates screaming. He knew about Cedar Haven. Everybody did. It was the place locals pointed to frighten children. When he moved his head back on the pillow the room was empty, only a kind nurse with his tray.

"Who was the other guy?" he asked her.

"Who are you talking about? Chief Kain was here, and Doc Leeds, of course."

"No." He shook his head. "I saw a man with a dark suit. He was over there." Logan pointed a weak finger to the corner.

The nurse fluffed his pillows and tightened the blankets covering him. "No, nobody was here. You must have dreamt it." She laughed. "How about I turn on the television?"

Logan shrank into the hospital bed, sullen and silent. He saw another man in his room. He saw a strange creature that night. Hadn't he? Everything was becoming jumbled, faded, like an out-of-focus photo.

The chief returned later in the day, his face angry and forbidding. His questions rattled off like a machine gun, the words making him blink as if bullets were hitting him. Logan shrank into the bed, wishing he could disappear. The chief filled the room sucking all the oxygen. *Where was the doctor, where was his family?* Logan shrank back into the pillows feeling alone and defenseless.

"I want you to tell me what happened to your dad," said Chief Kain. "You remember now, right?"

Logan stared out the window at the red brick outline of Cedar Haven. His stomach tightened. If he were locked in there, he'd never get out. The officer wanted him to betray his father and lie about what happened. He didn't want to do that. Logan warred with himself. *Had it been suicide or something else?* Was he being as obstinate as his father, believing what he wanted to?

Logan shook his head, wanting to erase everything. He gazed out the window, his mind exhausted. Doubt assailed him.

The memories replayed in his mind as if underwater. Images merged, fading into one another. He touched the bandage on his hand, where he knew strange puncture wounds were covered. He closed his fist around his palm, hiding them.

He watched the officer pace the room.

He firmed his lips, knowing he had to let it go. If he insisted on the events as he believed it, he ran the risk of them locking him up and throwing away the key. If he admitted his father killed himself, it wasn't the truth, and a betrayal of his father's life work. He had to lie to survive and escape.

He would live in two worlds, have two faces, he decided. He was used to it after all. *Didn't he do the same thing when he hid his father's condition?* He lied to protect him, and now he had to lie to protect himself.

He could tell them what they needed to hear. That would keep him safe. They couldn't get into his head. He made a promise, though. Once he got out of there, he would never lie again. Not for anything or anybody.

His brain ached with uncertainty.

He mumbled a response to the chief sullenly while he said a silent apology to his father's memory.

"What? I didn't hear you," the chief snarled.

"He jumped."

"Louder. I said, say it louder," the policeman ordered.

Tears smarted his eyes. "He jumped." Logan's voice quavered.

"Again."

"He jumped. He jumped!" he shouted, tears coursing down his face.

"That's right, and don't you forget it. He jumped and killed himself. Then the sharks got him. A big, fat tiger shark, ate him up."

Kain left the room. Logan turned his face into the pillow, allowing the cotton of the material to absorb his tears.

He'd bide his time and wait. Uncle Jack and Aunt Minnie would take him away from here soon.

Logan closed his eyes, shutting out the world. He

would find a better place and lose himself in it until the danger passed.

His aunt and uncle arrived the next day. They came as fast as they could. They had been in Alaska on a cruise and took a flight when they made the closest port.

They closed up the Hamptons house and moved him north to join his cousin. Logan waved farewell to his friends Penny and Rory; Aunt Minnie promising they were welcome to spend summers with him upstate. He'd miss them, but he needed to get away. He wanted to put as much distance between himself and Officer Kain as possible.

Logan devoted himself to working the farm, helping his aunt, uncle, and older cousin Nathan, grateful for the home, but his mind still tried to sift through the memories separating reality from his imagination. Hidden away in the mountains of upstate New York, he felt free to discuss his father's bizarre death. He became obsessed with the details, drawing recreations of the creature.

While the local kids could talk hours about monsters like werewolves, vampires, and zombies, Logan's fascination with a fishlike being unnerved them. The google-like eyes, scaly skin, and talon-shaped fingers had an otherworldliness that kids his age couldn't relate. With movies glorifying creatures with chiseled good looks, some of his peers found his drawings offensive.

Nathan grabbed the illustrations. "You have to stop. My friends think you are weird." His cousin stuffed them in the trash. "The guys don't want to come here," Nathan whispered.

Logan hung his head feeling dejected. "I'm sorry."

"No, no. Look, Logan I don't want to have to beat up

the neighborhood to defend you." Nathan smiled. "You're my cousin. I'm not going to let them talk crap about you. But can't you make it a little bit easier."

Nathan went to his desk and dug around the messy drawers for something. "I saved this for you. Ma didn't want me to give it to you, but I thought you'd want to have it. It won't make it easy for you, but it has to be the truth. It's written in a newspaper."

Logan opened his mouth to say that maybe you do have to argue. Just because something was printed didn't make it the gospel truth.

"I know it hurts, but the more you keep rehashing it, it's never going to heal."

Nathan showed him the *Hamptons Sun*, his old hometown's local newspaper. Logan scanned the front page. His father's picture was there, the headline about his suicide and Logan's near drowning. He pulled the paper close. They wrote that his father was bipolar or schizophrenic. It was all lies.

Logan shook his head. He glanced up at his cousin's hopeful face.

"Can't we just play ball instead of talking about things that crawl out of the swamp?"

He owed his new family a lot. He didn't want to make anything more difficult than it already was. Logan nodded, swallowing the thickness in his throat. It was finished. He clammed up about that fateful night, never talking about it again.

It didn't stop his interest in the subject. It stole into his dreams, waking him. He would be sweating. He silenced the screams with his fist held against his mouth lest they know what troubled him. Logan learned to keep everything to himself.

Logan sat on his bed, staring out the window, afraid to close his eyes and see the hideous face and bulbous eyes. He imagined the long, scaly fingers that grabbed his father and pulled him into the abyss. Night terrors about the accident woke him, dragging him from peaceful sleep, haunting his dreams.

The strange scars on his palm throbbed as if they had a pulse of their own. He held up his hand, his finger measuring the distance of the two puncture wounds, wondering how they got there.

How could they explain those? He caressed the twin scars that were quickly fading from their angry red. Nobody could. He knew rehashing the story brought unwanted attention.

Logan became a loner, spending his spare time in the library, going through its meager science section, compiling information. When he finished that aisle, he began investigating all the books he could find on mythology, creating a notebook containing observations of strange creatures from a variety of cultures throughout time. He scanned the computer for news articles; incidents that happened all over the world. He wasn't sure if he wanted to find the creature, but he couldn't stop the compulsion to look. He read about people who saw things, strange things that no one believed.

Hours turned to years in the library, but both the internet and the computer his aunt and uncle bought for his twelfth birthday made it easier for him to research. It called to him. Logan could hear his father's voice, pulling him away from this world to operate in the shadowy place of strange and bizarre creatures.

His anger at the situation dimmed, replaced by a growing curiosity about the netherworld of mermaids, bigfoot, phantom cats, and mountain gorillas. The list went on. *Come*, they called. They were waiting for him to find them.

Night became his time to escape into the universe of creatures not recognized by authorities. History was filled with stories of sightings and contact.

Mermaids alone, he discovered, existed in diverse cultures, from Chinese females that wept pearls for tears to African Mami Water or Mother Water spirits that lured men to their deaths.

He marveled at the coincidence that they were recorded in all different time periods, from the ancient Assyrians to the devious Melusine of European folklore.

He compiled notes and drawings in his notebooks, wishing he had just one of his father's diaries. They were all gone. Aunt Minnie and Uncle Jack had shuttered the house. They covered the furniture and locked the doors. It had been ransacked by vandals, they told him. Not much was left.

Did his aunt and uncle believe him? Logan wondered. He wasn't sure. The memory was as faded as his mother's features.

He still searched the internet. It made him determined to find proof, if not about his own mermaid, then for the truth about monsters that haunted other people.

He read account after account, his thirsty mind wondering why mythical beings could be found everywhere in so many different countries across over four thousand years.

How could these creatures keep reappearing without cultures having the ability to network and influence each other?

Since his discussion with his cousin, he kept his interest a secret. He knew instinctively that he had to be quiet about it. Strangely enough, in his second year of college, a professor brought up the Tilowanney Swamp incident.

The professor had a copy of his father's original paper. It was an article about the Loch Ness Monster. Logan hadn't known there were any of those around. He could find nothing on the internet of his father's work. It was as though George Osbourne had never existed.

Professor Haversham spoke, walking to the lectern, referring to a chart he'd made up, but Logan couldn't remember any part of the lecture. He sank into his seat, buried in the past, the professor's voice droning like an incessant insect.

A tide of memories washed over Logan. He spent the entire class trying to sift through the faint images. Twice he was asked a question, and both times, Logan failed to respond correctly. The words froze in his throat. He knew he must have resembled a deer in the headlights.

"Mr. Osbourne," the professor called at the conclusion of the class. "A moment of your time."

The student next to him rolled his eyes. He was in for it now. His wandering mind was going to get him in trouble once again.

Haversham stood by his lectern, his sparse white hair revealing a pink scalp. He was all angles, with a thin face dominated by a blade of a nose.

"There is a new field opening up, hardly recognized by most universities," he told Logan as he packed up his notes.

Logan looked up; surprise etched across his face. He was expecting to be admonished for not paying attention. "I like you, Osbourne. You remind me of your father."

"My father?"

"Yes. I studied under him at NYU. He was brilliant." The professor picked up a pipe and hit it against the wood of the podium. "Filthy habit." He shrugged guiltily. "But a habit nonetheless. Cryptozoology," Haversham continued. "Have you ever heard of it?"

"It's the study of creatures that have not quite been proven to exist, such as mermaids." Logan watched the professor's face for a reaction.

Haversham smiled and replied, "Exactly. It's not considered a legitimate field – yet. Most people think we're crackpots and don't take us seriously."

Logan gulped. He had so much to say, he didn't know where to start. "Have you ever seen a cryptid?"

Haversham rocked on his heels as he answered, "Altamaha-ha is a plesiosaur-like river creature you can find in the southern United States. I spent quite a few summers in McIntosh County waiting for Altie to show himself. I was laughed out of more than a few lectures by people I thought were my friends." He opened his book, leafing through the pages, until he pulled out a picture. It was an eight by ten printout from his computer. He handed it Logan who stared at the photo of decomposing remains of a dinosaur-like creature.

"Sir," Logan said. "Some performance artist claimed he created it out of a stuffed shark and papier mâché. It was branded a fake."

Haversham's eyebrows rose to reach his hairline. "Precisely Mr. Osbourne. That is exactly why we choose not to be vocal about it. We find more comfort studying from the shadows rather than exposing ourselves to be ridiculed. However, there are a few of us trying to get it into the curriculum." He looked at Logan straight in the eye. "We believe in this subject. We meet twice a week." The professor looked down his long nose at Logan. "Are you interested?"

Logan didn't take a second to answer. He knew he'd been waiting for this his entire life. "Hell, yeah."

Haversham took him under his wing and Logan went on to complete his doctorate, following with his postdoc work. Haversham provided him with a position where he was paid a nominal sum to teach classes and the rest of his time used for research.

Logan knew he had found a home, a place to discuss his thoughts with others who wouldn't scoff at his ideas. Though he finished his doctorate in animal behavior, he pursued questionable animals on vacations and summer breaks with other people with the same mission. That's how he met Elliot... *and Aimee.*

They traveled the world, backpacking on money raised by the group. Greece, Israel, Scotland, every country had a creature, and Logan was determined to find them. He went anywhere he could except the Hamptons. He swore he'd never go back there.

His uncle Jack complained that he was supposed to be thinking about livestock they could breed on the farm, but Logan sought other kinds of beasts.

Then came his first solo big break. The university was

willing to fund an expedition to search out the legendary Thunderbird. Two thousand to travel to Mexico with the possible bonus of five grand if he produced evidence. This was the first time they were willing to pay him. Haversham said the evidence was the most compelling they'd ever seen.

"Thunderbird," Uncle Jack scoffed, pulling Logan back into the present. "Go to Ricky's Garage. He has an old red '72 under a tarp there."

Logan laughed good-naturedly. "I was looking for the winged kind. From Native American folklore. There was a report that a farmer had killed an enormous creature with a gigantic wingspan."

"How big?" Uncle Jack asked skeptically.

"The report said it was over thirty feet."

"Yeah, sure. That's a mighty big chicken."

"Leathery skin, featherless wings like a bat, and a face like a reptile."

"Sounds like a pterodactyl." Aunt Minnie nodded. "Did you find anything? A feather, or maybe some humongous bird poop?"

Logan smiled. His aunt had indulged him when he was a child more than anyone else. Whatever interested him fascinated her as well. She could name fifteen dinosaurs and the era they lived in. She could tell you what you'd weigh on Mars. *Yeah, some people were better suited to being mothers than others,* Logan thought ruefully.

"Wait here." He ran up the steps to his room and retrieved his notebook. Returning, he slid into his seat at the table and opened the well-worn tablet to the middle. His aunt and uncle peered over his shoulder to see a thin scarlet feather lying in the crease of the book. Aunt Minnie exhaled with excitement.

"Is that color real?" Aunt Minnie asked.

Logan picked up the delicate quill, holding it in the light for them to admire.

"Looks like the one Mabel the stripper wears down at Juicy Lucy's," Uncle Jack said, breaking the reverential silence in the room. "Probably synthetic, made for the tourist trade."

Aunt Minnie slapped Uncle Jack on the head playfully. "Always a skeptic. Odd coming from a man who grows trees celebrating an overweight bearded elf delivering presents once a year." She looked at him sideways. "And how do you know what they're wearing down at Juicy Lucy's?"

They all laughed.

"Nope." Logan shook his head. "No tourists where I got this. It was in the nest about, well, high up on a cliff."

"Still looks fake," Uncle Jack said.

"We'll see. I sent a sample to the university lab I work with for DNA analysis."

"Oh, I bought Jack a DNA kit for Christmas," said Aunt Minnie. "It took a long time to get his results. You know, you've got quite a bit of Native American ancestry."

Logan smiled. "Really? I'd like to look at the paperwork."

Uncle Jack waved his hand. "That stuff is still under debate. Some people don't think it's accurate." his uncle raised his gray eyebrows.

"I don't know about that, Uncle Jack," Logan replied. "I think it's real."

"Oh, Logan. It must have been dangerous." Aunt Minnie's face was concerned.

"Only when I picked up the egg."

"So, what happened to your giant bat-bird? Mexican authorities confiscate it?"

"I never made it into the first village in Mexico. There was some kind of drug war. The whole place was deserted. The driver took us out of there before I could even start to question anyone."

"I don't like when you travel to those places, Logan." Aunt Minnie clicked her tongue. "Like that trip last year into the mountains of Turkey. Can't you look for Bigfoot in our mountains?"

"Another waste of time," Uncle Jack said under his breath.

"Yeti," Logan corrected with a shrug. "Didn't matter. I got a lead on the Thunderbird in the next town, that led to even another place. I found a guy who took me to an old couple. They told me about rumors of a nesting place in southwest Arizona. They had a map."

"Sounds like something out of a movie," Uncle Jack commented, then held up his hands at their impatience. "Hey, I'm just saying."

"It's not as glamorous as a movie. It's tedious, boring, back-breaking, but . . ." Logan paused, trying to find a way to explain it. "It can be exhilarating."

"You remind me of my brother," Uncle Jack said in a flat voice.

Logan ignored the comment, even though it rankled a bit. "I caught a flight and headed north. I saw it, Uncle Jack." Logan wanted his uncle to believe him.

"You did?! Is that where the feather came from?" Aunt Minnie glowed with excitement. "Will they give you a chair at the university now?"

"Something tells me it slipped right out of his grasp," Uncle Jack said, his eyebrows raised, a slight smirk on his face. "Like those sea creatures in Israel."

"I wish you could have seen it, Aunt Min. Its beak had to be eight inches long. It had a turquoise face and yellow beak, and the wings were leather like a bat. Its body had vivid green feathers. These red ones were tufted on its head like a crest." Logan paused and then added, "It was like a small airplane."

"When will you get the results?"

"Not soon enough for me."

"So, did you get any pictures of this... big bird?" Uncle Jack asked, his voice doubtful.

"The camera broke."

"Of course, it did, What about your cell phone?" Uncle Jack smirked.

Logan continued; his voice filled with wonder. He cupped his hands. "I held its egg right in the palms of my hands. It had life in it."

"What do you mean?" Aunt Minnie gasped.

"It means he's got a great bridge for sale in New York Harbor if you are interested." Uncle Jack laughed. "Nice story, Logan. So, it slipped out of your grasp, the bird attacked, and the mommy bird flew away with her hatchling."

"Something like that," Logan said dejectedly.

"It was probably a buzzard or condor. They have that

prehistoric look." Uncle Jack started to rise, dismissing the conversation.

"It was a Thunderbird. I held its egg in my palms."

"How big was the egg?" Uncle Jack asked speculatively, sitting down again.

Logan held his hands ten inches apart.

"About the size of an ostrich egg," Uncle Jack challenged. "Maybe somebody has an ostrich farm or something there."

"No way. I was high on a cliff. No ostriches that high up or even in this country. Besides, I saw it. It attacked me. It had a screech that would crack glass."

Aunt Minnie gasped. "How did you escape?" She placed a slice of strawberry rhubarb pie with homemade vanilla ice cream in front of Logan. He felt a note of satisfaction when she gave him a larger piece than his uncle. "You could have been killed."

He showed her the stitches on his hand. "Almost lost my hand. The chick attacked. Took a chunk out of my finger. It bled like a… well… let's say a lot. My leather jacket got the worst of the battle. You should have seen those talons. Her cry, it felt and sounded like the rotors of a helicopter. My guide lost the camera down the side of the cliff. I placed the egg back… very gently," he added, looking at his aunt.

"And your phone?" Uncle Jack asked.

Logan hesitated, then muttered, "I lost it somehow."

His uncle let out a laugh.

"I would expect no less of you. Still very considerate of you to return the egg in spite of the circumstances." His aunt smiled.

"I wish I could have taken it," Logan admitted with a lopsided grin. "In the interest of science, of course."

"You would never separate a chick from its mama!" Aunt Minnie was shocked.

"Get on with the damn story already," Uncle Jack growled. "They'll never believe that's real," his uncle added softly. "Not without more proof."

"I know," Logan agreed. "Still, the feather might be enough. If they can extract enough DNA."

"What happened next?" Aunt Minnie interrupted.

"I rolled down the mountainside, landing in a crevice that was too narrow for the creature to come after me. The chick chose that moment to crack open her egg. The mother scooped him up in her beak and took off. I have nothing to show for my expedition. Well, except for a feather and a bruise or two."

"Yes, the feather," his uncle said with an edge of sarcasm. "Too bad about your cell phone. That's what all your fellow creepologists use. The photos are never believable, anyway."

"Cryptozoologists. Yeah, and that's why I wanted to use the university's camera. I wanted to show the real thing, not some vague five-second video. But damn, even that didn't work out."

"Better luck next time," Aunt Minnie said soothingly.

"Nothing but a silly waste of time." Uncle Jack laughed, then added. "Like when you found that giant walrus. Made a big deal about nothing."

"It was a sea cow and was thought to be extinct," Logan said quietly. He wished his uncle accepted his choices better.

"Big deal, so it's not. What difference does it make?

They found it, and you were there and didn't get any credit. That *Aim-eeee* took all the credit."

"She found it first." Logan didn't understand why he felt he needed to defend Aimee.

"You were working together. You should have shared. She did the same thing time and time again. Besides, this kind of work won't put food on the table, Logan." His uncle punctuated each word by pounding the surface with his finger.

"I have my teaching job," Logan answered, feeling fatigue roll through him. He didn't want to have this conversation; he was tired of it.

"For how long? If you keep following these harebrained ideas, you'll ruin your reputation like your father."

"Yeah, alright, they didn't believe him, destroyed his life. Maybe things could have turned out differently that night if he could have brought proof."

"Proof of what?" Uncle Jack shouted. "Proof he had a breakdown? I know you are trying to validate that night."

"No, I'm not," Logan protested.

"There was no mermaid, Logan. You have to stop trying to justify your dad's suicide."

Logan shook his head sadly. He didn't want to fight. He loved his uncle, but things never added up. They still didn't fit together. Snatches of dreams came to Logan, making him question those times.

"Enough!" Aunt Minnie shooed them away from the table. "Go argue about the Cowboys and the Giants."

Ah, the age-old restorer of equilibrium, sports. Logan had spent many hours watching games with his uncle, lying on the couch without the need to speak or explain, just being present.

"Wrong season, woman." Uncle Jack gestured to Logan.

He knew his uncle was over it already. He wanted peace between them as well. Logan watched his uncle's eyes soften with affection. "The Mets are playing. Wanna watch them lose?"

"Let's take off the hardtop from the jeep before it gets dark. Then we can catch the game down at Sully's."

Logan couldn't help the smile that teased his lips. Uncle Jack might not have believed a single word he said, but he was home, and somehow the scrapes and stitches, and even his bruised heart, didn't hurt anymore.

CHAPTER 4

L OGAN FELL HEAVILY onto the mattress, inhaling the fragrance of the sheets. *She must air-dry them*, he thought absentmindedly.

He was so tired. He and Uncle Jack worked on his car. He helped with some chores around the farm. Then they went to Sully's Bar and had a few rounds while they watched the game.

Logan groaned with pleasure stretching on the bed, not missing the lumpy one he slept on in his apartment in Long Island. He wondered what drove him to live the way he did when he had a comfortable home if he chose. He could quit his teaching job and take over most of the responsibility of running the farm. He had an open slate. Uncle Jack and Aunt Minnie would be only too happy to hand over the reins to him. The farm was profitable. He knew they longed to move south to a warmer climate, but his dreams of finding new creatures called to him, not that he was able to do it full time.

He lived in the small town of Farmingdale, a mile from the campus where he taught classes on animal sciences. He was between semesters for the summer and had promised his uncle he'd stay for the season on the farm.

Logan closed his eyes dreamily, thinking about Aunt Minnie's Sunday roast and late-afternoon naps with the window open, letting in the upstate breeze. It felt like he had slept for hours when the persistent buzzing of his phone punctured his dreams. He fumbled as he tried to swipe its surface. He rolled over, looking at the illuminated display, perplexed at the caller. He finally got it to open and answered groggily.

"Penny?" He smiled at her voice, thinking of her pale blond pigtails. He rubbed his eyes. No, wait, the pigtails were gone. She wore her hair hidden, stuffed under her hat. She was a police officer now.

Penny and her twin, Rory, stayed in touch with Logan generally through social media. They didn't see each other much anymore. Aimee had taken an instant dislike to the twins and refused to socialize with them. They went from meeting frequently in Manhattan, to almost never at all. Logan saw them alone a few times. No matter what had gone on in their lives, they maintained steady contact through Facebook and Instagram, exchanging snarky remarks, hers about his 'fake' field of cryptozoology. Logan teased her about becoming a 'fake' cop on Long Island. She worked for a private police force contracted by the small exclusive community he used to live and somehow, he knew Aimee felt threatened by Penny's wholesome earnestness.

Logan glanced at the clock on the bedside table. "It's four o'clock. Is everything okay?"

"Well," she sighed, her voice thick as if she had been crying, "that answers my first question. You're on the East Coast."

"What?" Logan asked after a wide yawn.

"The time difference. You're on the east coast."

Logan laughed, "You called to tell me you made detective?"

"Don't be nasty," she said. "I need you to listen."

"Penny…" Logan asked. "Are your parents okay?"

"Well," Penny said in a high voice. "Sort of…"

This sobered Logan. "What's up?"

"You see, I thought you might still be in Mexico. I need you to come down," she said.

Logan went silent for a minute, then responded, "Nope. No way." Logan sat up, swinging his legs onto the floor and wrapped the sheet around his lean hips. "I hate the Hamptons. I never go there." He shivered at the thought of that place. It made him uncomfortable just picturing it.

Logan heard a shuddering sigh on the other end of the phone. "Yeah, I thought you might say that. Thing is… I mean…"

"What's going on, Pen?"

"We have sort of a situation going on." Her voice was breathless, urgent.

"What kind of situation?" Logan leaned forward, suddenly alert. An icy chill traveled down his naked spine.

"You know, like when your father… *um*, died."

"*What?* Sorry." Logan cut her off. "I'm not interested."

"But it's about the *mermaid*," she whispered. "You… you're still doing that kind of stuff."

"Anywhere but there," he said after a long pause. Penny was quiet. Resentment made Logan's lips tighten. "It's complicated. Look, even if I do come, they'll just stir up the old stories, and they'll discredit me. I can't do that now; it could destroy my credibility."

"Credibility?" Penny asked. "What are you talking about?"

"Legitimacy. My career. Cryptids. The field of cryptology." Logan sighed and replied, "Besides, you know I can't be objective about the Hamptons."

As if she sensed he was going to hang up, Penny interrupted him. "It's not the first incident. There've been two others, but they've quashed the stories. This is big, Logan. You need to be here."

She paused, and he heard the soft hiccup of a sob. "Pen?"

He waited for her to get her emotions under control. Penny was the tough one in the family; Rory was the more sensitive twin.

Logan stared out the window at the inky blackness. The soft hoot of a barn owl drifted through his window. He had known Penny Swanson and her family his whole life. Whenever he smelled the fresh ocean breeze he associated with the beach, he thought of Penny, her brother, Rory, and the times they spent exploring the dunes, swimming, fishing, and snorkeling the sound during the endless Hampton summers.

Penny and Rory kept him sane when his father relocated to the small town, blending the seasons until he stopped missing the city. He loved the quiet town and the musty old cottage they lived in until that fateful night his father died.

Logan never went back, but his friendship with the

Swanson twins never ended. Penny and Rory came north to visit him at his uncle's farm every summer. They stayed close, writing and calling. He had never been more surprised when she took on the job at the private police in the local precinct.

"Have you been following the town paper?" she asked after a long sniff. Her voice was stronger.

"Nope. I want nothing to do with that place. You know that." Logan picked up his watch and fiddled with it, the phone was resting in the crook of his shoulder.

"I can't hear you," Penny sounded hurt and angry. "Are you even listening?"

"I hear every word you're saying."

"I thought you read my reports. You look for stories. I always sent you the links." Penny said.

Logan didn't answer. He tossed the watch on the night-stand and stared moodily at the floor. He wanted a cigarette. He had an old pack in his backpack. He had pretty much stopped, promised his aunt he would give it up, but just the thought of the Hampton's made him want to smoke. So absorbed in those thoughts, he wasn't listening to Penny.

"Well, don't you?" she asked, her voice angry. "Or are you too busy-"

He focused on Penny.

"Come on, Pen. Don't be like that. You know how I feel about the Hamptons. I'll go anywhere but there," he interrupted her.

"Listen, two years ago, a rookie police officer disappeared."

"You mean one of your security guys?"

"Police, security, it's all the same thing. We protect the people of the town. Enforce the rules."

"Okay, okay. Penny, I respect what you do. I always have. You don't have to get hot about it." He was quiet for a minute. "Sly never mentioned it."

"When was the last time you talked to him?" Penny's voice held a note of accusation.

"I hate to admit it, it's been a while."

Penny exhaled heavily. "Yeah, when you get here, we can all have a nice reunion."

Logan pinched the skin at the bridge of his nose. "What can you tell me about the cop?"

"He vanished. No trace. His body was never found. There were several sightings a week before he disappeared."

"Sightings of what?" he asked with exasperation.

"Don't be obtuse. You know what," Penny hissed. "I sent you every article."

Logan sighed. "Did they say he committed suicide?" Logan's world-weary demand was met with a weighted silence that answered his question.

"Another vagrant went missing, too, but nobody cared enough to investigate."

"Been there, done that," Logan said bitterly. He glanced at the clock. He was up now. No chance of going back to sleep. He reached down, rummaging in his backpack to find a crumbled half-empty pack. He pulled one cigarette, lit it and inhaled deeply feeling his body relax. He exhaled toward the window, so the smoke curled into the darkness of the night.

"Are you smoking again?"

Logan smiled and crushed the cigarette. "No."

Penny cleared her throat. "You promised to stop." Penny sounded angry. "Listen, something big happened tonight. Really big. Two people went missing."

Logan grunted an acknowledgment.

"There was a ton of blood on the beach."

Logan absorbed the information.

"Are you listening to this?" Penny asked. The sob came back.

"Why should I care?" he asked.

"The girl was not a local. Logan, it's bad, really bad..."

"Technically, my father wasn't a local. They hushed it up."

"I know." Penny's breath hitched.

Logan swore. "What are you not telling me, Pen?"

"It was a couple. We think Rory was with her."

Logan straightened; his scalp tightened. "Rory? Are you sure?"

"He never came home. His phone goes straight to voice-mail."

"He's probably locked up somewhere writing. He doesn't want to be found. He's done this before. Did you check my place? He asked me to turn on the utilities a couple of months ago. He said he needed to get away from everybody."

"That was the first place I looked. He had been staying there on and off for a few weeks, writing. I found his clothes and some food in the fridge."

They sat silently together for a bit.

Logan said, "Was the food fresh?"

"It was leftover takeout," Penny said. "But it wasn't old."

"You said there was a woman. Maybe he went somewhere else," Logan said. "Somewhere more private." He heard her sniff on the phone again. "Pen?"

"I don't think so," she said, her voice hoarse.

All Logan could think about was Cedar Haven and Officer Kain. He hated the man. He pushed it to the dark recesses of his mind.

Penny needed him now.

She started speaking again in a ragged whisper, as if it hurt to speak. "They found one of his shoes on the beach. I'm worried. Really worried."

"Shit," he said. "How do you know it was his shoe?"

"I know," Penny said. "I bought them for him."

Damn you, Rory. He felt fear rising like a giant bubble in his chest. *Blood on the beach.* He was quiet for a long time. When the words came, they had to be dragged out of him, as if they were coming from deep inside him. "I'll be there sometime tomorrow."

CHAPTER 5

"**Y**OU JUST GOT here." Aunt Minnie put a plate before him with a little more force than necessary. "I don't understand what's so important you have to leave."

Uncle Jack waved his hand. "Oh, come on, Min, you loved the twins. He should be with people his own age having fun. Especially after what happened with *Aim-eeee*."

Minnie was thoughtful for a minute. She tilted her head and said, "I adore Penny. Good values. She's a sweet girl. I thought the two of you might make a thing of it."

Logan flushed bright red. He opened his mouth to respond but his uncle interrupted him. "Well, I certainly like her." Uncle Jack brought his coffee mug to the table. "She's pretty and smart. I like that blond braid she wears."

"Why are you noticing some girl's braid, you old goat?" Aunt Minnie cuffed him on the side of his head. Uncle Jack laughed good-naturedly. He grabbed her around the waist, pulling her, unresisting, onto his lap. Aunt Minnie's eyes softened; with a special look Logan knew belonged to his uncle. She stroked his gray ponytail.

Logan thought the conversation was finished and his aunt diverted until she added, "And it's the Hamptons, of all places! I'd rather see you looking for the *dino-bird* than go back there."

"Thunderbird." Logan shook his head. "I have to go. They saw something unusual."

"No, not that again." Aunt Minnie leaned over. "Don't you remember what they did to you? They wanted to put you in an asylum—the one on that island in the bay."

"They closed that place up years ago," Logan said without looking up. He couldn't meet their eyes.

"Yeah, well, we didn't let them do that, Minnie mine," Uncle Jack said affectionately. "Scooped him up and took him home."

For a minute, Logan forgot where he was. His hand touched his temple. A flash of a man with white hair seared his brain. It was Doc Leeds, his friendly face growing muddy. He hadn't thought about him for years. He had been in the hospital room too, along with Kain. How could he have forgotten that? His memory was hazy at best. He was having trouble distinguishing Chief Kain and Doc Leeds. Their faces became interchangeable.

Wait, he told himself. Doc Leeds was always so friendly, warm, ready with a treat, yet Logan shuddered, feeling cold.

Something niggled his mind. He bent his head. It felt heavy on his shoulders. There was more, he realized. Was his mind playing tricks with him, inventing new scenes? Could speaking with Penny and the thought of going there have jogged something in his mind?

All he could recall was talk of the asylum with Kain, but he realized with sudden clarity that there was more. He looked at Aunt Minnie's worried face and closed his eyes for a mere second, the memories rushing at him with the force of a hurricane. He sank deeper into the chair, letting the images play out in his mind. He wasn't on the farm anymore; he was locked in his old nightmare. The farmhouse faded and he was nine years old again, alone and defenseless.

"Logan." Chief Kain was so close, Logan could smell the liquor on his breath. "Your father jumped. You hear me? You said you saw it."

Logan shook his head stubbornly. Kain grabbed his face, his ham-sized hands squeezing his chin.

"You're hurting him, Red." The doctor called the chief by his nickname. The doctor *was* in the room that day… and someone else. Someone erased by time.

"Let go of the boy," a deep, gravelly voice said. Red Kain dropped Logan's head none too gently and moved away from the bed, his ruddy face paling.

Logan turned his head on the pillows to see a shadow detach itself from the wall. A huge man wearing a dark suit moved into the light. He had one of those haircuts men got when they entered the army. Logan focused on his nose, which was broken, as if someone had punched him hard. The bridge was flattened against his face, and his dark eyes were as sharp as the hawks that hunted by the bay.

"Doctor." He nodded to Doc Leeds, who gulped nervously. The older man leaned over. "Logan, I know it's hard, but if you insist on this silly story, we'll have no choice but to send you to Cedar Haven."

Logan saw Kain open his mouth to say something, but the menacing man exchanged a fearsome look with the chief. Red Kain's lips tightened. He put his beefy hands in his pockets and walked backwards until he bumped into the wall.

"You don't want that, do you, son?" the man said softly, sending a shiver up Logan's spine.

Logan shook his head. Words clogged in his throat. The man tapped his temple. "I can tell you're a smart kid. You know the difference between fantasy and reality, right?"

Once when Logan was young, his mother had shown him a conch shell. They were on an island; he wasn't sure which one. She blew into the shell, and it made a mournful sound. This man's voice echoed with that same timbre, low as if it were coming from the depths of the ocean.

Logan looked at the fierce eyes observing him. The room was silent. Perhaps not the bottom of the ocean but the bowels of hell. He understood two things at once: this man was not his friend, and both Doc Leeds and Chief Kain were desperately afraid of him.

Logan looked out the hospital window, watching the angry surf crash against the beach, its greenish-gray waves churning the sandbars, wiping away the footprints of people who walked there so no one could tell they'd ever existed. At this point, it felt as if father didn't exist anymore. He'd been erased. His mind went blank, as if all the thoughts, memories, and dreams had been sucked out. Survival made him put a protective wall up. If they institutionalized him, he'd be as forgotten as his father in a few years.

It wasn't Kain who had scared him. It was someone else. *Who was that other man?*

Logan fought the tears gathering at the corners of his eyes, nodding once. The man stared hard at him. His mouth thinned into a tight grin, as if he weren't used to smiling. "Good," he told the other two. "Let him sleep."

Later that week, while he lay in a netherworld caught between dreaming and waking, he saw his aunt's white face, his uncle's arm around her shoulders. The man was back. He heard the low rumble of voices, his uncle nodding, Minnie's cry before she covered her face with her hands.

When he finally awoke, he was alone with his aunt and uncle. The three of them looked at one another with silent assent that the subject was closed, and George's death would remain a family secret forever.

"Logan," his aunt said gently, bringing him back from the past.

He barely heard her until her voice changed. "Logan," she said more forcefully.

"I still don't like you going back there."

His skin prickled with a sense of unease. He shifted in his seat, the dark shadow of a vague threat hovering nearby. He closed his eyes, determined not to give in to it. He was safe now, he reminded himself, looking at his aunt's kind eyes. He took a deep shuddered breath. "Uncle Jack?"

His uncle looked up. "Yes?"

"Who was…?" He searched his aunt's and uncle's concerned faces and shook his head. "Never mind. I have a lot to do if I'm leaving today."

Logan picked up his leather jacket, marveling at the repaired tear near his arm.

"I took it from your room last night. You were dead to the world," Aunt Minnie told him.

After he hugged his uncle, Logan embraced his aunt warmly. "I'll be alright."

"Still… " Aunt Minnie started.

"I'm fine. I'm not afraid of what I'll find."

"That's not what I'm afraid of," Aunt Minnie said grimly.

He tossed his leather backpack into the rear of his jeep. It was an old one, his father's car. George had purchased it in the seventies while he was in graduate school. It was faded, dented, and beat up. Logan couldn't bring himself to sell it. It ran like a top and could do zero to sixty in a pinch. The thing had nine lives, was almost indestructible, but guzzled more gas than his eco-friendly mind liked to calculate.

Logan had called Elliot the previous night. He glanced at the dash to see it was almost eleven in the morning. He was picking up Elliot at LaGuardia in a couple of hours. Elliot had told him he'd catch the shuttle from Boston, where he was visiting his other half.

Logan and Elliot had both taught at Farmingdale College, researching for Professor Haversham in their free time.

Elliot had been in a long-distance relationship for two years and was waiting to see if his fiancé could transfer to Long Island.

Logan drove down the expressway, enjoying the crisp morning air. He stopped for coffee, deep in thought, memories of his father's last night distracting him. While he avoided thinking about his father's death, that conversation, the heated words, haunted him. He wished he hadn't snapped. He hated that it had ended up being their final exchange, the final memory he had of his father.

You can't change history, he thought bitterly. He remembered his younger self, replaying that night, wondering again how much of it was real or a product of the disordered mind of a nine-year-old. Could he have imagined the whole thing, the way Officer Kain had insisted?

Blinking, his eyes stinging, he saw her, his father's creature. He refused to give her an identity. He was sure of it, the bright yellow eyes as fresh in his mind, yet he still questioned his own memory. Hours of therapy had created a vast distance, blurring the image.

Logan reached for a cigarette, thought of Penny, crumpled the package, and threw it in the trash bag on the floor of the car. The smell of tobacco lingered on his hands the same way the feeling of unease clung to his skin. He blasted the radio, chasing the specters from the car. He sped past the lush farmland and hills filled with trees, barely noticing it, caught in his thoughts.

He pulled into LaGuardia Airport and waited on the same line as all the rideshare drivers picking up passengers. Elliot bounced out of the terminal, a smile on his face.

He was lanky, with a mop of curly brown hair that reached his shoulders. He wore jeans and a button-down shirt open at the neck, where he sported a leather cord with a Greek coin suspended from it. Elliot had found that coin when they were in the Aegean two years ago. He tossed his well-worn duffel in the open rear, then slid into the front seat.

"How's James?" Logan asked Elliot.

Elliot smiled, his white teeth gleaming. "Wonderful. The food tasting was amazing."

"Did you bring the cameras?" Logan questioned. They had to shout when they spoke since there was no buffer from the noise. It was like riding in a speedboat or open helicopter.

"Well, nobody's going to loan them to you anymore. I borrowed two of them from a friend. I scored a GoPro, but if you break this one, he'll have my hide." Elliot changed the subject. "There's a White Castle near here." His brown eyes were surrounded by a fan of lines reflecting hours of his skin being damaged by the sun. "Oh, come on." He rolled his eyes, throwing his head back dramatically. "I didn't have breakfast." He looked at Logan's shoulder, a question on his face. "Am I gonna see it?"

Logan smiled. He pulled aside a bit of his shirt from his neck, letting Elliot admire the partial view of the raptor tattooed on his shoulder.

"Color's off. You really should have waited until you had a picture."

"It's scabbing over, dude," Logan said. "You have to wait until it's completely healed. You don't know what you're talking about. I saw them. The chest feathers were as green as grass."

Elliot considered the flaking skin, then shook his head. "The legend says blue. Peacock blue."

"It flew right over me," Logan insisted.

"You're completely color blind, or you like to remember what you want to," Elliot said. Then continued, "I wish you'd managed at least one decent photo so I could prove to you how mistaken you are."

"I wish you managed to come with me and take the damn pictures. My hands were kind of occupied."

"Still," Elliot laughed. "I would have waited until I did a permanent ink."

"Maybe." Logan shrugged as if it didn't matter. "The tattoo can be fixed if I'm wrong," he said, then added, "Everything can be fixed." He thought about the last time he saw his father. "Well, almost everything."

"Then fix my hunger, man. I've been on the road since four. I'm *hangry!*"

Logan crossed over the highway heading for Northern Boulevard. "I'm not waiting on a long line," he warned, "so it's Mickey Dee's."

"Either way, I'm perishing!" Elliot shouted. "Hamptons, huh? Has to be something from the water." Elliot confirmed their destination.

Logan didn't answer him. He pulled into the drive-through, purchasing all of Elliot's fast-food fantasies.

Even without a roof, the car smelled of fried food. Elliot moaned in ecstasy.

"I know there is an aquarium out there. Did something wash up?"

Logan shook his head.

"Aren't you going to tell me? I left a warm bed and a willing—"

"Spare me your love life," Logan said loudly. "Mermaid." Logan swallowed, then was quiet.

"Mermaid… mermaid. I remember one they called the Mermaid of Minatuck?" Elliot asked, then seemed to realize something. "Oh, isn't that—?"

"Yep," Logan interrupted.

"They totally debunked that one," Elliot said.

"I know. I was there. They don't like to talk about it in the town."

"You'd think they'd use it to boost tourism. People love those kinds of stories." Elliot began another burger. He must have eaten three already.

Logan glanced at him.

"*What?* I said I was hungry."

"They don't like those old yarns about sea creatures. Not where I came from. They… never mind. It's not a popular belief there."

"Let me see what I can find." Elliot pulled his cell phone and started searching.

Soon they were cruising on the Long Island Expressway, driving east toward the Hamptons.

Elliot had to shout the information he found on Google. After a while, he got tired and stopped. "My eyes are burning." He observed the scenery. "It's nice out here," he said as they passed towns, the service road crammed with stores.

"If you like big box stores and strip malls," Logan responded.

They slowed near Jericho, traffic crawling for no reason. They moved at a slower pace, so conversation was easier. Music blared from cars around them, the sun made shimmering waves on the hoods of the surrounding vehicles.

"Hot," Elliot said, hiding a yawn behind his hand.

"Must be an accident." Logan searched the highway for an explanation of the traffic jam. "They'll stop just to look at what happened."

Elliot ignored him. He was back on his phone looking up information.

"There's not a lot of chatter anywhere about mermaid sightings on eastern Long Island… that is, except for yours," Elliot told him when they slowed right before a small knot of cars by some roadwork. He read silently for a while, then whistled softly. "Wow, you never talked about it." He looked over at Logan sympathetically. "I can see why."

"I still don't like to talk about it." Despite being in his field, that subject was usually off limits.

"There's the sighting in Haifa in Israel," Elliot offered. "I wish I could've gone on that trip."

Logan nodded. "Yeah, last summer. It was pretty well documented. A lot of witnesses. I interviewed a few."

Elliot was busy typing. "I read your notes," Elliot paused then added, "and Aimee's."

Logan looked away. "Yeah. It was one of our best trips."

It was quiet in the car for a bit.

Elliot laughed breaking the silence. "Did you know the Israelis offered a million bucks if anyone would bring proof?"

"Why do you think Aimee insisted we go there?" Logan responded with a cynical smile. "But you can't do much when you're investigating something for only a week."

"It would have been cheaper to research in the Hamptons."

"In the Hamptons, they'll probably give you a million dollars to keep your mouth shut," Logan said wryly.

"Have you noted any differences in the sightings?"

Logan thought for a minute. "The mermaid in Haifa appears always at sunset, never far from the surf... and is non-threatening."

"What do you know about your mermaid?" Elliot asked.

"First of all, she's not my mermaid. I don't know.... There have been some sightings. Nothing's been published about it. People make statements, then retract them right away. There are no descriptions. There's no rhyme nor reason to her."

"Logan, did you ever talk to Aimee about what happened?"

Logan stared straight ahead and shook his head. "No. She doesn't know."

"So, there's no chance she'll show up on this?" Elliot asked.

"There's nothing in the papers. I got the downlow from a friend. No, Aimee won't know anything about this. Hell, I don't know if I want to know anything about this!" He hit the steering wheel. "What is taking so long here?"

"Relax, Logan. It's just traffic. At least you can hear me read now."

They picked up speed, making conversation difficult.

"What?... What did you say? What do you remember about her?"

"Aimee?" Logan asked, his eyes distant.

"No, the Mermaid of Minatuck!"

"Nothing.... I remember nothing," Logan replied, but he knew Elliot couldn't hear him.

CHAPTER 6

"HOW COULD YOU want more food?" Logan asked after Elliot complained that he was starving. "We don't have time-"

"I'll die without sustenance. Besides, I'm sure you've got nothing for us for later."

Logan pulled off the exit ungraciously, insisting they use the drive-through window again at the first place they could find.

They finally stopped at a White Castle where Elliot ordered ten of the small burgers and ate them two at a time.

"You're disgusting," Logan said without heat. It was a long running joke between them, Elliot's insatiable appetite and Logan's lack of one.

"No, disgusting happens after digestion," Elliot replied with a smirk. "At least I function as a normal human."

"You're like a pygmy shrew. They can't go an hour without eating-"

"At least, I eat." Elliot would not be bested. He had two additional degrees in science, besides English Lit. "Your ancestor must be an olm. They can live up to ten years without eating." He pulled down his sunglasses to make eye contact. "How can you expect me to function on little to no sleep and not enough food?"

Elliot's food and alcohol consumption was legendary. After another food orgy, Logan continued his drive out east. Elliot slept in a belly-bomber coma.

Elliot could sleep in a pile of dung if he wanted. The man slouched back, put a hat over his eyes, and started snoring, whatever the circumstances.

Logan envied that ability. His own mind was constantly in high gear, as though it were afraid it would miss something.

An insistent beep of a horn interrupted his thoughts. He looked to the left to see a white Mercedes convertible in the next lane, the top down, and a blonde with expensive sunglasses behind the wheel. She was suntanned golden brown, and she kept turning her head to get Logan's attention. Logan looked at her, his first thought was that he didn't recognize her. She flicked off her glasses and winked at him. He looked at her with some regret and shook his head smiling. *Another time maybe.* He had sworn off women for now. His heart was too bruised from Aimee. Exhaustion always loomed nearby. He wasn't interested in resting either; there was too much to do. Too many places he needed to see.

He glanced over at Elliot, envious of the look of peace on his face. Much as Logan enjoyed research, there was a sinister side, almost a compulsion to do it. From the day he decided to dedicate his life to this field, he understood the risks. While it played an important role, he never let it slip over that edge into total consumption. At least, he told himself he wouldn't allow that. He had seen what that did to his father, and even Aimee. It was all about balance. Placing his hand on the steering wheel, he glanced at his friend. Elliot managed his career as well as a healthy personal life.

Logan grew thoughtful. He had friends, not that he saw any of them often. Aimee was difficult with people. Rather than force her, he lost touch with a lot of people, including Penny and Rory. He thought back to the last time he'd seen them. *Had it been two years?* Rory had been staying in Logan's place, but they hadn't spoken much. He knew Rory was struggling with his writing career, and the rejections were getting harder. He wished he'd taken the time to call him. But there were all these trips, then the breakup with Aimee, his classes. They were all busy. Each one of them had a life crammed with tons of activity he realized with sudden clarity, except for Rory.

"Did you ever really consider it?" Elliot asked, and Logan was pulled from his reverie.

"Who?"

"You know who, Aimee's people." Elliot spoke without taking the hat from his eyes.

"I thought you were sleeping," Logan said, and after a pause continued. "I told you then. Not my type of thing."

Elliot grunted and Logan went on. "It's not about the money."

"I know, bro. You don't have to tell me that." Elliot said.

It was never about the money. It was bigger than that. The past was never far from Logan's thoughts.

He needed to know: were his dreams the product of an overactive imagination, or were they based in reality? Did these strange and beautiful creatures really exist, or were they phantoms created to forget his father's alleged suicide? He clenched his fist. He knew in his heart the creatures that visited him at night were real. Logan opened his mouth to share his thoughts when a gentle snore made him laugh. He shook his head.

As soon as he could prove that they did indeed exist, Logan knew the elusive feeling of peace he envied would follow. *Validate and vindicate.* He could validate a new field of science and vindicate his father's reputation.

He rested his arm on the side window of the car. The sun beat down, warming his skin. Lost in thought, He looked up and smiled as a group of bikers formed a triangle behind him. They kept a steady pace, the roar of their engines like a group of jets. At times they seemed to be driving too closely. Logan sped up, watching as they increased their speed as well. He peered into his rearview mirror. Helmets with attached dark glasses obscured the bikers' faces.

Some instinct made his skin ripple. He really wanted a cigarette, but he had resolved, he reminded himself, to quit. He looked over to Elliot who slept on peacefully and wondered if he was being paranoid. Tapping his finger on the wheel, he fought feelings of panic. It had to be this place. It did it to him. He traveled into all kinds of dangerous situations, and never felt this sense of gloom.

Logan turned on the radio hoping the music would calm him. The radio spat back static. He twisted the knob, but the reception was spotty, at best. Impatiently, he shut it off.

Logan observed the bikers trying to define what was making him jittery.

They were all on Harleys—not choppers, fairly new models, the sunlight bouncing off the polished chrome. He watched the riders in the mirror, wondering what bothered him about this group. Perhaps it was their expressionless faces, the way they appeared to be communicating with subtle glances, or maybe… he thought it was about what wasn't there. There were no tandem riders, no girls. Logan considered the idea. Some gangs were just a bunch of guys…. Wait a minute, his mind raced. A gang. *Were they a gang?*

He looked up to see them hang back a car length. They weren't harassing him, but the dogged persistence in the way they kept pace with the jeep rattled him.

Logan was almost home… well, not home actually. He was approaching the Hamptons. His lower belly clenched tight, and his skin prickled.

The area had a way of reducing his confidence to a quivering pile of nothing. Each mile that brought him closer filled the car with impending doom. The Pine Barrens bracketed him, both sides of the highway becoming thickets of dense dark woods. It was quieter out here, as though the city were a million miles away.

Uneasiness trickled from his scalp to his spine, and while he was glad Elliot was next to him in the car, Sleeping Beauty did nothing to ease the tension Logan was beginning to feel.

Well, at the very least, I can catch up with Penny; her twin, Rory the idiot, when we find him; and Sly. Sly was an old family friend and owner of the scuba shop. Logan had spent a lot of hours with him and was looking forward to reconnecting. They hadn't seen each other in years.

Breathe, Logan told himself, sucking air in through his nose to fill lungs that felt compressed and stifled. His eyes were everywhere, but other than a doe grazing on the median, there was nothing. Pine trees, deer, a hawk coasting above him, no bogeyman, yet he could see his knuckles were white where he gripped the wheel. He loosened his hold with another deep breath and concentrated on the sparkling sunshine. He wasn't far from the sea. His nose twitched from the salty tang of the air.

Enjoy the serenity, he repeated like a mantra. *It's another job, just a job.* Israel, Turkey, Mexico—none of those places had unnerved him. He scanned the scenery. This was his occupation, he reminded himself. *I'm not afraid of anything I've explored in cryptozoology*, he said to himself, glancing at the bikers riding surrounding him. The road was wide open, he couldn't understand why they didn't use the opportunity to seize the highway. He reduced the speed of the jeep, his frown deepening when they slowed their pace as well.

Traffic was light. The tourist season hadn't started. Still, Logan couldn't quell the feeling of dread sweeping over him as the exit numbers grew higher.

The trees were clumped closer together. He recognized some burnt trunks from the incendiary blaze that had decimated the Barrens in '95. The fire had swept through, devastating fifty-five hundred acres as well as a dozen homes.

Logan was living in the Hamptons with his parents back then. He remembered the intensity of the flames, the destruction in the area. When he left in '97, it was a forest of blackened timber.

Time and nature had taken the Pine Barrens back. Logan felt the presence of the tall, dark trees towering over the road, guarding the beaches like silent sentinels. Increased clusters of deer nibbled grasses, darting into the shadows as his car passed. Dense groupings of overgrown bushes encroached on the land adjacent to the highway, blotting out the horizon, making Logan feel the weight of their growth. His world narrowed to those ominous trees and the miles of highway being eaten by his car as he propelled toward his past.

He fiddled with the radio again, but reception was still off. Elliot grumbled at the noise. Wiping his sweaty hand on his pants, Logan repeated to himself that he did this for a living and should feel right at home. It was just another coastline and another job.

By the time they turned onto Route 25, it was nearing five in the afternoon. He was relieved to see the group of bikes melting away. The single-lane road into the Hamptons was deserted but for his jeep. The constriction in his chest eased, and he realized he was being fanciful, what could they have possibly wanted with him?

It was Monday. Most of the weekend crowd had returned to their jobs in the city until the following weekend.

Logan had heard about all the wineries that had opened in the past twenty years. The land was perfect for growing grapes. Long fields of grapevines, the stunted trees held up by a series of wires, were on both sides of the road.

Soon he looked for the familiar signs of each town. The Moriches, Remsenburg, Quogue: each town held a memory.

Ice cream here, picking strawberries with his parents there. Renaissance fairs, fishing, the Hampton Bays were filled with sepia-tinted pieces of his past he thought long buried and forgotten.

Party rental trucks lined the westbound side of the road, a caravan of vehicles carting away the debris from wealthy inhabitants' gala-filled weekend. These were not his people, the folks he remembered. His friends were the fishermen who ran the marinas, the storekeepers from the many shops that sported everything from superior baked goods to the garbage they sold as antiques to the tourists.

Logan smiled as he passed the farm stands with their green cardboard cartons of luscious red tomatoes and fuzzy peaches. Sheep ate in the fields, their tender mouths mowing the lawns better than any machine. He fought the sweetness of memories, reminding himself of the homily that nostalgia was the way of remembering the past without any of the pain.

Despite fighting them, memories intruded. He replayed his feelings of hurt when his father had explained his mother's need to "find herself," leaving his eight-year-old self to live as a second child to his father's first love, his search for an undiscovered species.

He was a latchkey kid, a forgotten child, used to eating cereal for dinner while his father was lost in research or writing yet another paper. The Hamptons had no appeal for him. It stirred up the silt of his childhood, best left forgotten.

Logan's chest tightened with anxiety. The feeling of abandonment and neglect by his parents brought unwanted memories. Resentment formed a tight ball in the pit of his stomach, making him question why he actually cared about the perception of his father's death. Was this what it was really about? Did it matter that everyone thought his father committed suicide?

His father had been selfish, absorbed in his field, even a bit of a geek, but Logan knew, in spite of the fuzzy details, that his father did not jump into the water that night to take his own life. A driving need to prove it hummed to life from the center of his gut. He laughed at the bitter irony that his father's death was the reason he pursued the interests that had created havoc with his young life. He wondered what career path he might have chosen had his father lived, how different his life would have been.

It was just another coastline, another town. He said it like a mantra to himself, chasing the demons of his childhood away.

They passed two types of towns. The first contained small blocks of stores in Second Empire period buildings, their sad façades peeling; Italianate manors painted odd pastel colors; and old saltbox Colonials that were mostly home to tackle shops. Here and there, upscale eateries popped up, promising hand-rolled pasta or Thai specialties.

The other type of town was rich. Tightly packed storefronts with expensive shops were crammed with specialty items one can't live without. There was plenty of parking in these little towns. Women in short tennis skirts, carrying caramel lattes, climbed into sporty Mercedes convertibles, electric, of course, or oversized sports utility vehicles that needed ladders to scale the front seat. They raced down the two-lane road, driving too fast, next to the rusted pickup trucks or mud-splattered delivery vehicles of the locals.

Motels that looked like movie sets from the latest zombie

films popped up between the red barns and empty fields. Huge threshers sprawled across the farmland alongside bales of hay. Cows munched on feed in bucolic luxury.

Each town included a small police station, library, tall-steepled white church established in 1732 or thereabouts, and a cemetery sporting a biblical name with rows of crooked tombstones that sprouted on the grass like broken teeth.

Logan passed the local bait shop, followed by the diving rental store, his excitement growing when seeing Sly's building. He couldn't wait to visit him. He'd definitely get the lowdown on Rory, and maybe now Sly could give him a different perspective on his parents.

They had all been friends once upon a time. Logan never saw Sly after that fateful day when his father disappeared, but he kept up on him through Penny.

It had never occurred to Logan to ask Sly if he believed his father had committed suicide. Maybe he was afraid of what he'd hear. Perhaps if the truth didn't match his own, his whole world would be in question. He had trusted the old guy; at least he had when he was young. Trepidation lodged in his throat, but the search for the truth made him push open the door to his past.

Sly's shop was a town institution, supplying diving equipment to the area for over forty years. Logan pulled into the three-car parking lot, then glanced at Elliot, who slumbered on.

Sly was a crusty old sailor, maybe even an ex-Navy SEAL. Logan opened the door. A bell tinkled his arrival. The shop was barely three hundred square feet.

The wooden planked floor was worn away, bowed in

the center. A young kid no older than eighteen manned an ancient register. Photos of a tanned Sly in diving gear adorned the walls. Smiling celebrity faces shared the frames.

The clerk was ringing up a pair of guys with a load of equipment on the counter. The kid wore a torn tank top and cutoff shorts. Logan smiled when he saw his tanned feet were barefoot. He couldn't wait to take off his boots himself. Tanks were lined up behind the counter with manila tickets attached, identifying the rentals.

Logan waited patiently, perusing the black and white photos on the wall. He smiled at Sly's ruggedly tanned face and the huge Breitling watch on his thick wrist. Logan loved that watch. Sly had let him wear it whenever he came into the shop. He told him it was a sailor's watch. If you were lost at sea, it had a device to pinpoint your location.

Logan turned, spotted what he was looking for, and walked toward the corner of the room. It was there, just as he remembered, a picture of himself with Sly and his parents.

He'd never forget that day. Five-year-old Logan, his parents, and Sly on his boat, a bucket of chum between them. He leaned close, a chuckle escaping him. There, on his skinny wrist, the Breitling hung, along with Sly's worn captain's hat on his head. Logan's parents were gazing at him, their arms linked, his mother windblown and carefree in her peasant outfit, his father holding his ever-present notebook.

Sly had taken them whale watching, or something; Logan wasn't really sure. He remembered only the intensity of the sun and strong breeze that kept the boat ride lively. They had discovered a great white shark nursery. *Must have been the chum*, Logan mused, lost in the memory of the salty air and the sound of his parents' laughter.

"Can I help you?"

Logan looked up, surprised to see he was the lone customer in the shop.

"Where's Sly?" Logan moved toward the counter.

"Not here," the teen answered evasively. He glanced at a clock on the wall. "We're closing in five minutes."

"Oh." Logan pulled his lower lip. "I… never mind. You work for him?"

"Duh," was the snarky reply.

"Yeah." Logan bristled. "That's pretty obvious. Do you know when he'll be back?"

The clerk lowered his eyes and shook his head.

"Is everything okay?" Logan asked.

The boy paused, then said, "Yeah, perfect. Just tell me what you want, and I'll get it for you."

Logan flitted around the store, his eyes resting on the merchandise as if he could gather clues.

"Look." The kid slammed the drawer of the register. "I told you, he isn't here and I gotta close. Do you want to rent something or not?"

Logan shifted from foot to foot with uneasiness. "Well, okay, then," he said, finally giving his order.

Logan went over the items, every so often looking up to see the boy's troubled gaze. He ended up spending a small fortune on diving equipment, wetsuits, weighted belts, and underwater lights. At the last minute, he put two daggers with straps, on the countertop. The boy looked up at him. His eyes weary. Logan ordered it to be delivered to his back door early the next morning.

"Tell Sly I said hello," he called out as he left the building. The teen never answered. He turned to grab an ancient dial phone on the wall. Logan heard a muffled conversation as he slammed the door. He'd talk over the amount of the bill with Sly when the old man was in, he thought, dismissing the rude clerk. As he walked to his car, he saw the clerk flip the sign in the window to say *closed*.

Logan got in the car, smiling at Elliot, who had slept through the entire stop. He pulled out backwards, his grin fading when he saw a trio of Harleys parked at the side of the store. They were the same bikes that had appeared to be following him earlier. A large burly guy walked up the steps to the shop, opened the door and disappeared inside as though the sign didn't apply to him.

"Wow," Logan said.

"What?" Elliot asked sleepily.

"I'll tell you later," Logan muttered to himself.

Logan took off through the main street of the town, his eyes darting to the mirror to see if the bikes were behind him. He took a quick left, the layout of the local streets coming back to him as though he'd never left. He made several turns, knowing his confusing route took him out of the way, but he relaxed once he realized he was not being followed.

Lost in thought, he crossed over Pickett's Bridge, the water to the right, an eagle's nest on the top of a tall pole. He slowed. The predator stared at him as he passed, the ripped shreds of its meal hanging from its beak. The squiggly coastline revealed one of the many bays and inlets of the Hamptons. Tall grasses grew in abundance, waving from the dull-colored waters.

Logan knew each waterway like the lines in his hand. He had swum and fished in them with Rory and Penny. He slowed to a crawl, knowing Cowpath Road was up ahead.

A row of aluminum mailboxes gathered on a corner like neighbors discussing a crime scene. He made a right onto the road, hearing the crunch of gravel and rocks as he drove down its long, twisting blacktop.

Elliot stirred as Logan turned into the old beach house.

"We're here," Logan said, looking at his former home.

It had sea-green shingles with an old roof that sagged in the middle. Glancing up, Logan wondered if he cared enough about the place to fix it or if he should let nature take it back.

Low and squat, it had been built seventy years ago as a bungalow vacation home. He knew his father hadn't paid much for the place when he'd purchased it in the seventies. It was dilapidated then. The story went that his mother fell in love with it. It was a perfect retreat for her painting. She was an artist.

Logan's memories were always of the scent of patchouli; long, dangling silver earrings; flowing skirts; and oversized tie-dyed peasant blouses. She had rippling wheat-colored hair and looked completely at odds with his buttoned-up professor dad.

George Osbourne wore khaki pants and drab-colored shirts as a uniform when he wasn't teaching. While he was in school, tweeds covered him from head to toe, often competing for domination to swallow him whole. He had a funny gray mustache that sat on his lip like a contented caterpillar. He was the epitome of an absentminded professor, and a part of Logan was not surprised when his fey mother left his dowdy father.

Yet memories of her sitting on the floor, a rapt expression on her face listening to his father speak, teased him. She was much younger than her husband, but Logan remembered… he remembered her saying she loved to learn, and George was full of engaging stories. They had met in school. She was a student. Logan shook his head, thinking of the inappropriateness of it. He couldn't imagine falling in love with a student. Maybe that's why the marriage ended badly.

The surf crashed noisily behind them, bringing Logan back into the present. He stood on the sun-heated sand, looking at the perimeter of the property. Low bushes that never seemed to grow hid the foundation of the house he knew was cracked. His uncle wanted the place demolished, said it was nothing but a bad luck house. Once Logan became of age, Uncle Jack handed him the keys and told him he'd be better off selling the cottage as is or taking a wrecking ball to it.

Seagulls screamed, diving low, as if threatening him for trespassing. The garden was overgrown, the window screens black with filth. He turned to face the street, Elliot following him. Three motorcycles raced down the block. He ducked behind the corner of the house, pulling Elliot with him. He was sure they slowed as they passed his home. He waited until the roar of their engines grew fainter.

"You know them?" Elliot asked.

Logan shrugged and made his way to the front of the house. "No." He turned to scoop up a handful of flyers in indestructible plastic sleeves that littered the front stoop. The screen door was stuck. He pulled at it, but it wouldn't budge.

"Kick it," Elliot added helpfully.

"I would if that would work," Logan answered.

Putting his shoulder into it, Logan yanked hard, and the rusted aluminum screeched noisily as it gave way. An avalanche of restaurant take-out menus cascaded onto his feet.

Elliot grabbed one. "Yum, sushi." He read the folded paper. "And they deliver."

Logan dug into his pocket, producing an old key, and opened the door. "We can Door Dash if you're hungry again. There's a place in town I want to take you, maybe tomorrow. You're going to love it. They have the best fried clams on the island." Logan's face grew dark. "Rory and I loved that place."

He saw Elliot watching him with a frown.

"Are you OK?" Elliot asked.

Logan took a minute before he answered. He ran a hand through his long hair. "I'm hoping that Rory is holed up somewhere with this girl."

"I'm sure he's fine. Anyway, I'm in."

"You're in?"

Elliot smiled, "The clams. The clams." He pushed past him, groaning when he entered the vestibule. "It's freakin' hot in here. Turn on the air."

It was stifling inside, with the stuffy smell of ratty carpet. Venetian blinds obscured the outside world. An old television with rabbit ears stood opposite a faded Naugahyde couch, its surface cracked and peeling.

"What air? Open some windows," Logan said quietly.

"How can you not have air conditioning?"

"I lived with a teacher and a free spirit. They believed in creatures, not creature comforts."

"That explains a lot."

Logan turned around. "Like what?"

"Like how nothing rocks you. It's like you're used to roughing it."

"I wouldn't call this roughing it."

Elliot took a long look around the shabby room and laughed. "I would. Is there electricity in this dump?"

Logan shrugged. "Should be. I left the utilities running. Rory liked to crash here."

Elliot threw his bag onto a recliner and asked, "What now?"

"Open the blinds," Logan said.

Logan searched the house, beginning with the living room. Someone had dusted recently. The tile smelled of pine cleaner. He saw the back door had been opened, the shade raised. While his friend let the warm sunlight into the rest of the cottage, Logan walked through the rooms, his face as shuttered as the house.

His father's bedroom had been straightened up. The bed was made. The cabbage-rose bedspread covered the queen-sized bed as though the old man were returning tonight. The room had an odd quality of a museum, like those staged quarters when they sell a house.

Logan walked over to the hulking antique roll top desk in the corner of the room. It looked like a relic from the Victorian age. He played with the slats, rolling them backwards to reveal his father's last workspace.

Neat piles of blank paper stared up at him. He picked up a square milk carton cut in half and covered with shells that he had made for his dad for Father's Day when he was in elementary school. The scalloped shells were glued in great translucent globs, carefully stuck to the cardboard container. One of the shells dangled, then fell onto the rust-colored shag rug. It created a vacant space on the crowded surface of the carton, looking like a smile that had lost a tooth. He touched the spot where the shell had been, feeling only the grainy remnant of the old glue. Loneliness swept through him, making his breath catch. He wondered if he looked down on the carpet whether he'd find pieces of himself littering the floor.

Vague memories flitted through his mind like an old-time movie projector. He saw himself giving the gift to George for Father's Day and making a cake with his mother. He remembered the table was covered with unlikely ingredients. She had humored his five-year-old imagination by baking a gummy worm confetti cake. The table was dusted with flour, gummy worms dangling from the edge, the confetti sprinkles dotting the floor as if a party had occurred.

He looked out the window and saw them all seated on an old army blanket, celebrating the day as the sun dipped into the ocean. He asked his father if the water doused the heat of the rays, recalling how he had pulled him onto his lap and explained the rotation of the earth in a way he could understand it.

They had watched the stars pop out that night and sat in wonder with the idea that the earth was always traveling, circling the sun so that the view was ever-changing. "Don't ever take life for granted," his father told him as he stroked his head. Logan looked up sleepily, a question in his eyes. "As long as the earth spins, you can look out your window and see something new. Never lose that curiosity."

Logan stood in the kitchen twenty-three years later, his eyes drifting shut as he tried to remember how his parents had looked. Was the timbre of his mother's voice high or low? She had long hair the same color as the shafts of pampas grass growing rampant on the beach. Had his father always been silver-haired? Could his hair have been as brown as Logan's own? He knew he had his father's eyes, but he couldn't recall the exact color of his mother's. There was not a single photo of her left in the house. He was sure Aunt Minnie had one somewhere. He'd have to ask to see it when he went back to the farm.

The desk was filled with rows of small compartments and secret drawers. He ran his fingers down the smooth wood until he located a lever. It creaked loudly, then gave when he pressed it, springing open. A smile tugged at his lips. A stale Tootsie Roll lay inside the hidden spot, just where his father always hid them for him to find when he was a child.

That desk had always been crammed with mountains of papers, stacked and stuffed on the entire surface. Now it looked abandoned, the blank sheets wiping it clean of its history. *Oh, the stories this desk hid in its many drawers and compartments*, he thought with a wry grin.

Notes and illustrations, photos and newspaper articles had cascaded from the desk's surface. It was a vast storehouse that had contained everything that had been valuable to his father. Now it stood naked and empty, with a history that had been wiped clean.

Logan looked around the room, wondering who had

taken his father's journals and why. There were dozens of note-books, huge boxes filled with thousands of pages. He hadn't thought about them in ages. After he'd left this place, he told Uncle Jack and Aunt Minnie he never wanted to come back again. He didn't want anything the house had to offer.

Who had taken all his father's work? What value did it have to anybody? After all, they all said his old man was a crackpot, and if he hadn't killed himself, there was a nice padded room with his name on it over at Cedar Haven.

Elliot poked his head in. "Nice place. Why didn't we ever stay here during spring break?"

Logan placed the childlike pen container down carefully on the desk. "You can take my old room."

"Cool. I like the *Star Wars* bedspread."

Logan smiled, his face looking boyish. "Who'd you have, Inspector Gadget?"

"How'd you know? … Whose room was this?" Elliot opened a door at the end of the hall.

"Leave it!" Logan ordered a minute too late. The warped door screamed as rusty hinges squealed open.

His mother's easels and art equipment lay in dusty piles. A shrouded piece of furniture was shoved haphazardly in the corner.

Elliot looked back at him with a question in his eyes. He cocked his head. "You're creeping me out, dude."

Logan cleared his throat. "It was my mother's studio. We never went in there after she left." He walked over to the lin-en-draped piece, pulling off the cloth, revealing an old sewing machine. "She used to do craft projects with this." He ran his hand along the smooth side of the antique Singer. He tapped the pedal with his foot, and the machine jumped to life, the bobbin moving up and down, the noisy gears filling the room.

"Officially creepy. What is that, like a hundred years old?"

"Probably more. It belonged to her grandmother." Logan glanced around the room again, then said, "Just close it up."

They walked out toward the kitchen. The screen door slammed with a whack. A petite girl with an ivory braid hanging down her slim back stood in the doorway, her face hesitant. Her mixed heritage was evident with her caramel skin. She had her father's Nordic hair and her Caribbean mother's chocolate eyes. She wore a beige uniform indicating she was local police.

Those eyes were red now, her skin blotchy. It didn't take a detective to know she had been crying. She carried a bag of groceries in her hand, a notebook in the other. Her wide mouth broke into a winsome smile. Her chin wobbled with emotion.

Logan grinned warmly as she entered the room. He saw relief and something else on her face. He could feel her tentativeness. He watched her glance at Elliot, then back at Logan, her emotions sliding back in check.

"I figured you were going to need this." She held out a plastic bag filled with necessities.

Elliot relieved her of the groceries. "I'll take care of it." He exchanged a look with Logan and left the room.

"Put the milk in the fridge. I came here this morning and cleaned it up a bit," she added to his retreating back.

"Henny Penny," Logan said affectionately, calling her by her nickname, holding out his arms to her.

"The sky is falling," she responded, walking into his embrace. She fit under his chin.

He hugged her, feeling her quaking body.

"It's alright. We'll find him." Logan heard a sob that was quickly suppressed.

"I don't think so. Not anymore. I'm scared for him."

Logan clasped her hand; his fingers caressed her thumb. He looked down at her hard-bitten nails. Penny pulled them away, hiding them in her pockets.

"Your parents?" Logan asked as he sat down.

Penny joined him on the sofa. She shrugged. "Mom has hope." She looked away. "Dad thinks… " She swallowed convulsively, her eyes brimming with tears.

"What does Kain say?... No, never mind. I don't want to know. Is the meathead still working there?"

"Mitch?" Penny asked. "Yes. I forgot about your history with him."

"How could you forget?" Logan stood and paced the room. "He tortured Rory and me for years."

"He's not so bad now. He's just a big stupid lummox. He keeps asking me out." Her lips turned up in a mischievous smile.

"Really?" Logan felt his chest tighten. "Did…?" He paused at even asking the question. "Did you go out with him?"

Penny laughed. "Don't be silly. I made it clear I'm not interested. Why? Would it bother you if I did?" She searched his face.

Logan cleared his throat. "Of course not. Why would it bother me? You can go out with whomever you want."

Penny picked at her fingernails, her voice small. "Oh, that was a while ago anyhow." She shrugged. "He leaves me alone now. He's not a bully anymore."

Logan snorted with disbelief.

Penny went on. "I can handle him. Anyway, I'm sick with worry about Rory. He's all I can think about."

"Rory will show up like he usually does." Logan kissed the top of her head, trying to reassure her.

Penny leaned backwards to take a look at the long scrape marring his jaw. She reached up to touch it with her fingertips. "That's nasty."

Logan ducked his head self-consciously. "It's nothing. Don't make a big deal of it."

Her eyes went soft, and her lips shifted into a sweet smile. "Looks like you got dragged ass-backwards down Main Street again."

"Ass-backwards?" Elliot asked.

"Not one of Rory and my more successful stunts."

"What did you guys do?" Elliot joined them in the living room.

"Shhh." He held a finger to his lips. "Don't want to talk about it. They never caught us."

Penny's smile faded. "Shall we get down to business?"

They all sat on the ancient couch. Penny sighed, recounting what she knew. "They are planning to hush it up again." She brushed a tear from her eye.

"I thought you said they wouldn't be able to," Logan responded.

"Rory's a local. They're saying he took off because he couldn't find work."

Logan's lips turned downward. "He's done that before. Many times."

"His sneaker was on the beach." She covered her face with

her hands. "I've seen lots of things in this job. This totally unnerved me."

"There could be an explanation for that," Logan told her.

She took a shuddering breath. "I've prepared myself, Logan. I had to." She looked out the window, her dark eyes bleak. "Nobody seems to care about his companion. I thought they would, but her husband acted kind of relieved. He didn't even file a report. He said she probably left with Rory."

"You talked about blood on the beach?" Logan prodded.

Penny was silent for a minute. "Everything's gone. The report and anything related to it. But I saw it. It's all stored up here." She pointed to her head.

"That's not going to help," Elliot responded, walking back to the kitchen. They heard the fridge open and the sound of a beer opening. "Want some?"

Penny ignored him.

"No thanks. Was there a witness?" Logan asked.

"I can't get to him anymore. His parents won't let me talk to him."

"What about the chief of police?" Elliot asked as he walked into the room and fell onto the sofa.

Penny looked up at him, then turned to Logan with a question in her face. "Oh, sorry. Elliot, Penny; Penny, Elliot. Elliot goes everywhere with me."

"Mexico?" Penny asked.

"Not there, but Alaska and Hawaii," Logan said slowly.

"Don't forget the China Sea. Yeah, this time I had to go to the food tasting for my wedding," Elliot added helpfully.

Penny paused. Logan said, "Anything you want to tell me you can say in front of Elliot."

"This morning Kain informed me the case was closed. Permanently," Penny said, her voice cracking.

"Like that is he?" Elliot asked.

"Red Kain's older than dirt, and covered by it too," Penny spat.

"He was the officer in charge when my dad disappeared. He wasn't helpful then either. Seen anything unusual lately?"

"But he's not a real policeman," Elliot stated.

Logan and Penny exchanged looks. "It's a private police force, overlooked by the town. There is a Suffolk County precinct not far from here, but generally they leave it up to the locals to oversee everything."

"That's crazy," Elliot said.

"Think of us as constables," Penny said with a shrug. "The chief is elected and then he hires his force." Penny produced a black and white marble notebook.

"Who do they report to?" Elliot was never one to let things go.

Both Penny and Logan gave him a pained look.

"Talk about older than dirt," Elliot laughed pointing to the notebook. "Is that from grade school?"

Logan glanced up, his face alert as the sound of a group of motorcycles intruded on the street. He peeked around the blinds to look out the window. He motioned for Penny to come join him. "You know them?"

She shook her head. "Never saw them before. They're not from here. I could ask Mitch." She bit her bottom lip.

"Mitch? Why?" Logan asked, his mind returning to earlier that day trying to see if he recognized any of the bikers

"He has a bike and rides with some friends but only on the

weekend. We don't get a lot of bikers, so he stands out a little bit. They do pass through occasionally but don't stay here."

They watched them turn down the street. Penny wrote something in her book. "That's not him. I know his bike. I'll run their plates."

They returned to sit on the old couch. Penny put the notebook on the table. Her head was down, her shoulders slumped. Logan looked at the straight part of her hair, thinking she looked so vulnerable, so young. He reached out to squeeze her hand reassuringly.

"You said there was a witness?" Logan asked.

She nodded. "Some high school kid on Patricia Lane. He was walking his dog."

"Give me his info," Logan said.

Penny jotted it down on a scrap of paper.

"David Wagner." He read the information aloud to confirm it. "Old-timers?"

Penny smiled. "They are fairly new. They redid the old Shelby place."

Logan nodded. He knew exactly where they lived.

"Speaking of old-timers," Logan said, "I stopped by Sly's shop. Has a kid working there."

"Robbie, a grubby looking guy?" Penny asked.

"Yeah, well, I asked him where Sly was, and he was downright strange. Anything going on?"

Penny sighed. "Sly took off a couple months ago. Hasn't come back. Chief said he was visiting his sister down in Key Biscayne or something. You know Sly, he's always going somewhere."

A stray thought niggled at his brain but flitted away before he could grab it.

Penny inched closer to him, placing her head on his shoulder. He watched her close her eyes, letting her stay there for a long moment. She sat up, turned to face him as if she needed to share something, then picked up her book again, her voice all business.

"I've been working on this awhile. I spent a lot of time at the library going through the local flyers from the last two decades. I made a chart. You recall when your dad died, there was a surge of house pets—dogs and cats—going missing. Like four or five all at once."

Logan shook his head. "I don't remember anything like that."

"Well, I went back and checked. Four families along the beach lost pets. Three dogs and a cat, a couple of nights before your father's incident."

"Pets don't generally run into the surf, especially cats," Logan said quietly.

"My brother wasn't swimming either," Penny said.

Elliot stretched his bare feet onto the coffee table, making himself comfortable.

"You don't know that, Penny. What's a mermaid going to do, get out of the water, hop up, and pull him into the surf?" Elliot asked. "The ones observed in Haifa come in with the tide and are pulled back out with the water. They can't walk and are actually quite helpless. They are harmless."

Penny looked up. "Who says it was a mermaid?"

"Well, I assumed when you called Logan, that's what you were going for," Elliot said.

"Have you seen one?" she demanded.

"Not yet," Elliot snapped. "Not for lack of trying," he added with a slight chuckle and a look at Logan. "He spent a week last summer on a beach in Haifa waiting for one to wash up."

"It isn't funny. That thing pulled Logan's father into the water," Penny shot back, her face dark with anger, her eyes hurt.

"I'm not sure of what I saw," Logan said. "They told me I had a wicked concussion. I might have dreamed the whole thing."

"Then why do you keep searching for them?" Penny asked. "If you believe in something long enough, it becomes true." Penny dashed a tear from her cheek.

Elliot laughed. "That is the biggest crock of—"

"Stop," Logan said. "I might have seen a mermaid. I'm not sure. For a while I thought I was crazy, and I wanted to know if other people had seen things too. Maybe it has something to do with my dad.… I don't know. More than likely Rory and the woman could have met with foul play, a robbery or something. Maybe the disgruntled spouse did something. The missing animals could have run away or been hit by a car, even poisoned. The list goes on and on."

"If they were poisoned or hit by a car, we'd have found their bodies. You don't believe that," Penny said quietly. "I know you… and I don't know you." She nodded to Elliot. "One thing I am sure of is that you both don't believe that; otherwise, you wouldn't go playing Indiana Jones all the time."

They sat silently, and nobody talked.

"Look," Penny stated, "I checked the records. In July of 2002, a vagrant disappeared. They thought he might have just left. But I knew him. He liked it here. He wouldn't have gone without saying goodbye. I nosed around and discovered there was a rash of missing animals, on the other side of the estuary. Then it happened again when the rookie I told you about disappeared. The same thing, missing house pets."

Logan sat back.

"They were all from homes backing the sound. For a while they were saying we might have a rogue alligator or a coyote loose."

"But there are no coyotes or alligators on Long Island," Elliot added helpfully. "Why hasn't anyone else brought this up?"

Penny looked at Elliot. "This is a tourist town. We depend on people spending summers here. Each time an episode happened, it was around the first week of July, the height of rentals. Nobody wants to ruin the town's financial prospects. What?" she asked Logan, who was pulling his lip thoughtfully.

Logan's shrug ended in a slight shudder. He said, "When I was in the hospital, I remembered another person, a man. Not from here, a stranger. I don't know where he came from, but he kept at me until I was so confused, I wasn't sure what had happened. The weird thing is, I just remembered that the other day. For a long time, I thought it was only Chief Kain."

Elliot whistled *The Twilight Zone* theme song, breaking the tense atmosphere of the room, then announced he was ordering sushi and asked who wanted what.

CHAPTER 7

DISCARDED CARTONS LITTERED the coffee table. Logan, Elliot, and Penny sat on the floor eating with chopsticks, the heavier feeling from before having dissipated.

"My guess is we don't have Wi-Fi here," Elliot said as he left for the kitchen.

"We'll use my cell as a hotspot," Penny replied.

Elliot returned with a dusty bottle of wine, which Penny politely refused. "On duty, later."

Her belt and holstered gun lay on the edge of the couch where she had placed it. She sat back, pushing her half-eaten carton of food away. A notebook sat on the table beside her right hand.

"The night Rory disappeared, what was the date?" Logan asked, sipping a nice red from a paper cup.

"It was Saturday the ninth." Penny wiped her face with the paper napkin.

"The ninth. I was on my way home from Arizona. Elliot, google it. See if it was a supermoon."

"Supermoon? There was no moon that night at all. I remember it was dark as pitch." Penny shook her head, her hand thoughtfully pulling on her braid.

"Yup," Elliot called looking up from his phone. "New moon. It was the fourth supermoon this year."

"What does that mean? Sounds like something out of a comic book," Penny said.

"A 'Supermoon' refers to a full moon and the closeness of its orbit. When the moon reaches its perigee—"

"English please?" Penny pleaded.

"It's closest point to Earth in its monthly orbit," Logan explained.

"It comes to about 224,000 miles from here," Elliot murmured.

"You two are such geeks. You probably never get laid." Penny smiled sweetly.

"I'm engaged," Elliot replied defensively.

"You still probably never get laid." Penny laughed huskily for the first time since they'd arrived. "So why is that important?"

Logan smiled at her, his teeth flashing white, then turned to Elliot.

"Check the tide charts," Logan ordered. "You see, when the moon is that close, it plays havoc with the tides."

"Like how?" she asked.

"For a girl brought up around the water, how could you not notice that? Supermoons are responsible for unusually high tides. Give me the exact dates of the other disappearances."

Penny tore them from a page in her notebook, then handed it to Logan.

"What kind of moon was July 3rd, 2002?" Logan asked.

"The night the vagrant disappeared," Penny whispered.

Elliot snatched the paper from Logan. "Full moon," he said, then added without being asked, "Spring tide and full moon." He typed some more, then looked up at them. "It was a supermoon as well."

"It wasn't in the spring. It happened in July," Penny interrupted.

"Spring tide as in jump or burst forth," Logan explained. "The spring tide brings the most extreme tides and always happens around the full or new moon."

Elliot whistled softly. "It wasn't just a spring tide; it was a perigean spring tide. An extra-large tide." He typed furiously and then turned to face them. "It was the same on each night of the incidents." He caught Logan's eyes. "Even yours."

"What does it mean?" Penny asked, standing up.

"It means we are seeing a pattern." Elliot closed his laptop with a snap. "Ready?" he asked Logan.

"Ready for what?" Penny looked at Logan, her dark eyes shadowed. She stood, grabbing her belt from the couch. Logan watched as she strapped it on. She paused, and they stared at each other, the silence heavy in the room.

"We're going to take a walk on the beach. Where are you going?" Logan replied.

"I'm on duty," said Penny.

"Be careful," Logan responded.

Penny stopped where she was walking, turned to face him, and replied. "No, you be careful. Knowing what we know, isn't walking on the beach dangerous?"

Logan put his arm around her. "Danger's my middle name, ma'am." He casually walked her to the door.

Penny leaned into him; her fingers fiddling with the button of his shirt. Their chests almost touching, their breathes intermingling.

Penny asked, "I'm afraid for you. I don't want anything to happen to you."

"I'll be careful," Logan said. "I know what I'm doing."

"I'm glad you're here," she told him, her eyes meeting his.

"Ditto," Logan replied, meaning it, squeezing her hand.

"I know this was hard for you. You know, coming back here." Penny looked at the floor.

Logan tipped up her chin, so their eyes met. "There's nothing I wouldn't do for you or Rory."

He searched her face and saw something new there. She seemed shy with him, and they had a minute when the silence felt too heavy. Logan cleared his throat to say something to fill the void, but Penny spoke first.

"I have to leave," she said, glancing at her watch. She turned toward the screen door, and Logan grabbed her wrist gently, pulling her back.

"Penny? Did you say Sly went to Florida to visit his sister?"

"Yes," she replied.

Logan shook his head. "He couldn't have."

"I'm sure that's what Chief Kain said. Why?"

"His sister died the year before my… a year before my mom left and my father died."

"How could you remember that?" Penny looked at him. "You barely remember anything from those days."

"I remember it because we were with Sly when he scattered her ashes at sea. He said she had a wasted life, that she'd missed all her opportunities for happiness."

"Are you sure?"

Logan nodded. "I'll never forget it. My mom booked out the next morning."

Penny thought for a moment and replied, "Maybe he was visiting her kid… you know, a niece or nephew?"

"No, she didn't have any. He sold everything in Florida. He told us all about it. It was like she was erased from the planet, and it made him sad. He is not in Florida."

"Then where is he?" Penny whispered, her eyes huge.

"I'm not sure." He took her hands and looked her straight in the face. "Keep your eyes open and be aware of everything."

"I could say the same to you. I've been trained to protect myself."

He leaned in and hugged her, missing her expression. Penny clung to him with an intensity. He gave her a reassuring squeeze then held her at arm's length. "We'll find him, Penny."

Penny opened her mouth as if she was going to respond. Instead, she turned and ran down the front stoop.

Logan stalked to his room and rummaged through his backpack looking for his cigarettes. Elliot passed by, a towel around his neck.

"Lose something?"

Logan thought about all his losses, his parents, his cousin, Aimee. He dropped his bag. "Nah." He shook his head remembering he'd thrown them away in the car. He'd have to keep in the mind the difference between losing something and tossing it away.

CHAPTER 8

THE SUN WAS making its slow descent into the western horizon, painting the sky pink with streaks of apricot.

"She's got it bad for you," Elliot told Logan as they left the house.

"Who? Penny?" Logan looked at his friend. "Nah, she's like my sister." The minute the words left his mouth, he felt his face flush. It didn't feel like his sister when she was going to work.

"I don't think so, bro."

"No way." Logan brushed off the thought with a twinge of guilt. "I've sworn off females since Aimee. She annihilated me."

"Ah, the fair *Ah-mee*." Elliot nodded.

"Besides, her brother would kill me," Logan added. He felt his gut twist with the thought of something hurting

Rory. "He's alive. I'm sure of it. Rory was never responsible. He takes off every now and then, disappearing for a bit. He writes books. He's probably locked away somewhere in the middle of a story."

"What about the woman who went missing?"

"The best-case scenario is that she is with him," Logan said hopefully. "It's not like it hasn't happened before."

"Still, there's blood on the beach and his sneaker," Elliot persisted.

"You know, El, sometimes you're really annoying," Logan said, walking faster.

"Where are we going?" Elliot trotted after Logan behind the house.

A rusted swing set took up a corner of the yard on one side, a small shed on the other.

Elliot stopped in his tracks and whistled softly. He stood still taking in the entire ocean lapping against the shore. "This is awesome. The Atlantic Ocean is your backyard." He turned to look at the dilapidated house, then the view behind it.

"It may not look like Disneyland, but the view is incredible." Logan smiled.

The yard opened up to reveal a sprawling coastline, the churning water changing from dark blue to a lighter foamy green when the waves met the beach. White sea caps curled toward the shore. The warm wind caressed their faces.

Logan held his hand over his eyes, scanning the horizon. Far out, they could see the freighters bobbing on the waves. Seaplanes crisscrossed the sky. They both looked up, instinctively ducking when the rotor of a helicopter flew over their heads. The water sparkled like it had been dusted with diamonds.

Exchanging a grin with Elliot, Logan smiled, thinking of the flapping leathery wings, knowing his friend would be thinking about it too. "I wish you had been there."

"I wish I could have been there too. I can't believe you didn't take the egg."

Logan shook his head. "Come on, Elliot. You don't mean that. We would never destroy a habitat."

It was quiet between them for a minute, and Logan knew they were both thinking of Aimee.

"She would've taken it," Elliot said, his voice angry.

"Maybe not," Logan said too quickly.

"You're such a sap. You would've given it to her," Elliot laughed.

"You would have stopped me."

It was like that between the two of them. They could pick up on each other's train of thought as though they had been together forever. Logan enjoyed Elliot, and he knew Elliot felt the same way about him. They had an easy friendship, the kind not often found. If he ever had a kid, he'd probably name him Elliot, he liked the guy that much.

"What could I do? I had the tasting."

"Oh yeah, *the tasting*," Logan said with exaggeration. "You missed the discovery of the century to eat rigatoni ala vodka… like you don't know what it tastes like," he said with a laugh.

"Hey, it was mac and cheese with lobster, okay? And it tasted great."

"I'm surprised you left the chocolate fountain to join me, now."

Elliot grumbled a response, but Logan didn't hear him. He trotted closer to the shore.

They walked about a quarter of a mile down the beach; their feet sinking in the warm sand.

"Here." Logan paused, pulling out a handful of plastic bags and sealed swabs they used for retrieving DNA. "You hold them. They're annoying me."

"Do you always walk around with specimen packets?" Elliot said, grabbing the envelopes.

"You never know when you're going to run into Bigfoot."

Elliot tried to stuff them into assorted shirt pockets. They didn't fit, so he held them in his hands as he walked. "If we're looking for mermaids, we're supposed to go *in* the water."

Logan was already twenty feet ahead of him, lightly jogging on the sand.

"If we are going in, we'll need diving equipment," Elliot called, trying to catch up.

"It's being delivered tomorrow." Logan turned to face him but continued walking backwards.

Elliot shoved the remaining specimen envelopes into the pocket of his cargo shorts. "Where's the estuary? This looks like open sea." Elliot observed the coastline.

Logan oriented himself from east to west. "The old lighthouse is down that way." He pointed in a direction where the water narrowed, the beach becoming grassier, almost marsh-like. The lighthouse stood on a spit of land in the middle of the water. It was constructed of red brick and had a huge panoramic window with three-hundred-sixty-degree views.

"How old is that?" Elliot asked, pulling off his sunglasses.

"It was built in the early eighteen hundreds, but it's been refurbished over the years."

"I bet you saw some good times in that place." Elliot smiled.

"Don't you know it. We," Logan swallowed hard and continued. "Rory and I painted the bulb red one year. They never caught us." Logan stopped, stuck on a memory, then said, "The estuary is—"

"I see where it starts. The estuary. Is that where it happened with your father?"

"Yes. It's that narrow inlet that opens up to the sea." Logan gestured in the direction of the reedy marsh.

Logan started walking down the beach. Houses lined the dunes. Most were on stilts, new construction rebuilt bigger and better after Hurricane Sandy had washed away their old homes.

The house next door to his cottage was completely new, a McMansion, gray-shingled with turrets and a copper dolphin weathervane, green from corrosion by the salty air and moving with the breeze from offshore.

Logan whistled softly at the long jetty and fancy toys bobbing in the water at the end of the pristine dock. There was a Sea Ray that must have cost a pretty penny. Attached were four Jet Skis in primary colors.

"Rich neighbors?" Elliot asked.

"New people. Many are buying the old homes and putting up these monstrosities."

"Why didn't you sell this place? I bet the land is worth megabucks," Elliot said.

Logan shrugged. "I never thought about it."

"You should. I would."

"I know you would. You're not sentimental about anything." It was a long-standing feud between them. Logan for all his bravado was a softie, while Elliot was the more cynical of the two. "Besides, you were brought up around this. You would know what to do with it."

"You bet I would. You could travel on your own dime instead of taking those crappy jobs in the summer."

"I like those crappy jobs."

"And meet crappy people like Aimee to break your heart."

"She didn't break my heart," Logan said and then added when he saw Elliot's expression, "She just bruised it a bit."

"If that's what you want to call it. Still..." Elliot said, admiring the mass of windows and patio doors of the large house facing the water. "You could take a mortgage on the land, build a party palace, and rent it out. You might be able to give up your day job."

Logan shook his head. "And give up working with you?" Logan compared the two houses and said in a more serious voice, "In all honesty, I never thought about it."

It now occurred to him that he'd never even checked on the house after the last hurricane until Rory called and told him the house was fine. Not that he cared. It could have been completely washed away, and he wouldn't have known. Rory offered to clean up the debris and then asked for him to reconnect the utilities. He knew Rory stayed there from time to time, especially when he was working on a project.

Logan turned and looked at his dwarfed cottage, the shingles from another century, the rusted swing set. It looked abandoned. He was lucky he didn't have squatters.

"What are you looking for?" Elliot asked. "On the beach? Sun's setting."

"Not sure," Logan answered absently, his gaze returning to the sand. Tufts of feathers rolled on the grainy surface. "But I'll know when I find it."

For a quarter of a mile, they followed the trail of loose feathers blowing in the bracing breeze. Logan stopped, his feet planted, his face down. It was getting dark, shadows moved in as the air chilled.

"A dog attack?" Elliot caught up to him, stopping short at the carnage.

The carcass of a Canadian goose lay dismembered, its organs exposed and glistening in the sand. Nearby the mournful sound of his mate honked loudly. Logan fought the bile that rose to the back of his throat. He crouched down to get a better look. It was starting to smell. "Definitely a predator."

"Maybe an eagle," Elliot suggested. "I noticed one on the way here."

"An eagle wouldn't have left it. It's pretty fresh." The bird was ripped to shreds, but there was a definitive shape to the bite marks. "It was not a dog attack, or eagle for that matter," Logan said quietly. The teeth marks were in the shape of a perfect circle.

Elliot bent over. "That's the weirdest bite mark I've ever seen. It looks almost like a—"

"Cookiecutter shark," Logan finished.

"I was going to say suction cup. I never saw a fish bite like that." Elliot stared at the strange shape.

Logan had one knee in the sand, and he was using a stick to poke around the body. "The cookiecutter or dogfish shark takes circular bites out of its prey," he said.

Elliot bent down and peered into the bird's body. "It looks like a plug was pulled out. You think the shark did this? Could it have washed ashore?"

"I didn't say that." Logan looked at him. "Dogfish sharks never travel this far north. You only find them in the warm water down south, especially near the islands in the Caribbean."

Logan got to his feet when he saw a four-wheeled vehicle speeding toward him, the oversized tires throwing up sand as it zigzagged over the dunes. It pulled to a halt too close to him, a foot from their bare toes. Elliot backed away as if he were being squeezed out of a picture.

It was an official vehicle. Two muscled cops were driving, their arms resting on the truck doors. They slowed as they neared Logan and Elliot. Logan recognized the driver immediately. It was Mitch Gordon.

Mitch had tormented Logan and Rory while they were in grade school together. Logan hadn't seen him in years. He stood slowly, taking in the changes in the man he had known as a boy. Logan smiled at the exaggerated orbital ridge where Mitch had an over plucked eyebrow that ended up spacing his eyes very far apart. He looked a lot like the missing yeti he'd hunted in Turkey a few summers ago. Logan opened his mouth to share that thought, then decided not to escalate the encounter.

"What are you two doing out here?" Mitch demanded, his face hostile.

"Hey, Mitch," Logan greeted him. Mitch cocked his head as if he didn't recognize the shaggy-haired stranger.

"Logan Osbourne," Logan introduced himself. "I used to live over there." He pointed vaguely in the direction of his old home.

"Logan Osbourne?" Mitch narrowed his eyes as if deep in thought. "Nobody lives in that dump. Oh yeah, I remember you."

The other cop asked, "That the roadkill those people called about?"

"It's not roadkill. What people?" Logan said.

"What's it to you?" They stood assessing each other in charged silence, then Mitch added, "Your neighbors called. Their kid spotted it on the beach." He stood taller, and his voice became official. "Chief likes to keep things nice here."

Logan fought the urge to laugh and said, "Yeah, it's real nice."

Mitch ignored him. "Cobb, bag it. Damn coyote must've gotten it."

Elliot strode to the body and bent over to look at the dead bird. The other cop named Cobb got out of the vehicle to dispose of the body. Logan moved in front of the corpse.

"Do you mind? I was examining it," Logan asked.

"I think your goose just got cooked." Mitch laughed at his own humor. "Sorry, official business. You can't tamper with it."

"Why is it official business? It's just a dead bird. I'm sure you get your share of those."

Mitch scrunched his forehead as if he were in pain. Cobb stood frozen; he didn't know what to do. Mitch pulled himself out of the truck, his movements quick. He moved around the side of the vehicle, one hand resting on his revolver.

"Got a problem with that, Osbourne?" He puffed out his chest. Logan would see he was sunburned everywhere on his face except the skin around his eyes. He looked like a racoon. He stood toe to toe with Logan. "I told you to bag it, Cobb!"

Logan refused to back away. They looked at each other, neither blinking, and Logan knew they were both thinking about the time Mitch beat up Rory in the schoolyard. Logan came after him like a fury that day, resulting in each of them sporting black eyes.

Logan and Elliot watched the officer shovel the carcass into the black plastic trash bag and toss it in the back.

"That was no coyote," Logan said, gesturing at the bag.

"You some kind of expert or something?" Mitch leaned heavily on one leg, crossing his arms over his chest. He looked Logan up and down, a smirk settling over his features. Logan felt like David to Mitch's Goliath. Mitch poked him in the chest, then laughed as if Logan were an idiot. "Chief says we got a coyote on the loose, so we got a coyote on the loose."

"No coyotes on Long Island," Elliot informed him.

Mitch turned an unfriendly glare on Elliot, then looked at Logan, a slow grin spreading across his face. "The Fire Island ferry is a few exits back."

"What's that supposed to mean?" Elliot asked.

"He's insinuating that we're gay." Logan laughed.

"Nobody cares about that anymore." Elliot shrugged.

"I do." Mitch scowled at them both, then gestured for Cobb to get in the vehicle. "Let's get out of here." He walked back to the driver's side of the truck and hopped in; Logan had to admit with fluid grace for such an ape.

Mitch turned on the ignition of the truck, revving the engine. Ignoring Logan and Elliot, he made a wide turn and raced back the way he came, spraying them with a shower of sand.

"Did you get it?" Logan asked without looking at Elliot.

Elliot held up his cell phone and a plastic bag. "DNA and pictures. I swabbed it while you were sizing each other up. Man, the testosterone exploded all over the beach. Watch out before you step in some. Are we done here?"

"For now. We'll have to get them submitted tomorrow. I have a few things I want to look into."

Logan punched him on the arm good-naturedly. They started walking back to the house.

Logan held back. He looked at the depression in the sand where the body had rested with a puzzled expression.

"What?" Elliot asked.

"I feel like I missed something," Logan said absently.

"It's getting dark," Elliot said. "You're not gonna see anything now."

Logan marched to the hollow where the goose had been found. Elliot shined the flashlight from his phone on it.

Logan's eyes scanned the ground, as he walked around the spot. He dropped to his knees. A huge clump of feathers lay in a pile. Gently, he brushed them out of the way. He heard Elliot's rapid intake of breath.

"You see it?" Logan asked, a memory poking at him. He looked down to the old scar of the puncture wounds in his palm.

"How could you miss it?" Elliot snapped a bunch of pictures, the flash illuminating the sand.

It was almost a foot and a half. The balls of the feet on the footprint dug deeply into the wet sand. Six sharply shaped holes showed where the toes went on each oversized foot. Logan held his scarred palm near the print. He compared his scar to the toe marks on the sand. It was getting too dark to see and Logan cursed the setting sun.

"Wow. It's a perfect match," Elliot whispered. He held a pen next to Logan's hand, then compared it to the space between the claw marks. "I don't think that belongs to any mermaid I've read about."

The black stitches from his injury stood out sharply on his thumb. The skin around them looked red and angry. They itched. He had to get those out soon. He stood brushing the sand from his hands.

Logan gauged the distance to the water. The tide was coming in, the water inching closer. "The tide's turning now. This thing would not have been deposited so far up the beach. It had to have walked here."

"Don't just sit there ogling it; take measurements before your friend the goon comes back," Elliot said.

"He's not my friend," Logan responded.

Elliot touched his shoulder. "I know, Logan. I was only kidding. You know that, don't you?" Elliot looked at him with troubled eyes. "It couldn't have been easy for you after your mother left."

Logan swallowed hard, having trouble with words. He forced them out. "You have no idea."

The surf surged, bringing a frothy wave that bubbled around their feet, filling the small depression of the footprints, then wiping them away as it raced back out to sea. They both watched the depression fill with seawater, becoming invisible in the sand once again.

"Where's the post office? We have to get this over to Vadim to run some tests," Elliot said, changing the mood, the plastic bags gripped tightly in his fist.

"Tomorrow, bright and early. I want to make a stop first thing in the morning," Logan said, his eyes far away.

CHAPTER 9

THE DAY STARTED sultry, the hot sun burning off the overnight haze. The next morning Elliot got busy cooking bacon and eggs, while Logan searched the beach for more evidence. He found nothing unusual, no other dead animals. He returned to the house to find Elliot putting two plates of food on the table.

Logan was scrolling through his computer. Without looking up, he said, "I want to see that kid David Wagner and find out just what he saw."

"OK. Find anything?"

Logan shook his head. "Nothing. Usually an animal will continue to feed where it finds food, or unless it's scared off."

"You want this?" Elliot asked, pointing to the eggs on Logan's plate.

Logan shook his head. "I swear you have worms. You know what's bothering me?"

"You don't like my cooking?"

Logan ignored him. "There's no pattern to the location of the attacks by this creature. They are rarely in the same spot."

"Sounds like this animal is comfortable and knows where the best feeding occurs."

"Like it's premeditated," Logan said thoughtfully.

"Eating is a reflex for animals, they don't hunt for fun."

"You called it an animal. I called it a creature," Logan stood up. "You ready? We have a lot to do."

The drive to Patricia Lane was about twenty minutes. Each house they passed was deeply set behind rows of overgrown but manicured arborvitaes, their dense greenery hiding all who lived there. The air smelled of a mixture of cedar and the sea. Logan and Elliot were quiet, each lost in his own thoughts.

They pulled outside of a large Dutch Colonial with four cars parked in the gravel driveway. It was a new house with a welcoming porch that led to red double doors that stood out against the artificially weather-beaten gray shingles. Open windows revealed billowing white curtains. The garage door was lifted, with six or seven bikes spilling out of the entrance.

Logan smiled thinking of the family inside. It presented such a stark difference from his own home. He wondered if the children felt cherished and protected. He doubted anyone was dragging a kid into the bay at night searching for mythical creatures.

Yet for a minute he had to stop and examine his own thoughts. Did he resent it as much as he thought? Those adventurous expeditions fueled his imagination and ignited his curiosity. His mother's freewheeling spirit lifted his soul from the ordinary and taught him to pursue his dreams. The world shifted as if the sand was moving beneath his feet. He had never considered it this way before. Awareness that perhaps someone might want to be in his childhood shoes brought him up short. For years, he considered himself a victim, and now, he realized he wasn't.

His mind raced over this change of perspective. He looked at his palm, the roadwork of lines that were exclusively his, wondering how much his parents had shaped his personality and laid the groundwork of who he would become. Logan shook his head.

"Something bothering you?" Elliot asked.

"Nah, just trying to organize my thoughts," Logan responded, knowing he wasn't.

Visiting the Hamptons brought up the silt of his childhood that lay long buried in the deep recesses of his mind. It was the stuff of nightmares mixed with things he didn't want to explore. Some questions were better left unanswered. Logan took a steadying breath, suppressing the thoughts roiling in his head.

"You know you're scowling, don't you?" Elliot commented.

Logan rearranged his face, relaxing it into a smile that felt fake.

The double front doors of the house were open, with a screen door keeping the bugs out. Logan searched for the bell and pressed the button. He was rewarded with a set of chimes that rivaled the organ of the Mormon Tabernacle Choir.

A dog barked. It was the deep bark of a large dog, either a shepherd or Lab.

"*Ooh*. Big one." Elliot took a slight step back, rocking on his heels.

There was the sound of running feet and children laughing. A man's voice called a woman's name, but Logan couldn't make out what he said. Logan pressed the doorbell again.

"Everybody has those kinds of dogs here. They're all… whoa." A Great Dane hit the screen, his huge head eye to eye with him. It panted, making chuffing noises, its platter-shaped paws stretching the screen.

"Down, boy," Logan said. The dog answered gruffly, a chain of saliva attaching to the screen.

A delicate hand dragged the resisting dog away by the collar. A woman he guessed to be in her mid-forties watched him through the safety of the screen. She didn't open it. She was polite but eyed him suspiciously.

"Mrs. Wagner?" he asked.

"Yes," she answered, not saying anything else.

"My name is Logan Osbourne, and I was wondering if I could speak to David."

Her expression shuttered; her lips thinned. "Regarding what?"

"I'm looking into the disappearance of Rory Swanson."

Her eyes opened wide, and she backed away as if threatened. "He has nothing to say."

Logan persisted. "Wasn't David on the beach the night Rory Swanson and his friend disappeared? I just want to ask a few questions."

She looked at the street, searching frantically. "Ben…

Ben… " She turned her face away, and Logan supposed she was calling her husband. He sincerely hoped it wasn't the dog's name.

She started to close the heavy oak door behind the screen. Logan put his palm on the handle as if to stop her.

Her face changed to resemble a painting he'd seen of Medusa once on a wall of a ruin in the Mediterranean.

"Go away from here and leave us alone. He has nothing to say."

"Wait, he has nothing to say to me?"

"To you or anyone else," she said shrilly, slamming the door in his face.

Elliot looked at Logan. "Dude, you have to work on your delivery. A little charm might have gotten us further." They heard a window being rammed shut as well as the sounds of a garage door being closed, the sensor stopping just short of the bikes. A hand reached out to push a tire away, and the garage door slammed with a thud.

"Okay, smart-ass, next time you charm them with your Boston accent and winning smile."

Elliot grinned his response. Logan shoved him as they walked toward his car.

Logan stopped when they reached the jeep and turned to look back at the house. As welcoming as it looked before, it was as if the inhabitants had left town. It appeared deserted— no breezy curtains blowing from the windows. Every window was closed as tightly as a clamshell, revealing nothing.

They stopped at the post office overnighting the sample to

the lab. Logan paid extra, ensuring it would arrive early in the morning so Vadim could start working on it right away.

"When do you think we'll get the results?" asked Elliot.

"If I know Haversham, they should start coming in by tomorrow evening. Frankly, I'm surprised I didn't get anything on the Thunderbird feather yet."

"When did you mail it?"

"Before I picked you up." Logan was staring absently at the assorted stores along the main street of town.

"They might have had to run more tests," Elliot said.

Logan shrugged. "Haversham is not going to sit on it. He'll let us know as soon as he has something."

"Have you spoken to him?" Elliot asked.

Logan shook his head. "Not since I left Arizona."

The entire village consisted of a long two-lane thoroughfare filled with white storefronts that had exclusive shops lining the quaint street. It was mid-morning. Cafés and restaurants were filling up.

Logan felt his phone vibrate. He looked at the incoming call and said, "Give me a minute."

"Haversham?" Elliot asked hopefully.

"No, Penny." Logan ducked into a brick alleyway between two ancient buildings to answer it.

"What did you do to Mitch *Gorgon*?" she demanded.

He laughed at the childish name they had given him.

"I know of a famous pictograph of a gorgon in Greece, and I think we got that one all wrong. I discovered they are all female. We're going to have to come up with a new moniker for him. Besides, he's uglier than they were."

Penny snickered. "Well, he's pretty ugly right now. He's still stewing about yesterday evening. Carrying on something fierce about outsiders. Not real fond of Elliot, called him something nasty."

"What?" Logan demanded.

"I don't want to say. It's homophobic."

"A leopard doesn't change its spots. Mitch is a creep."

"I'm not arguing with you," Penny said then added. "He's in with the chief. What happened?"

"Found a half-eaten Canadian goose."

"*Ew.* Gross. But that's nothing new. It could have been a dog, or even an aggressive cat," Penny offered.

"Not with round bite marks," Logan murmured.

"Round bite marks?" Penny was thoughtful. "I think I read about something like that in a file. Let me poke around."

"That would be useful. We'll meet up later after you get off duty?" He paused as if he remembered something. "Did you run the plates on those motorcycles outside the house?"

"Huh!" she replied. "Really funny about those. They are not registered anywhere. I'll have to pull those guys in… that is, if we ever see them again."

"What kind of cops do you have out here?" Elliot asked when Logan eased out of the alley.

"You're thinking about the spectacle on the beach yesterday?"

Elliot nodded.

"It's a small town. The chief rules it like it's his own

personal fiefdom. You know, like a security detail for the rich people," Logan explained.

"I didn't realize the area was that wealthy."

"Don't judge the town by my cottage. My parents bought it when they were newly married. My mother liked to paint there." Logan stopped abruptly as if he'd said too much. His palm itched, reminding him of the stitches. He looked up and down the street, spying the swinging doctor's shingle a few doors down. "You hungry?"

"I thought you'd never ask. Where's the clam joint?"

Logan pointed to a white-washed cottage with blue accents. "Over there. Get us a table. Start eating if you're hungry."

"I'm starving."

"I'm not surprised. It's been three hours since your last feeding."

Elliot laughed. "Hey, that's part of the package. I can't help it if I'm hungry. I burn a lot of calories. Where are you going?"

"I have to get these stitches clipped. Doc's office is right over there." He pointed to a tiny two-hundred-year-old salt-box of a house that was in desperate need of a paint job.

Elliot eyed the dilapidated building with distaste. "You sure you want to go there. It doesn't look especially... modern."

"It's not, but I know the doctor. He took care of me until I was nine. It'll be fine. Besides, I have a few questions." Logan's face clouded as he stared at the physician's office.

"You sure you want to go alone?"

Logan gave him a pained look. Elliot threw up his hands. "No argument from me. I'm hungry."

Logan's stomach gave a rare gurgle, sending Elliot into a fit of laughter. "Will wonders never cease? Could it be that you're actually hungry? Logan," Elliot called. "Logan… you look like you've seen a ghost."

Logan snapped out of his reverie and replied, "We don't believe in ghosts."

"Yeah, only mermaids and Bigfoot." Elliot waved and walked toward the clam shack.

Logan turned in the opposite direction and crossed the street. A woman holding a toddler opened the door to leave as he arrived. The baby was wrapped in a blanket, his feet dangling against his mother's hips. He held an orange lollipop to his tear-stained face.

"Doc still in?" Logan asked, holding the door for her.

She looked him up and down, then behind him as if looking for his child. "You caught him just in time. He waited for us. He's about ready to leave for the hospital." She looked puzzled. "Are you new here?"

Logan shook his head. "Just passing through. I'm an old friend of Doctor Leeds."

She smiled and hurried down the steps toward an SUV parked in the empty lot next door.

Logan opened the door to a small reception area with a pudgy woman sitting on the other side of a half wall with a cloudy glass partition. She looked up, her glasses sliding down her nose to halt on the rounded tip. She had three pencils tucked into the untidy bun on the back of her head.

"Is the doc in?"

Without looking up, she muttered, "It's Tuesday morning. He's about to do rounds at the hospital."

Logan cleared his throat. "Does he have a minute to see me?"

She studied him, then typed on a keyboard, as if looking for something, then eyed him. "Do you have an appointment?" she asked tartly, knowing he did not. "The doctor is not taking new patients right now. We are about to close the office for the day."

Logan's response was cut off by a booming voice.

"Indeed we are not!" Doc Leeds stood in the doorway, his large size dwarfing the low ceilings of the old house. "I would recognize that face anywhere. You're the living spit of your father. Don't you remember Logan Osbourne, Hetty?"

"Logan Osbourne," she repeated. "George and… what was her name? Oh yes, George and Samantha's boy? Oh, my!"

The doctor enveloped him in a warm embrace that left Logan perplexed. He wasn't expecting this reception. He wasn't sure exactly what he was expecting.

"Come in, Logan. It's been a long time. Last time I saw you, you were flat on your back." The doctor looked at him keenly. "Well, never mind about that." He held out an arm in welcome, ushering Logan into his office. "Hetty, call the hospital and let them know I'm running late." The receptionist's mouth opened in astonishment. She nodded curtly, then reached for her phone.

The doctor's inner sanctum was a cramped room with an oversized desk. Plastic models of body organs were scattered around. Each replica had the name of a medicine printed on it. Every available surface was filled with hundreds of files stacked in haphazard towers. The room smelled faintly of tobacco and Logan had a pang of longing for a smoke.

He suppressed it, noting with surprise it was happening less often.

The doctor caught Logan's eye and laughed. "I'm not computerizing. Hetty uses one, of course, but not me. Few more years and I'll retire. I've got everything right up here." He pointed his finger to his temple. "Don't need a computer when I have a very successful filing system. It's been an age, son."

Logan gestured to a pile of paper on a chair. "May I?"

"Of course. Here I'll do that." The doctor moved his considerable bulk forward, but Logan was faster. He removed the column of files, placing them on the worn carpet on the floor and sat down.

He looked at the doctor, seeing him as if for the first time. He thought Doctor Leeds was an old man twenty years ago. He couldn't have been more than forty then, barely eleven years older than Logan was now.

Doc Leeds's hair was a cloud of white around his head, and with his glasses, mustache, and goatee, he had a strange resemblance to Colonel Sanders. Logan stifled a laugh. *How had I not seen that before?* The memory of a frightened boy sobered him instantly. The next question from the doctor, though it was perfectly innocent, startled him.

"What brings you home?"

What brings me home? Logan asked himself, memories assaulting him like crashing waves. He closed his eyes and swallowed. The confidence he had earlier evaporated. For some reason, he felt nine-years-old again. It was almost too much for a second. He saw his father's feet flying over the bow, the sparkle of a green iridescent arm flashing, all mixed with a primal fear that froze his bowels.

Half rising from the chair, Logan raised a shaking hand to his temple. Doc Leeds grabbed it, running a gentle finger along the row of stitches. He put on a pair of old glasses hanging from a thin chain on his chest. He studied the healing stitches for a good amount of time. "Crude. Very crude. Who did these?"

"I was in Arizona. Local place," Logan told him. He was faintly annoyed that his voice sounded reedy. He cleared his throat. "It doesn't hurt at all."

"Nasty looking. Want them out, do you? When did you get injured?" Piercing eyes looked over the bifocals, watching Logan intently.

He squirmed uncomfortably. "Almost a week ago. It's about time they were removed," he admitted. "I didn't plan to be here."

"Penny called you." It was a statement, not a question. "Sit down."

Before Logan could respond, the doctor left the room. Logan could hear him rummaging around in a closet.

"I knew she would. She never listens." He returned with shiny surgical scissors and the antiseptic smell of cotton doused in alcohol. He pulled Logan's hand a bit too roughly, then grumbled something about not enough light. He twisted to yank a gooseneck lamp, bending it over his shoulder, illuminating the room. "They're a bit overdue." He snipped carefully, absorbed in his work.

"Never listens to whom?"

Doc Leeds pierced him with a disgruntled "ahem."

He cleared his throat. "Did I say that? I don't remember saying that."

Logan looked closely at his doughy visage. He was much older than the man who had treated him twenty years ago. The doctor's face was lined, tired, softened by age.

Logan watched him intently, then said, "You don't believe Rory left town, do you?"

Leeds stopped, his lips thinning. He looked directly at Logan. "I told Penny he was unhappy. He couldn't catch a break." Doc Leeds closed his mouth allowing the words to settle in.

Logan widened his eyes, and he asked, "Are you insinuating he killed himself?"

"People on the drugs that he took often end up suicidal."

The scissors pinched his tender skin. "*Ow.*" Logan pulled away, but the doctor held onto him in a surprisingly strong grip. "Drugs?" Logan asked.

The doctor's bushy brows furrowed. He turned his attention to Logan's hand, avoiding eye contact. "You know I can't share that with you," he said, his voice gruff.

"You were treating him?"

Doctor Leeds blew a long breath through his nose. "I treat just about everybody here." He looked up, his eyes floating above the half-moon glasses. "I treated your father, too." He looked pained, as if he was struggling with something. "Logan, you know Rory. He's been unhappy for years." He shrugged. "There's medicine for that. Sometimes that medicine has bad side effects. Rory had his share of demons."

"What are you insinuating, Doctor? Where is he?" Logan demanded, unsure if Rory could be diagnosed as depressed.

What did he mean by other demons? He had never thought his friends had that issue. "Rory wasn't depressed," he said at last.

"Where'd you get your medical degree?" the doctor snorted. "When was the last time you saw him or even talked to him? You can't bulldoze your way in here after, what, twenty years and think you know everything." The doctor gave a disgruntled "harrumph" and continued, "Things have changed in town. A lot has changed."

"Like what?" Logan asked, his voice soft.

The doctor ignored him, as if he were absorbed in his work.

Logan thought for a minute. While he had spoken to Rory here and there, they really hadn't seen each other for years. He knew Rory was frustrated with his writing career and wanted to move to LA. He was stuck, *but depressed?*

Logan sat in stony silence, then blurted, "Where's his body, then, and the woman's… and all the animals that went missing as well? Where is Sly Shaw?"

"Sly Shaw?" Leeds's head shot up. "Sly Shaw went to Florida to visit his sister." Logan waited a minute and paused, then added under his breath, "*Where's his body?*"

Doc Leeds snipped fast, piercing Logan's skin, causing a bead of blood to appear. He wiped it with the alcohol, stinging Logan's hand. The doctor's face was shadowed, his eyes evasive once again.

What had happened to the doctor's oath, Logan wanted to ask, the one about do no harm?

It felt as if they were in a tug of war for his hand. Logan pulled away, making the doctor look at him impatiently.

"What do you know, Doc? What do you know that you're not sharing?"

"I know that Chief Red Kain has everything under control and well in hand. Don't meddle, Logan." He grabbed Logan by the fingers and snipped the final stitch. He squeezed Logan's hand, then patted it.

"Is that a threat?" Logan asked.

"Consider it advice from an old friend."

Logan stood. He wanted to get out of there and as far from the doctor as he could.

"How much do I owe you?" Logan asked coldly.

"No charge for my services, or the free advice. Eat a lobster and go home. There is nothing going on here. There was nothing twenty years ago, and there is nothing now." He dropped the scissors into a metal tray, where they clattered loudly in the silence. Logan noticed the doctor's hands were stained with his blood. He looked at his finger to see a smear of red staining his palm.

The doctor handed him a gauze pad. "Good as new."

Logan studied the jagged line of his scar. "Sometimes when there is a scar, it's never the same."

The doctor watched him, his eyes cold and reptilian. "You used to pick at your scabs when you were a boy. Do you remember what I used to warn you?"

Logan's mouth formed into a tight line.

"You're just as stubborn as I recall," Doc said. "I told you if you pick at an old wound, you'll make it worse. Don't make it worse, Logan."

Logan nodded once and left the office, thinking that some wounds never heal.

He met up with Elliot in time to finish the last of the clams and an ice-cold beer. He watched the condensation form on the bottle as it sweated from the heat.

They sat outside on plastic chairs on a patch of beach at the rear of the establishment, watching the birds fight at the bread tossed by the patrons.

"Should we tell 'em that it gives the birds diarrhea?"

Logan shook his head with disgust. "They won't listen. They never do." He stared moodily at the water, unsure of what he was looking for, wondering if he really wanted to find it.

"Stitches?" asked Elliot.

Logan held up his hand sporting the angry scar down his finger. His face was closed, his eyes bleak. "Removed."

"Was it bad?" Elliot probed. "Did the doctor know what he was doing?"

"Oh yeah, he knew exactly what he was doing."

"What's up? You look pissed."

Logan dismissed the remark with a wave of his hand. He couldn't process it, didn't know where to start. It didn't feel right. Something had passed between him and the doctor, stirring up all the hated memories of that night and this place. The doctor had threatened him, of that he was sure. Though the words were cloaked by the patina of goodwill, the undertone of menace was there, like a predator stalking him.

Gritting his teeth, Logan watched the sea roll in, caressing the shore. Seagulls screamed, diving for the clams that littered the beach, grabbing them to hold in their beaks, then dropping them on the rocks to crush them. Then they swooped down for the kill, devouring the exposed meaty flesh of the clam.

A dog ran along the beach, his owners walking behind it. The canine came upon a horseshoe crab. He buried his nose in the sand and flipped it. Logan heard the dog's owner yell, but the dog had the black shell in its mouth like a Frisbee. He took off down the beach, his paws throwing clots of sand into the air.

There were predators all over. A large gray seagull swooped down to gobble a clam, his cry triumphant over its prize, reminding Logan that everybody was a member of the food chain, even him.

Elliot's phone pinged with a message. He put down his fork and made a noise deep in his throat. "*Huh*. You were right, they must have gotten right to it." He waved to the waitress and ordered another dish of fried clams.

"What?" Logan spoke ignoring the girl but kept his eyes on the waves lapping the shore.

"It's Vadim. He probably worked all night. He got the DNA reports on the feather."

Logan sat up in the chair. "The feather?"

"Duh, the Thunderbird. What's wrong with you, man?"

Logan's face reddened. He was still going over his confrontation with the doctor. "That was fast. What's it say?"

He watched Elliot's face fall as he read the email.

"I don't understand," Elliot mumbled.

"What?" Logan shouted.

Elliot held up his cell for Logan to read it. "It says unknown amino acids."

"Did Haversham add anything else? Another text?"

"Nope, just Vadim."

"Let me see." Logan held out his hand impatiently.

"Crap." His eyes scanned the report on Elliot's phone. "This has to be a mistake. Not enough tissue or blood on the feather…" He read the rest silently.

Elliot said, "I knew it might be a problem. Would have been better if you'd plucked it from its body."

Logan gave him a sour look, his eyebrows sliding to his hairline.

"Only you would have picked a molted feather. It was useless, Logan."

"Next time I'll make sure to yank it from its tail," Logan said sarcastically.

Elliot shrugged. "Just sayin.' You were right there."

CHAPTER 10

BY TWELVE NOON, the front of the restaurant filled with a rowdy group of college kids. They took over the small space, gathering around the aged-wooden bar, even though it was clear they were too young to be drinking. It was a mixed group, all monied and sun-tanned, wearing the latest trending fashions. The sounds of their banter drifted outside, but it was not disrespectful, and patrons were in a mood to be lenient. The round plastic tables had filled with groups of sunworshippers, oiled up for a day at the beach. Waitresses in cut-off shorts walked around with trays of overstuffed lobster rolls, Long Island Ice-Teas, and the ubiquitous clam dishes that made the restaurant famous.

Logan let the sound of people enjoying the day waft over him, and for a minute he allowed himself to watch the crashing surf and clouds scudding across the sky. The constant roll of the water made him drowsy, his hands relaxed.

The hypnotic sounds of the ocean, the bright sun, the crystal sky lowered his defenses. The associations of the night his father disappeared were incongruous with the peacefulness of the beach.

A kite floated overhead, the long string connecting the rainbow-colored silk diamond to a young boy and his father. The older man's head was bowed, their hair almost touching. A hand rested on the child's shoulder, the gentle touch giving the boy confidence, Logan could hear the father's encouraging words and wondered if in some way they were directed to him. *Don't bunch your shoulders, relax the tension, if you hold on too tightly, you'll lose it. Step backwards so you can see what you are doing.* Perhaps he was holding on too tightly and it was coloring his judgement, affecting his decisions. Maybe he needed to step back so he could analyze the data. He needed to remove the emotion, the sting of his anger in order to be able to distinguish truth from myth. He had to stop making it personal, it would be the only way his scientific mind could uncover what had to be right in front of him.

Despite his disappointment in the DNA results, he could feel himself unwind. Taking a cleansing breath, he let the clean air fill his lungs then released it slowly as if he was meditating. He loved the smell of the beach. That light fresh scent brought back all that was good about this place. He sat back in the chair, his body going limp.

"You going to sleep or something?" Elliot's keen eyes observed him.

Elliot was on his third order of fried clams, the used cardboard serving plates were stacked to make room for Key Lime pie.

"What?" Elliot asked, looking at Logan. "I like Key Lime."

Logan made a face.

"You should have had the clams. You were right, they were amazing."

Logan reached over and snagged the last strip in the greasy dish. The summer breeze caressed his face, his feet were itching to get out of his boots. Logan wiggled his toes imagining the sand cushioning his steps, the water lapping at his skin. At this moment there was no creature, no murders or disappearances. It was all about summer in the Hamptons, no cares and a great place to just be.

Logan heard the name David twice, and only when someone shouted "Wagner" did he put it together. He scooted back his chair and rose.

"Where are you going?" Elliot asked.

"I'll be right back."

Logan wandered inside. The restaurant was packed. Dishes clanked. Busboys in white tees and cargo shorts rushed with the dirty plates while servers brought out armloads of steaming seafood.

Logan walked up to the bar, on the fringe of the group of boys, trying to figure out who David was. He realized they were younger than he'd first thought. They were drinking sodas.

He didn't have to wait long. Two of the boys grunted, then acted like a pair of apes in a lousy imitation of the creature from the Black Lagoon.

"Cut it out," a thickset boy said from the middle of the group. He looked around nervously. "Stop it, Jason." He punched his friend in the arm.

"Ow." Jason winced. "You thought it was funny yesterday."

"What was funny?" Logan asked in a friendly manner.

The boy eyed him distrustfully. He turned back to the bar, ending the conversation.

Logan squeezed in, motioned the bartender, and said, "A round of whatever they're drinking."

It got quiet. The bartender said, "They're underaged, dude."

Logan looked at their glasses and said, "I said a round of whatever they're drinking. Doesn't have to be beer."

"In that case, I'll take a scotch," one of them shouted. Foaming glasses of more soda were placed before the group. Logan picked one up and took a long swallow. "Anything interesting ever happen in this town?"

One boy turned a shade paler. "I'm going home."

"Dave! Come on, the guy bought us drinks."

David shook his head. "I'm not even supposed to be out. I gotta go." He melted into the sea of people crowding the bar.

Logan put down his soda and squeezed into the crush, catching him as he walked out the door.

"David," he called. "David, please hold up a minute."

David stopped just outside the entrance; his face blanched of all color.

Logan put his hand out as if to halt him, the boy shrank away. "You are David Wagner, right?"

The teen looked around nervously, then reached into his pocket taking out a pack of cigarettes. He fumbled with a lighter that refused to spark. "What's it to you?" he said his voice filled with false bravado. He had his feet planted, and his shoulders back as if he decided to take a stand. Logan thought he looked incredibly young, like the boy on the beach flying his kite.

Logan watched him, forcing his voice to remain neutral, then said, "Can I talk to you for a minute?"

"Who are you," David said and tossed the lighter into a trash can with disgust. The cigarette followed. "I'll get in trouble if they see that."

"They usually know just by smelling it on your clothes."

David tilted his head, a sneaky grin on his face. "Yeah. But what are they going to do about it. I'll be back at school in the fall."

"Boarding school?"

David gave a curt nod.

Logan remained silent; his stance relaxed.

David considered him, "What are you, a reporter or something?"

"A reporter?"

"Yeah. Because every time I leave the house, they keep bothering me."

"I'm not a reporter," Logan said. "Do you want to go to the corner where we can talk?"

David looked around, his eyes tense, his hands clenched into fists. A group of twenty-somethings swept passed them, bumping into them as if they weren't there.

"City trash," David said contemptuously. "They think it's all fun and games. They don't know what's really going on here."

"And you do?" It was said without judgement. Logan kept his expression impassive, but he searched the boy's face.

For a moment, they exchanged a long look. Something passed between them.

They stepped from the entrance. The building was sandwiched between a parking lot and another restaurant. It was also packed with loud clusters of patrons enjoying lunch.

Logan walked toward the back of the parking lot. "My name is Logan Osbourne."

The boy nodded once, his eyes widening when he recognized the name. "I know who you are. I googled you. It was all there, your story. The Mermaid of Minatuck."

David's voice was flat.

Logan made a face. "It was a long time ago."

"You were at my house today." It was an accusation.

"I wanted to ask some questions."

"I didn't see anything," David said too quickly.

"I don't believe you," Logan said after a bit. "You have to tell someone if you saw something." Logan paused again, then added, "I know you saw the same thing as I did."

"If you know that then you don't need to ask me any questions." David started to walk away.

Logan stopped him with his next sentence. "It's a monster. It's deadly. It will kill again."

David was breathing heavily, his back to Logan. He could see the teen was trembling. "You need to tell somebody about it," he said urgently.

David spun to face him. "No, I don't. You just want someone to tell you it really happened. You're afraid you imagined it."

The words hit a raw nerve, and Logan fought grabbing and shaking the boy.

Barely controlling his anger, Logan ground out, "It murdered my father."

David backed away, his eyes round with fear.

Logan forced himself to calm and regulate his voice. *Here it is, proof.* He needed corroboration. He waited a lifetime for this. "What did you see? I need to know," he whispered.

David looked up and down the street. He was silent for a long time, his Adam's Apple working as if he was fighting off tears. The teen was wrestling with the information. "They came to my house. Secretive people. Like, you know, like in the movies. Told me what to say. Why do you think they did that?"

"They don't want the truth to come out." Logan sighed. "What are you going to do about it?"

"I'm more afraid of them than *it*." David's voice was hostile. "I have to go. This is dangerous."

"For whom?"

"Who do you think? If you were smart, you'd stay out of it."

Logan's face folded inward with disappointment. "It's a killer," he said simply. "It will kill again."

David turned and went back toward the front of the restaurant. Walking a few yards, he stopped, his head down, his shoulders hunched. Hands deep in his pockets, he stalked back, his movements jerky. He approached Logan, his eyes gleaming fiercely, stopping when he was almost nose to nose with him. "Listen," David said, his voice a harsh whisper, as he cast a furtive look around. "You didn't imagine it. Everything you saw was real." David Wagner walked down the street disappearing as if he never existed.

Logan paid their tab, then walked to the lot where they had

parked the car. He approached the curb, one foot in the street in order to cross it. A car barreled down the road, causing him to jump back onto the sidewalk. It barely missed him. The vehicle came to an abrupt stop.

The passenger's window slid down. A blast of cold air hit Logan's midsection. He heard his name called by the person inside.

Bending down, Logan saw Chief Red Kain, his auburn hair threaded with gray now. "It's been a long time. I thought you gave up the Hamptons, Osborne," he said in a friendly manner. His fleshy face was split in a sneer that belied the words. Logan noticed his thinning hair had been pulled over his head in an unattractive combover, as if he was hiding his baldness.

"Not when you get all the great weather," Logan drawled.

"What are you looking for?" the chief demanded.

"What do you think?"

"Don't be a smart-ass with me. I have a crew that does fine without any interference. You remember that. Do what everyone else does when they come here. Get drunk, get a suntan and keep your nose outta my business." He pointed a thick finger close to Logan's face. "And don't go bothering people in this town with your stupid questions." He peeled out, his tires shrieking on the asphalt.

Elliot came up behind him to watch the retreating cop car. "Maybe we *should* have gone to Fire Island," he said with a heartfelt sigh.

CHAPTER 11

"WHAT WAS THAT all about?" Elliot asked.

"He's been chief here for about a hundred years." Logan laughed. "He runs a tight ship."

They got into Logan's jeep and headed in the opposite direction from Logan's home. Elliot held onto the roll bar above his head. "Isn't your place in that direction?" He pointed the opposite way.

"I want to make a stop," Logan said. He slowed the car. "If I remember correctly, it's not far from here. Just down one of these streets. He lived, down... there somewhere... Sand... Sand Dollar Path. I used to go there all the time with my parents." They were inching along the main street, traffic filling the road with rentals of convertibles, and fancy sports cars in bright colors.

"That's odd," Elliot looked in the direction of Logan's gaze. "They look out of place."

A trio of black SUVs with official license plates were lined up outside the city hall.

"Yeah," Logan agreed. "No Taxi and Limousine Commission plates which means they're not a car service. They look governmental. I don't recognize them, do you?"

Elliot shook his head. "No idea. You think they're out here for your mermaid?"

"Not my mermaid," Logan responded absentmindedly. "Can you see anyone?"

"Windows are dark, but I can tell each vehicle is filled." Elliot looked up. "Light's green, we got to get moving before Rosco Purvis Coltrane comes back and impounds the car."

"Who?" Logan looked at Elliot.

"The sheriff from the Dukes of Hazzard, didn't you watch any tv when you were young?"

"And you call me a nerd?" Logan laughed.

"Where are we going?"

"I want to check out Sly's place."

"Who?" Elliot looked at his watch. "Did you hear from Penny yet?"

Logan shook his head. "The guy who owned the scuba shop. Penny will stop by later. She's bringing some reports she's found."

"Why Sly's?"

"Something's not sitting right with me. Someone's lying."

Elliot agreed. "It appears to be an ongoing problem with the people of this town."

They passed a small church on the corner. The graveyard was filled with crooked tombstones packed tightly together. The road was uneven, the street broken from many cold winters. A large pond split the road in two directions. Logan moved toward the right. The path they turned onto was bumpy, the sides overgrown with bushes. Cicadas sang, their strange songs mixed with the croaking of bullfrogs.

"Anyone ever tell you your town is plain old creepy?" Elliot said as they navigated their way through the tangle of greenery. Branches reached through the sides of the doorless jeep, scratching them.

"I never said it was Mayberry."

"Ow!" Elliot complained.

"This is no worse than Brazil," Logan grumbled.

"Yeah, but the beach there made it worth it," Elliot shot back.

Sly lived in an old cabin not far from the pond. The house was on a small hill that looked out over the sound. The roar of the ocean was a constant thrum. They pulled into a drive that looked like a cow path, the sun baking the whitewashed shingles of the three-hundred-year-old cottage like dry bones. Sycamores dwarfed the tiny building.

Logan rolled next to a faded building that looked almost like a toolshed. The outside was covered with green lichen. The gravel driveway crunched as he slowed to a stop. They could hear the sound of the waves more prominently crashing against the shore below the structures.

Logan got out of the car, stopping to stare at the majesty of the water. It stretched as far as the eye could see, with clusters of reeds near the shore.

"Come on," he said to Elliot, his voice low.

"What are you looking for?"

Logan shrugged. He wasn't sure himself.

Logan spit on his hand and rubbed the dusty glass pane in the window of the small house. Moving closer, he squinted, peering into the darkness.

"See anything?" Elliot came up behind him. "I'd go around back if I were you, before your friend Kain finds you peeping in some old guy's window."

"First of all, Kain's not my friend. One day I'll tell you a little story about him."

Logan walked on the springy turf toward the rear of the house. There was a double-door garage that once might have been a barn.

They heard a cat meow loudly. Elliot choked back a scream.

"Really, Elliot? It's a cat." Logan walked in the direction of the animal. He saw a calico tabby peeping out from under the house. The green eyes glowed in the shadows of the foundation of a rotted-looking porch. Logan leaned down, holding out his hand making soft purring noises. It skittered away from him as if afraid, vanishing around the back of the building. Logan followed, stopping when he saw it scratching the green painted door to what he remembered as the entrance to the kitchen.

"That his cat?" Elliot asked.

"He loved animals. It might be his, or maybe it's a stray." Logan stood deep in thought. "An animal lover wouldn't leave it without food," Logan murmured.

"I'll check out the garage." Elliot walked toward the right. "It's open," he called a minute or two later. He was back after a few moments adding, "Well, if the old guy went to Florida, he definitely flew."

Logan cocked his head. "Car's still here?"

Elliot held out a filthy hand. "It hasn't been used in a while. The car is covered with dust."

Logan turned the knob on the back door. It was locked. He spied the cellar door and jumped off the steps, bending over to swing it open.

"It's a felony, guy," Elliot warned.

"Call me if you see the coppers."

"What kind of signal do you want?" Elliot asked, but Logan had disappeared inside the slanted doors. "I'll whistle," Elliot called after him.

Logan's head popped up a minute later, his brow furrowed.

"What's up?" Elliot asked.

"If he went anywhere, he didn't take luggage. His suitcase is still in the closet."

"He could have more than one," Elliot said as they walked back to the car.

Logan shook his head. "I know Sly. He's a simple guy. Something's not right. It's just not right." He stopped dead in his tracks. "Did you hear that?"

They both watched the sparkling water of the ocean, the surface like rippling silk.

"Are we done here?" Elliot asked.

Logan nodded, his eyes still searching the water. He shivered. It was at least ten degrees cooler in the shade of the trees.

"Why do you care where this guy is? Maybe he doesn't want to be found."

"Like Penny's brother? Something smells rotten. I can't put my finger on it," Logan answered.

"Well, that was a dead end. Any other ideas?" Elliot asked.

"I want to see the reports Penny is bringing. Maybe we'll find something there."

The clouds had taken on a dark ominous color. "Looks like we're in for some rain." Elliot looked pointedly at the bikini top on the jeep. "I don't feel like getting doused."

"Okay, home." Logan studied at the sky. "I'm tired. Let's call it a day."

"No arguments here, buddy."

The sky opened up as they pulled into the drive. They raced in their shirts and shoes soaked.

The house was clammy when they arrived.

"I'm going to change." Elliot went straight to his computer in his bedroom. After a few minutes, Logan could hear him typing furiously away knowing his friend was researching any number of things. Later, he heard Elliot on the phone, his low voice intimate. He knew it was personal. Soon, the talking ceased.

Logan's finger ached. He stared at the long weal. It was tender to touch. He rummaged the kitchen cabinets, found a box of bandages and put the largest one he could find over his finger.

Logan changed into dry clothes, his laptop on his stomach as he looked up incidents from nearby towns. He checked local newspapers, each village had one, and Facebook pages. He typed in *mutilations, Long Island, disappearing pets* and came up with nothing substantial.

Logan's eyelids drooped, He lay on the couch, the day,

as well as his feelings catching up with him. His finger throbbed where the stitches had been removed.

"Bring Tylenol," he texted Penny, then dozed off on the sofa, his phone falling onto the floor.

Logan was startled when a soft hand caressed his arm. Instantly awake, he didn't know where he was.

Penny sat next to him, her eyes luminous in the growing darkness. For a minute, he didn't recognize her. It was early evening.

"You alright?" she asked, her voice filled with concern. "You both fell asleep. I could have ransacked your house. You left all the doors open."

"You just got off?"

"I pulled a double shift," she said with a shrug. Penny was looking at his bandaged finger.

"I had some stitches removed earlier. Hurts like a mother… never mind. Did you bring Tylenol?"

She placed the plastic bottle in his hand, letting her fingers linger against his palm.

Logan looked down at their hands, a strange feeling overcoming him. He resisted the urge to squeeze her hand and pulled away.

Logan went to the kitchen, filled a glass with water, and swallowed two pills. "Did you find anything in the reports?"

Penny patted the couch. "Not sure. Come take a look at these." She turned on the light.

Logan noticed the blinds were still open from the afternoon. He walked over to shut them. As he lowered them, he saw a black SUV pull away from the curb across the street.

"Did you notice anything when you arrived?"

Penny shook her head. She reached over and turned on a lamp. "It's so dark in here. What are you guys, vampires? I know the people next door are in for the summer. They arrived today."

"You know that because…?" Logan asked, his eyebrows raised.

"They alerted us because they thought squatters were in your house." She laughed. "The son is a little wild. It's a real party house when he's home from school."

She held a folder in her hand. Logan fell onto the cushion next to her. Penny moved closer as she gave him the police report.

"See, this is a complaint. It's the Richardsons over by Tidewell. It's one of the reports I told you about earlier."

He read the paperwork. They had complained their dog had gone missing. "Read this." She handed him a sheaf of official-looking papers.

"Yeah, it's all routine."

"I know. The strange thing is, they said there was no recovery of the body."

"Yeah, so? What's so intriguing?" Logan tossed the papers onto the coffee table. He had the beginning of a headache despite the medicine. "It feels like Chief Kain makes up all the rules as he goes along."

"I know that, but you see, I found this." She held up a folded letter written on onion skin stationery. "It was stuck to the back of a file."

Logan read it. Here it was, just the kind of thing he was looking for. The Richardsons were horrified that their dog had been mutilated. They demanded answers. They asked if it was a ritual killing because the dog had several round marks on the corpse, circular wounds where pieces of flesh had been ripped from its body.

Logan combed through the papers, and nowhere was there evidence of finding the corpse of the dog.

"Do you know where this Tidewell house is?"

"They built it at the end of Dune Road, right on the ocean. Why?"

Logan shrugged. "I was thinking of talking to them."

"Don't show them the letter." Penny sounded nervous.

"Don't worry. I know what I'm doing." He was still going through the files.

He finished to find Penny sitting glassy-eyed, staring at nothing. "Want some tea?" He placed his hand over hers. "This has got to be hard for you."

She replied, "It's hard for all of us."

"You're thinking about Rory?" he asked gently. "Can I ask you a question?"

Penny nodded. "Sure."

"Was Rory depressed?"

"Rory was frustrated. He couldn't catch a break." A tear rolled down her cheek, and she punched her hand with her fist. "I don't know why I'm talking about him in the past tense."

"Last I spoke to him he was working on a script. He asked if he could stay here," Logan told her. "I turned on all the utilities for him. Pen, was Rory taking drugs or something."

Penny got up and walked to the bathroom. She returned with a balled-up tissue in her hand. "Yes."

"Why didn't you call me?" Logan's face fell.

"What could you do? You were traveling and I knew Aimee gave you crap about seeing us."

Logan felt his jaw twitch.

"Don't get mad. I didn't like her too much either. Dad put him in Miracles, you know the rehab place. When he got out, Doc Leeds prescribed antidepressants. He was okay and wanted to write, again. Things were looking up. Some network was considered one of his scripts for streaming." Penny shook her head. "No, I think he was getting better."

"And the drugs?"

"As far I know, they were under control."

Her bottom lip trembled. Logan could feel the coiled tension in her body. He put his arm around her, and she settled in next to him. She was so quiet; he thought she might have fallen asleep. He bent low to peer at her, and she reached up to kiss him. He moved his head sideways, catching the kiss on his cheek.

"You want to crash here?" His voice was low.

She mumbled an answer but didn't move. They sat quietly together until he heard the slow rhythm of her breathing. Logan eased her out from his side and laid her gently on the couch. He went to his room and brought out a cover, then tucked her in. He watched her sleep, the fan of her lashes covering the gentle swell of her cheeks. He leaned down, brushed the hair from her face, and closed the lights, plunging the room into blackness.

Padding to his room, he touched his cheek where she'd kissed him. It still tingled.

CHAPTER 12

LOGAN'S DREAMS WERE vivid, making for a restless night. He was in the boat with his father, who
was leaping in and out of the craft with the grace of
an Olympic diver. George dove into the murky waters only
to resurface, pieces of his body missing and round bite marks
covering his torso where his hip or shoulder should have been.

Logan lay in a tangle of sheets, sweaty, irritable, and
waking every hour, his heart beating wildly. He dreamed
of Chief Kain and a figure behind him, menacing from the
shadows. His aunt's and uncle's worried faces haunted him
until they too were gobbled up with round bite marks.

He gave up on sleeping sometime after four but stayed
in his bed, going over the details again and again. At six, he
put on jogging shorts and a tee and left the house to run
on the beach. Logan knew Elliot would kill him and Penny
would call him an idiot, but he wasn't afraid, and he knew
all the answers would be found on the beach.

He ran down the unrecognizable shoreline, passing new house after new house. Everything had changed. He could tell by the hulking structures lining the water on stilts. His house alone sat on the sand; a dwarf surrounded by an army of giants.

It wasn't until the sun crested over the water, dazzling his eyes, that he realized he had not heard a single dog barking from any of the homes he passed.

He made a wide circle, coming back to run in front of the monstrosity next door. He heard a friendly shout and paused, breathing hard, his hands on his knees as he tried to catch his breath.

A man hobbled down the steps of the deck, his beefy arm waving. He was a big guy, his stomach a hard basketball combined with his stocky legs to give him the outline of a sumo wrestler. He was wearing shorts, and an open bathrobe flapped behind him. His chest was covered with so much hair, he could have easily been a distant cousin of Sasquatch. It was everywhere but his head, which was sunburnt and peeling. He wore dark glasses that he pushed onto his forehead. A large gold chain with some sort of medal nestled in his chest hair. He was holding a mug in one hand, a folded newspaper in the other. A golden lab trailed behind him.

"You're from next door?"

Logan was breathless from the run. He held out a hand, which was engulfed in a warm handshake.

"Norman Preston. You're Osbrook?"

"Logan Osbourne." Logan nodded.

"Just get into town?" Before Logan could respond,

Preston continued. "Staying long? I hope so. I'm glad we're finally meeting. It's about time. We just got in yesterday."

Logan felt his gaze regarding him, as if his neighbor was sizing him up.

Preston moved closer; his voice lowered. "Look, you've got to do something about your house. Do you mind? I mean, it's an eyesore."

Logan smiled. "Yes, I noticed. I haven't been here in a while."

Logan turned around to the water equipment bobbing at the end of the dock in the water. "Nice toys." He nodded toward the assorted jet skis.

"Kids like them." They walked to the water's edge. "I'll kill that little snot." Preston reached forward, yanking keys from one of the jet skis. "That son of mine. He always forgets to take in the keys. I'm gonna kill him."

The dog went near the surf. Preston's voice rang out, "Molly!" The dog whimpered and moved back to circle the sand near her master's feet.

"Labs are water dogs, right?" Logan asked, keeping his voice neutral.

"Yeah, they like it. But you above all should know the water's not safe."

Logan looked at him, holding his gaze, willing him to continue.

"I mean, you know how it is. The sea is full of predators."

"Sure. Sharks are known to walk on land and snatch small animals and children," Logan said.

Preston's eyes grew wide. His mouth dropped in shock. He stammered, "I didn't mean anything, really." He recovered quickly. "Look, you have to start taking care of the house. It's an invitation to vagrants. I'd be willing to buy it."

Logan watched the gulls wheeling across the sky, as if he were considering it. He looked back at Preston, keeping his voice neutral. "A friend of mine said there had been some dog disappearances of late. They find remnants of the body with circular bite marks."

Preston glanced around. "Chief Kain doesn't want anyone to talk about it."

"You know, I jogged this entire beach. I haven't heard a single dog bark."

"Yeah, well, nobody lets their animals out anymore. It's a thing, you know? We all follow it."

"What do you mean, a thing?" Logan asked.

"You know, an understanding. We all get it. It's not safe."

"Was there ever an official document?"

Preston laughed. "No. Just one too many mutilated pets. We're keeping our kids and pets close. You know what I mean?""

Logan was thoughtful for a minute. "Have you seen the bite marks?"

Preston gulped. "Yes, horrible." He put down his coffee on the piling at the dock, the newspaper next to it, then held up his two hands, making a circle. "This big they were. Gruesome. I think that Swanson kid—you know, the police girl's brother—I think something happened to him too." He pointed to a looming house two doors away. He had stopped making eye contact with Logan. He kept his gaze downward. "See that house? Those people lost both their cat and dog. They got the body of the cat back, but there was so little left, you couldn't even see the round marks."

Logan did his best not to show emotion. He was finally getting somewhere. His heart pumped wildly in his chest. "Got any ideas about what kind of animal did it?"

Preston shrugged and leaned closer. "Matter of fact, I've got a theory."

"I'd love to hear it."

"Satanism. It's ritualistic murders. I'm telling you, there's a coven of witches here. Your house is an open invitation for them to move in. Gonna ruin the neighborhood. Listen, Morgan, I'll give you a good price for your place."

"Logan."

"Yeah, whatever, Logan. I'll give you all cash, with a thirty-day closing."

Logan laughed to himself. He had no idea what that meant. "Well, nice meeting you." Logan held out his hand watching as it was swallowed by the other man's huge paws. "Gotta go," he said and resumed his one-man race.

Logan made himself a cup of tea and sat on the rear porch, drinking in silence. He watched the sun burn off the morning haze, the mesmerizing ebb and flow of the waves calling him. He knew they held all the answers to his questions.

"We had company last night?" Elliot asked, a toothbrush in his paste-filled mouth.

"Penny left?" Logan asked.

"You and Penny a thing yet?"

Logan fought the surge of anger, his fists clenched. He made himself breathe deeply. He knew Elliot didn't mean anything. He interrupted him. "No, she's like a kid sister to me," he said, wondering why the words sounded so hollow. "Hurry up. I'll be waiting in the car."

"What about breakfast?"

"We'll get something in town," Logan said as he walked toward the door.

"What's the rush? It's not even eight-thirty," Elliot called.

Logan didn't answer.

Logan waited in the jeep for Elliot. He had a bunch of errands planned.

They stopped by Sly's shop. This time the door was locked despite the notice in the window saying they were open. Logan jiggled the doorknob.

"There's nobody there. The shop is dark," Elliot said in a bored voice. "No matter how hard you rattle that door, nobody is going to answer."

Logan hopped down the steps.

"Can we eat?" Elliot whined. "I'm starving."

"You're worse than a five-year-old." Logan rolled his eyes and took off for the diner in the center of town.

They grabbed a corner booth and slid in. Their order was taken by an older waitress. Elliot gave complicated directions on how he wanted his eggs cooked while she scribbled on her pad, cracking her gum.

Logan looked at her name tag, asking, "Hi… Bertha?"

She nodded. "You need anything special for your eggs?"

Logan shook his head and smiled. "Is Eddie still the cook here?"

"Eddie? He passed away ten years ago." She took off her glasses and looked at him. "Do I know you?"

"We used to eat here all the time. My parents and me. My father was Professor Osbourne."

Logan watched her closely for a reaction. She hid it well. He saw her shoulders stiffen; her chewing slowed. She considered him a long minute and asked, "You're that kid Lonnie?"

"Logan," he corrected.

"Right. Logan." She was observing him warily. "That was a long time ago. What brings you back?"

"Home?" Logan continued. "I missed the place. Thought it was time to visit again."

She looked around the diner and moved closer to him. "What'd you really come back for?"

"What do you think?" Logan leaned in close to her as he asked it.

He could swear he heard her hiss. He was so close; he saw where her red lipstick bled into the tiny lines that surrounded her tight mouth. Their gazes locked for a bit, and she broke it away first.

"I'll get you those eggs."

"What the heck was that about?" Elliot asked as soon as they were alone. "It's like we're in some movie-of-the-week town where everyone is hiding something."

"Yeah," Logan said thoughtfully. "It sure does."

Bertha brought them their food, practically throwing

it at them. The diner had filled with people. The place hummed with noise.

Logan chewed his food, his eyes watching for the waitress. She wandered to check if they were happy with the food.

"Bertha, do you know where Sly's gone off to?"

She leaned over, her face nasty. "Do yourself a favor, Osbourne, and go back to wherever you've been hiding all these years." She stood up. "You see this place? It's busy, the way we need it to be so we can all make a good living. We don't need no troublemakers here, no sir." She slapped the check on the greasy table.

Logan took out a crumpled twenty from his pocket and placed it next to his empty plate. He picked up the bill to pay by the register. He noticed the place had gone quiet. The patrons were watching them as they left the diner.

"That was spooky the way the place went all silent when we were leaving. Do you have that effect everywhere you go?" Elliot shivered.

"Lately," Logan responded.

"Where are we headed?" Elliot asked.

"Tidewell House. The people there lost a dog. It had those same round bite marks."

They drove for a half hour, entering a part of town where the homes were half-hidden by rows of overgrown cedars. Logan slowed the car, not remembering exactly where Dune Road was located.

"That's it." Elliot pointed to a half-bent street sign.

The Richardsons of Tidewell house lived off a sandy lane down one of the many roads that faced the beach. If the new homes by his beach were big, these were enormous. Some had their own helicopter pads.

"Oh em gee! Elliot exclaimed. "We're in rarefied air here."

The uneven road opened to a giant compound that looked like a Hamptons cottage on steroids. Logan pulled into a court, got out of the car, and walked up to double doors. There was a giant bronze sculpture in the yard. It was a circle with a type of girder running through the center. Nothing appeared to hold the steel beam up; it looked like it was floating. The sculpture was placed on a cement platform in the center of the emerald grass of the yard.

Elliot walked up to the artwork. He stood studying it for a minute. "You know this is a Calder?"

"Really?" Logan replied.

"Yeah. It's signed."

"Wow." Logan nodded, impressed.

The driveway was made of large squares with the same bright green grass bordering each square. A lot of thought had been put into the design of the house. It had amazing details, as if crafted with loving hands.

It was made to last, yet as they got closer, Logan could see a neglected air about the building. A shutter had fallen and lay propped against the shingles. The top of an antique-looking lamp was missing, making it look like a hatless leprechaun.

The sun was full out, beating down on their heads mercilessly.

The door swung open. A college-aged girl was holding the brass doorknob, her windswept blond hair half covering her face. She was in a bikini top and cutoff jeans the size of a postage stamp.

"Are you here for Tarik's party?" she asked, her eyes lingering on Logan and the tattoo sleeve covering his arm.

"Is Mr. or Mrs. Richardson home? I need to speak to them."

"No. They don't live here anymore."

"They moved?" Logan asked, looking over her shoulder into the entrance hall.

"No. They rent it now. A bunch of us have taken it for the season."

Logan peered into the cavernous living room; its terrazzo floors bare of furniture.

"Do you know where I can reach them?"

She held open the door. "Come on it."

Both Elliot and Logan followed her inside. The house stank of weed. People sat in clusters around the empty room. There were cots and bedrolls everywhere. Outside by the pool, Logan counted over twenty people lounging or playing in the water. The house was elevated so that the bright blue Atlantic filled the wall of windows that made up the back of the house.

Sailboats and watercrafts bobbed on the choppy waves.

"How many people are renting here?" Logan asked.

"Depends on the week. It's a big house. We all live in the city and come out here for the beach. We're having a party tonight. Do you want to come?" she asked, her eyes sparkling.

"It's a beautiful house. Big."

"Yeah," she replied. "It's over ten thousand square feet."

Elliot whistled softly. "That's bigger than the whole floor

of my apartment house. Do you know why the Richardsons stopped living here?"

There was a shout followed by a scream. Logan took off, running though one of the open patio doors followed by both Elliot and the girl. He stopped at the railing to look down a steep incline to see a knot of people on the pale sand pointing at the beach. He turned his gaze to the direction a bystander was pointing to see the knobby head of a humpback whale break the surface of the water, then gracefully arc upwards. The whale crashed back into the ocean to the delight of the observers.

Cheers erupted from the bystanders, along with crows of delight.

"Wow. What a view," Elliot said. "It's like having your own personal aquarium."

Logan stood transfixed, his eyes glued to the spot where the whale frolicked, his breath in his throat. The mammal rose again, making an even bigger splash. A smaller humpback rolled onto its back, waving its baby flipper. Logan fought the urge to wave back. The whine of a high-powered motorboat intruded, and Logan's gaze was drawn to an expensive cruiser plowing through the waves. It was bigger than most of the boats he'd seen and was headed toward the estuary.

The boat was traveling directly in the path of the whale, it's bulky back glistening in the sun. The whale rose again letting loose a blast of air from its blowhole that looked like a geyser. The partygoers yelled indignantly at the careless driver of the motorboat.

Logan shaded his eyes, squinting. He made out several

males and a single female on the deck, holding onto the backs of cushioned seats on the speeding boat, the long strands of the woman's brown hair fanned out like a pennant. She had on dark glasses; her profile was startling familiar. Logan blinked once, then rubbed his eyes. It was something in the way she stood. *Turn your head,* he urged. Her rigid stance didn't change.

Logan's scalp tightened; his skin tingled as if someone walked on his grave.

"Is that-?" Elliot burst.

"I can't tell. It can't be. What would she be doing here?" Logan responded too quickly. He wasn't sure. He didn't want to think it was her. There was no reason for Aimee to be in the Hamptons.

Two other girls strolled over and joined them. "Who are your new friends, Daisy?"

"They're not my friends... yet?" she asked Logan and Elliot.

"Do you have a way to contact them?" Logan ignored her comment.

"I told you. They don't live here anymore. If you want to know the truth, I rented it from them for an amazing price for the size of this place. I dunno. The realtor said something about the house having bad memories for them or something. Are you gonna come back for the party tonight?"

"Can't wait," Elliot replied.

Logan studied the expanse of beach, but his eyes kept darting to the disappearing wake of the speed boat. "Who is the real estate agent?"

She eased her phone from her tight jean shorts. "If you give me your number, I'll share it with you." she smiled.

Logan pulled out his phone and said, "Just read the realtor's number to me, and I'll put it in my phone."

Daisy rolled her eyes, gave him the number, and stuffed her phone back into her hip pocket. "Oh, her name is Marion Humphries, and the company is… Ella, what is the name of the realtor we used for this place?"

Ella shouted back, "Quayle Realty."

"Well, that got us nowhere," Elliot said as they got back into the car. "But the humpback was spectacular. Do you think that was Aimee in the boat? It sort of looked like her."

Logan titled his head. "I'm not sure. It was far. It could be anybody. I did however get the realtor's number." He paused; his brow furrowed. "It doesn't add up. That's a ten-million-dollar house that the Richardsons left to rot. There's no way they're charging enough to cover the cost of the house."

"They're probably shitting money. Maybe it's a loss leader."

"Real estate in the Hamptons is not a loss leader. That house was built with a lot of care, and now they've abandoned it."

"Yeah, and who would abandon a Calder if they weren't going to live there?" Elliot pointed out.

"It's as if they don't care about the house. Something made them leave it to the beach rats," Logan said as he turned on the car.

A shout from behind him stopped him from moving. Daisy was bounding down the steps.

"Stop!" She bounced up to the window, breathless. "I just remembered something."

The car was running, Logan shut the engine.

"It was something the wife said about Plum Island or something. They were here the day we took over. They were leaving."

"Go on," Logan told her.

"They said they didn't want to stay here anymore because of the experiments at Plum Island. That's silly, right?" she asked, her eyes huge in her face.

"I'm sure it's nothing to worry about." Logan smiled back.

"Well, come back for the party tonight. We'd love to have you. Tarik is hiring a DJ, and we're gonna have food trucks."

Logan nodded, and they pulled out.

"What do you think of that?" Elliot asked.

"Not much," Logan shook his head. "They all blame Plum Island for everything."

"Plum Island? Why does that sound familiar?"

"Back in the fifties, they did some biological stuff there. I mean, it could be related," Logan said thoughtfully.

"Oh, right. It was an animal disease research center. Do you think anything funky is going on there?"

"Anything is possible, but…"

"But what?"

"That thing I saw, those bite marks." Logan shook his head. "It doesn't make sense." He handed Elliot the card. "Call the number and let's see what she has to say about the house."

"What do you want me to say?' Elliot took the card.

"I don't know. Tell her you want to make an offer. See where that takes us." Logan laughed. "Yeah, tell her you'll make an all-cash deal with a thirty-day closing."

"What's that mean?"

Logan shrugged. "Who cares, just say it and see if she bites. Maybe we'll get some information."

Elliot punched in the number. A recording answered, so he left a message for the agent to call him back. They pulled out of the driveway, each lost in his own thoughts.

Logan sped through town. As he pulled up to a light, he realized the realtor's office was on the opposite side of the road.

"Quayle Realtors." Logan nodded to the quaint building. It was a gingerbread Victorian painted pale blue with violet trim. They drove onto the crushed-shell driveway and walked up the flagstone path to climb the steps to the front door.

Elliot looked at the architecture and muttered, "Looks like a postcard."

Logan agreed. "The area is a conglomeration of all types of styles. This is original to the area. It used to be a preschool back in the eighties."

"I like the modern jobs, like the house we just left. When I buy a house, that's what I want."

"Yeah, right. On our salaries. You're lucky you have two incomes between the two of you, plus your trust. I'll be a renter forever."

"Not unless we discover something really big."

Logan's face changed. "I told you, Elliot. I'm not in this for the money."

"I know, I know."

Inside the entry was a narrow hallway with two rooms on either side. What must have been a living room and dining room now housed two desks each. There was a row of Windsor chairs lined up in the hallway.

One office was empty. In the other, a woman sat absorbed in her computer. Her desk was covered with papers. She looked up, her glasses magnifying her eyes, so she looked like a fly.

"May I help you?"

"I'm looking for Marion Humphries."

She scanned them from the tops of their heads to the tips of their shoes. "Are you looking for a place to rent for the season? I can assure you everything's booked for the season."

Logan shook his head. "I just want to ask Marion a few questions."

She put down her pen, stood up, and held out her hand. "I'm Marion. What kind of questions?"

"You rented out the Richardsons' place?"

"If you want to squeeze in there, you'll have to talk to the kids renting the place." She looked at them both and smiled. "I'm sure they'll find room for the two of you."

"No," Logan interrupted her. "I wanted to ask a few questions about the house."

Marion put down her pen, her eyes shrewd as if she was sizing the two of them up. "Are you interested in buying something?"

"Yeah, we'd like to make a deal. All cash," Elliot said.

She stood and dragged another chair over to her desk. "Please sit down. Is this an investment property?"

"We've been thinking about it for a while," Elliot said, warming to the charade. "Right, hon?"

Marion smiled a warm toothy grin. "Mr.?"

"Elliot, and this is-"

Logan interrupted, "And we'll close in thirty days, too."

The realtor started typing on her computer forgetting the introductions. "Very attractive incentive, but the Richardson place is not for sale. I could show you something a little further-"

"Why won't they sell?" Logan asked.

She looked up at them owlishly. "I'm sure I don't know. I have a nice place that's even bigger just down the block." She printed up a listing and held it out to Logan. "Seven bedrooms, six baths, and a pool house."

"Do you think I could speak to them?" Logan took the paper without looking at it. "Maybe I can convince them."

Marion placed both her palms on the desk, her eyes guarded. "I'm not happy the way this conversation is going." She glanced at the door. "I don't think you are here to buy anything."

"Do you have their phone number?" Elliot persisted.

Marion rose then walked around the desk toward the door. "I can't give out that information, Mr....?"

"Wayne. Bruce Wayne." He held out his hand but lowered it when he saw her frosty eyes.

"If you are not interested in renting or purchasing a property, we have nothing further to discuss, *Mr. Wayne*." She opened the door, letting a blast of heat penetrate the room. "I think you should leave."

"I haven't finished asking my questions."

"Well, I certainly have nothing more to say to you."

They left with no more information than when they arrived.

"Bruce Wayne? Elliot said. "You couldn't have come up with something more original than that?

"What would you have picked?"

"Lannister. Tyrion Lannister."

Logan snorted and said, "Oh, that's real original."

Logan pulled into a small red shack advertising lobster rolls. There was a line by a window where a clerk handed out trays filled with food. Picnic tables with umbrellas surrounded the building. A large oak tree gave more coverage from the punishing rays of the sun.

"You're kidding me, right?" Elliot asked, eyeing the stand with distaste.

"It's going on eleven. I figured you were hungry already."

Elliot laughed. "Yeah, but you think Long Island can compete with Boston with a lobster roll?"

"Who said I'm competing? Are you hungry or what?"

Elliot hopped out of the jeep. Logan held up four fingers, and a minute later the clerk handed him four potato rolls stuffed with lobster meat.

"There's no mayonnaise," Elliot complained.

"Just eat it. They douse them with melted *buttah*," Logan said, parodying a Bostonian accent. He went back and returned with two water bottles. They navigated around a crowd of people to sit at the end of a table across from each other. Elliot took a bite and nodded with appreciation. "Not bad."

"You guys up north don't hold a monopoly on these things."

"You still haven't shown me anything that comes close to Boston baked beans," Elliot responded.

"Somehow I don't see the need for… " Logan stopped their banter when someone blocked the sun, casting a shadow over the table.

"Food good?"

Though the encounter was not confrontational, Logan felt his back stiffen. Chief Kain stood next to the table, his sunglasses on, his eyes hidden.

Elliot, never one for caution, must have felt the threat because he responded, "Just enjoying the sites of your cozy little town."

The air became decidedly cooler. The chief nodded, his mouth a grim line. "That so? Make sure you take him past Cedar Haven, then, Osbourne. I bet he'll find that real cozy."

The last word was said with such menace, the food turned to dust in Logan's mouth. He balled the paper in his hand, stood, and took his trash and empty water bottle to the garbage, tossing them in.

"Cedar Haven's closed," he said quietly.

"That's a fact. The building is still standing as a reminder, though." The policeman's voice was soft but held no warmth. "You have to stop bothering the folks here, Osbourne. If I get one more complaint, I'm going to have to charge you."

"With what?" Elliot shouted.

Logan stood frozen, staring at the officer. He couldn't have moved even if he'd wanted to. He was back in that hospital bed and a little boy of nine once again.

"Well," Elliot rose taking his trash to the receptacle, "if the place is closed, sounds like there's nothing to worry about, then, right? Let's blow this joint, Logan. I know you liked it, but for me," he added, patting his flat stomach, "something smells a little fishy here."

A laugh bubbled up Logan's throat, coming out as a cough. "Right. Let's go, then."

They jumped into the jeep. Elliot turned to Logan. "That was friggin' weird. What's all this crap about Cedar Haven?"

"It's an old mental institution."

"For a small town," Elliot said. "You got a lot of crap here. What' up with the nut house?"

"It's not actually in the town, it's on a small island isolated from the area. You can't get there except by boat."

"You're white as a ghost." Elliot put on his seat belt. "The place is closed. You make it sound like something we read in English lit."

"Sometimes a thing doesn't have to be real to scare you," Logan murmured as he peeled out of the dirt parking lot onto the main drag. "I'll show you."

They drove for a bit, the salty breeze ruffling their hair. Logan picked up speed on the causeway. To their right, homes stood on high cliffs overlooking reedy marshes bisected by the road. The other side was a short beach with a jagged coastline of water. The bright sun bounced off the waves. Both Logan and Elliot put on sunglasses.

"Where are we going?"

"Oyster Point."

Logan rounded a bend and came to an outcropping with a metal barrier at the edge. Logan stopped the jeep. "Come on."

They got out. Logan pointed to the foggy horizon. "Look northwest. Over there." Logan shaded his eyes.

"I don't see…. What is that? Looks like something you'd dream up in a zombie apocalypse."

"Exactly," Logan agreed. "It's Cedar Haven. It was a mental asylum built at the end of the nineteenth century. They used to scare us with it all the time."

"How gothic. Wait, it was still in operation when you lived here?"

Logan gave a curt nod.

"Was the Sheriff of Nottingham threatening us with that? That's absurd. It's closed. This place is just a little too bizarre for me," Elliot said in disbelief.

Logan didn't answer. The water lapped against the pilings; the breeze plastered their clothes against their bodies. Gulls cried mournfully. Logan was staring down at the swirling eddies of water.

"He didn't get to you, did he?" Elliot's voice softened.

Logan cleared his throat. "When it happened, you know, with my father, I told them I saw a mermaid." He turned to Elliot. "I haven't talked about this in twenty years. I was so sure of what I saw, but they made me question myself. They said they were going to bring me to Cedar Haven and throw away the key." Logan lowered his head. "In the end, I changed my story. I kept thinking and thinking about it, and soon I wasn't sure about anything anymore."

"You were nine years old."

Logan's eyes searched the ocean. "They say when the wind is right, you can still hear the ghosts of the inmates screaming."

Elliot put his hand on Logan's shoulder. "Come on, man. You don't believe in ghosts, do you?"

Logan gave a half-hearted chuckle. "No, just mermaids."

"Well, be that as it may, by the time we finish here, we'll prove it. About the mermaids." Elliot pointed to the hulking silhouette of Cedar Haven. "That place is closed. We don't have to worry about it. The T-1000 over there"—he pointed back toward the town where they left the sheriff—"is skating on thin ice. A lot of what he's doing feels illegal. Next time he starts, I'm going to film him with my cell."

"Elliot, he's nuts. I stayed away from here for a reason. Don't mess with these people. I just want to find out what happened to Rory and get the hell out of here."

They walked back to the car.

"Can you take me to the estuary? I'd like to see it," Elliot asked.

"We should." Logan pulled a hard right, his face tight, his eyes a million miles away. "I want to look at those police reports."

They headed back to the cottage, Elliot checking emails while they drove.

"Did you hear from Vadim yet?" Logan inquired.

"No," Elliot said. "But that's not unusual. He's probably waiting for the lab reports. Don't you want to take a look at the estuary?" he asked as they pulled onto Logan's street.

Logan gazed out the window at the view of the crashing sea. "Yeah. Later when it's dark. I don't want our friend Chief Kain seeing us there."

CHAPTER 13

THEY RETURNED TO the house; Logan flopped on the sand on the narrow strip of beach to watch the surf as it rolled against the shoreline. Ten minutes later, Elliot joined him.

"Where were you?"

"Checking tide tables. Someone's got to work on something other than their tan," Elliot said with a laugh.

Logan nodded, "Anything from Vadim about the specimen?"

Elliot sat on the sand. "Nope. Nothing yet."

Five jet skis roared across the waves, driven by the neighbor's son and his friends. Their shouts cut up the peace, and the group entertained themselves by circling the area by Logan's place, doing silly tricks that caused them to fall into the water.

"You remember being young like that?' Elliot asked,

handing him his cell phone. "Go ahead. I know you want to look."

Logan shook his head. "No."

"No, to what. No, you don't remember being that young?" Elliot looked pointedly at the iPhone.

"I'm not looking."

"Why? I'm sure if you Google her name-"

"I'm not searching for Aimee!" Logan sat forward ignoring the cell. "She deactivated her Facebook page."

Elliot smirked. "Ha! You looked already."

"You're an asshole." Logan paused. "No, I mean, yes. A while ago."

Elliot raised his eyebrow. "She just does something to you."

"I don't know what you're talking about," Logan snapped, then paused. "Okay, I looked last week, but that was because I thought I saw her in Arizona."

"Well?"

Logan shook his head. "Nothing. Last I heard she was working in Singapore. Something about a giant squid. It's weird."

"It was weird that we both thought it was her when we saw that passing boat."

"No, that's not what I was talking about. We broke up last summer. When she took that job."

"You could have gone with her to Asia." Elliot sat hunched over, his forearms on his knees. "It was a good offer."

Logan stared out at the horizon.

"It was a lot of money," Elliot continued.

Logan's lips tightened. "She's been to three of the sites we've visited."

"Four and five," Elliot counted off on his fingers, "If you include Arizona and today."

Logan shrugged. "That's inconclusive. I fell about fifteen feet from the beak of that Thunderbird. I was concussed. I could have imagined her."

"I know I didn't dream her up today. Logan, they're searching for the same things as us. You got a homing device on you, or something?"

Logan was thoughtful. "That's the thing, other than the thylacine, they haven't brought in cryptids of note."

"I don't consider the Tasmanian Devil a genuine cryptid. It's extinct, not based in myth. They were hunted to death. Now, if she brought in a bunyip or a Jersey Devil, that would have been something."

"Aimee and I spent two weeks with an Aboriginal tribe in Australia looking for a bunyip." Logan smiled at the memory. "She was relentless."

Elliot nodded. "She's a maniac. Her students call her Taz."

"What?"

"Yup, behind her back, because they think she's as crazy as the Tasmanian Devil. I remember the stories about Haifa, when you two were searching for the mermaids. You almost ended up in an Israeli prison," he laughed.

Logan nodded. "Her temper gets the best of her. That's what's strange. She can

be aggressive, nothing stops her from the truth, and now that she has all the funds she needs, why can't the Obsidian Corporation discover anything?"

"You still didn't answer my question, why didn't you go with them?"

Logan's jaw hardened. "Gut feeling. Haversham is easy with rules. I didn't like the way Obsidian approached me."

"And it cost you your relationship." Elliot looked down. "Not that we all didn't see it coming."

"Really?" Logan asked.

"She's impossible. You're a saint."

Logan snorted. "Hardly."

Eliot continued, "Vadim refuses to have anything to do with her. Haversham won't even mention her name."

Logan took a breath and answered thoughtfully. "She's difficult. I understand, but that's part of her and when you get to know the whole person, you understand that passion she has is incredible, so you take the good with the… not so good."

"Maybe you do," Elliot laughed. "Too high maintenance for me. If you loved her so much, why didn't you go with her?"

"She went down her road, I went down mine. Neither one is better than the other. Just different."

"Oh, no pal, we're the white hats. They are definitely the bad guys."

Logan gave him a penetrating stare. "What makes you so sure of that?"

"She would've taken the egg."

Logan couldn't argue. Elliot was right. It was one of the disagreements that fed the fires of their relationship. He would never disturb a living creature. DNA and film footage was fine for him, Aimee argued they needed proof of life, the real deal. Logan looked to expand cryptids as a subject to be studied, not exploited. Aimee pushed for something bigger, a television show or working for a large corporation that would pay the bills. Their final fight was brutal.

"You don't understand!" she screamed one evening last summer, smashing her cigarette into an overflowing ashtray. He had never smoked, not until he met Aimee. He associated his last days with her in a haze of smoke and brimstone.

Aimee lived in a state of anger and when they argued, it was epic. The lower her patience, the more agitated she became. He recalled their last fight, replaying it in his mind hundreds of times. How it escalated to the point of no return.

"No, you don't understand." He modulated his voice, first for the neighbors, the other to bring down the velocity of their argument.

"We'll work for them for two years, that's all. Then we'll have enough to produce something for network television or even the streaming services."

"To what end?" he asked with maddening patience.

"I hate when you get like this." Aimee was fiery about her interests, including him. He loved that side of her, except when she pushed too far and became obsessive about the subject.

"What has Obsidian done so far? They have quite a team, Gregory Rushmore, Seymour Hauser, and Jennifer Rivera." He ticked off three of the biggest names in the field. "Why haven't they announced anything of significance? I think they're hiding something."

"That's ridiculous. You're being paranoid." Aimee dismissed his grievances.

"Jennifer Rivera's been searching for a Dingonek for years. She discovered that tusk near Lake Victoria. Why'd she leave that project to bring in a domesticated Okapi. Anybody could've done that," he said with disgust.

"They'll pay us to travel and discover strange new creatures," Aimee snapped. She started to pace the room.

"An Okapi is not a new creature. I want to look for the ones that exist in the shadows. The undocumented creatures. Monsters."

Aimee stopped and smiled in a way that turned his insides to jelly. "I love when you talk like that." She had a small mole on the outside of her upper lip. It lifted when she grinned, drawing his attention. He couldn't stop staring at her.

He smiled. He loved the slight French inflection left over from her childhood in Paris. It charmed him from the minute she spoke to him. She had won any number of arguments, disarming him completely. Most of the time, he gave into her whims. It seemed harmless, and ultimately not worth the argument. Pouting Aimee was no fun for anyone.

Steeling his conviction, he shook his head. "Not gonna work this time. I don't want anyone dictating what I can find and write about."

"That's silly, of course they'll let you write about it. Obsidian will pay a bounty for every new cryptid we bring in."

Logan covered her hands with his own. "That's the other thing. I don't want the creatures' habitats disturbed."

"Neither do they," Aimee exploded standing up. "They are transparent in their conviction."

"You call this transparent. Read the contract." Logan held up a sheaf of papers. "They own anything we discover, lock, stock, and barrel." He slammed the papers on the table. "Check out section fifteen, part seven." He rifled the papers until he found the spot. "Said creature will be retrieved and be the sole property of Obsidian. No photos, drawings, or descriptions are to be duplicated or revealed… blah, blah, blah. They'll own the creatures and us. I'm not interested."

Aimee went into the bedroom, banging doors and then returned, her face fierce. "I don't want to spend the rest of my life wanting to do things and then worrying about how we are going to pay for them. Look at this place, too hot in the summer, too cold in the winter." She pointed to the dingy walls with peeling wallpaper. "We can't afford to buy our own habitat, no less visiting a cryptid site will be impossible. If your classes get cut next year, our trip to search for the Chuchuna is never going to happen."

Logan didn't care much for his surroundings. He barely noticed them. For the most of their four years together they lived for fieldwork, and academia. He thought she didn't care about the material aspect of where they lived, or how much money was in the bank. Sure, it'd be nice to have unlimited funds, but somehow, they managed to get where they needed to be. It wasn't important, it never was. "Haversham assured me I have a place."

"But I don't!" It was a sore point between them. He was assigned his classes in the fall. Her schedule had been reduced. "The school year is over."

He was about to remind her the light schedule was the result of an unfortunate incident where Aimee's volatile nature got the better of her, but then snapped it shut letting sleeping dogs lie.

He walked to the kitchen table that served as a desk. It was overflowing with books, papers, and magazines. "I can't leave. I have papers to grade. I have some things to finish up. I can take another job for a few weeks and make enough for both of us to get to Russia this summer." He pulled out a chair to sit down.

"That's not what I'm talking about, and you know it," Aimee shot back. She stalked across the room. "This is our chance. No more youth hostels, or traveling on a shoestring budget, begging for capital. We'd be respected, corporate. Logan. I mean, what do you really want to do when you grow up?" She gripped his forearm, her brown eyes appealing. "Just a year or two of this and then we would have enough to open a cryptid zoo, if that's what you want."

Logan opened his mouth and no words came out. He felt himself deflate and said quietly, "We've been together four years, and you still don't know me." He stood to face the window. "It's not about money, or a zoo," he said with derision. "I don't want to destroy them. I want to prove they are real, legitimize the reports that have ruined people's lives."

"Not everything is about your father," Aimee snapped.

Fury roiled through him. Logan didn't answer her. He rose quickly, grabbed his jacket.

"Where are you going?"

"Out."

Aimee sniffed. "I'm not finished."

Logan didn't answer her. He was finished. He didn't want to discuss it. He left the apartment to clear his head, walking to Elliot's.

"Fight?" Elliot asked when he opened the door.

Logan shrugged.

"Want a beer?" Elliot grabbed two long neck bottles

with one hand, snapping off the caps with the other. He handed the icy bottle to Logan. "I'm listening if you want to talk about it."

They collapsed on the olive-green couches that took up most of the space in the cramped apartment.

"You don't like her-" Logan started.

"I may not like Aimee, but I'm fair."

Logan recounted the argument. Elliot listened without saying a word, then flicked on the television. They watched ten minutes of a tennis match until he said, "You could try working it out. Make it for a very limited time. Change the contract to protect your finds. If they want you badly enough, they'll agree to your demands." He added, "Logan, dude, it's nothing new. You know she's compulsive and driven. Aimee always gets what she wants."

Logan opened his mouth to defend her then snapped it closed. She was all of those things, it was a part of her charm, what attracted him to her. Aimee never did anything by halves. Her enthusiasm for her projects was infectious. She had a way of making everything fun and exciting.

Aimee taught him to step outside the box, take chances. He had changed since they'd been together, and he liked to think that he had influenced her as well. She pulled him from the quiet place he existed, dragging him to explore things he never thought possible. If he had to admit it, her free-spiritedness reminded him of his mother. Logan felt like he understood her, tempering her impatience, he was able to curb her wilder impulses. They were perfect as a pair, balancing each other out.

Logan put the beer on the table.

"That's going to leave a ring," Elliot complained.

Logan smiled at Elliot's fussiness. "Then you'll have tangible proof that I was here."

Elliot went into the kitchen, bringing a towel to wipe down the coffee table. "I'm not looking for proof that a human was here. I have enough of those. Don't be so hard on her. She probably feels stuck."

"Do you? Logan asked.

Elliot shrugged. "I have my trust, so money is not a problem." Elliot had inherited a sizable fortune from his grandfather. He didn't have to work for money.

"My uncle is always asking when I am going to start making a living doing this," Logan said grimly.

"You're not doing so badly, Logan." Elliot said. "Once you make professor, the money is kinda good. It's the grants that are a problem. No one wants to fund our research because they don't believe--"

"I know," Logan interrupted. "Cryptozoology is a real science."

"If you want stability," Elliot told him. "Then you should have picked high school biology. I hear the medical is great. What do you want to be when you grow up?"

Logan sat down, his face glum. "Aimee asked the same thing."

"Try to see it from her point of view. Look, the fact is, even though sometimes I find her irritating, I understand where she is coming from."

Logan's head shot up. "Would you leave and work for Obsidian if they offered?"

Elliot sat down next to him. "They have and I told them no, I wouldn't."

"They tried to recruit you? Why didn't you mention it?"

"I thought about it. I figured they contacted you to. They've been hiring everybody. I didn't want my decision to affect yours. I can eat and maintain my scruples. I don't need them, but I won't blame you if you do."

Logan left Elliot's that night willing to think about a compromise. Taking Elliot's advice, he mulled over the idea of negotiating for a year.

He arrived to a dark and empty apartment.

Aimee had packed her things and left. He checked the drawers and closets in their bedroom. Everything was gone. He took out his cell to call her, stopped and stood in the pitch dark. He was angry, his face tight with hurt. His gut churned. He looked at the face of his phone, pulled up her number, then swiped it back to the main screen. He rested it carefully on the bedside table with measured movements refusing to give into the impulse to throw it against the wall. He lay down flat on his back. Staring at the ceiling. Bitterness thinned his lips, his heart felt like a dead weight in his chest. Logan squeezed his emotions into a tight little ball, the way he did when his mother left. Putting a protective shell, he buried them deep in a dark space never to be examined. He placed his wrist over his mouth, a sigh escaped him. He had papers to grade, an article to write. He rose feeling like an old man, went to his desk and turned on his computer. The blue light illuminated his stark face. Pulling up the papers of his students, he read but the words made no sense. He kept returning to Aimee and the fact she'd abandoned him, and their dreams.

Maybe he hadn't seen it coming. Perhaps she didn't love him as much as he thought he loved her- like George and Samantha, history was repeating itself. Aimee was gone, and in making her choice, it allowed his conscience to clear. As if he had sudden clarity, the world rotated back on its axis, everything became focused. He did not have to compromise his values for love. Still, her last words stung. The sharp bite left his skin slightly thicker, his heart a little cracked.

None of his decisions were about his father. If it truly consumed him, then he wouldn't have spent his time or limited funds in Indonesia searching for the hominid, Ebu Gogo, or froze his ass off looking for Selma, the lake monster, in Norway last winter break. If he was only thinking about his dad, he'd be in the Hamptons. He never returned to Long Island, and for him it brought a measure of peace that her words did not ring true. He left the next day for his uncle's farm, submitting his student's grades electronically.

Logan shook off the memory. A gull screech brought him back to Elliot and the present.

"Logan, you still there," Elliot prodded him.

"Lost in thought for a bit." Logan laughed. He shook himself and looked at Elliot. "There's no way she's here. You see for yourself the town has buried the information. I doubt anything leaked out. There's no reason for her or Obsidian to be sniffing around."

Elliot agreed. "True, but still, you gotta admit it's weird that we both thought we saw her."

"It could have been anybody."

"Whomever it was, that was an expensive boat."

Logan frowned.

"What are you not telling me?" Elliot asked.

Logan turned to face Elliot but stopped when he heard a loud voice carry over from the water. It was the strident call of someone over a bullhorn. "I said, pull over!"

The jet skis were doing figure eights, the kids grasping bottles of beer, as they zigzagged across the ocean backing Logan's property. A police cruiser with that ape, Mitch at the helm roared passed. Logan saw Penny seated next to Mitch.

Mitch slowed the boat allowing Penny to exchange a smile with Logan. She waved, but a scowl from Mitch made her turn front, the expression wiped from her face. A siren filled the air, and the group of raucous boys burst out in drunken laughter.

One by one, they split up, moving in different directions, the cruiser in hot pursuit.

"I got to give it to your town, between the whales, mermaids, and Keystone Cops, it's vastly entertaining. What do you think they'll do when they catch them?"

"Penny will let them off with a warning." Logan smiled.

"What about the other guy?" Elliot pointed to Mitch. "Cro-Mitchdom."

Logan didn't answer, he was caught up in the chase. They both broke out in laughter as the wily teens moved closer together waiting for Mitch to approach them, they peeled off like a firework display in opposite directions. They could see Mitch pause in indecision, not knowing which jet ski to pursue.

"Yeah, he's a creep and a bully. But the father of the kid on the blue ski is loaded and will buy them out of trouble."

"I mean, I know the water is empty here, but they are a menace," Elliot said. "It's dangerous."

"You never did that?" Logan waved a hand. "They're just kids, having fun."

"Yeah, well, I wouldn't want my kid doing that. I'm hungry."

"You can't be serious."

"Serious as a heart attack. Want a sandwich?"

"I'll stay here."

Elliot left. Logan watched the police boat catch one of the boys. Penny climbed over the ledge of the boat and drove the jet ski back to the floating dock next door. She stood as she passed him, waving, her blonde braid unraveling as she flew past him.

Logan waited until she was out of sight, then picked up his discarded phone. He typed in Aimee Dupree and started to search the internet.

CHAPTER 14

DUSK WAS FALLING when they left. They cut through the town, and a couple of country roads later, they came to a stretch of street covered by sand. It was getting darker, the sky now revealing pinpricks of stars in the distance. It deepened to a teal blue, clouds scudding the horizon. Bullfrogs croaked a noisy concerto, fireflies floated lazily in the heavy night air.

"It's down there." Logan pointed to a small incline where tall grasses and cattails covered the sand.

"We're not the first to be here." Elliot pointed to fresh tire tracks.

Logan dropped to one knee and looked at them. "Big tires. An SUV." He looked up at Elliot. "Well, they're gone now." He stood.

They left the car on a patch of grass and walked casually toward a spit of sand that ended with a marshland.

The ground was spongy as if waterlogged. The further they walked, the more the growth thickened until they were hip deep in tall pale reeds. Logan could feel liquid seep into his boots. The water covered his ankles. The tidal pool lay before them like a small pond. It stretched far out, ending with a narrow passage leading out to sea.

Logan paused in the dense growth. He gestured toward the southwest. "The watershed is approximately forty-seven square miles. It receives freshwater from the Tide Mill Creek as well as a bunch of small rivers. We used to come here all the time, my father and I." He paused as if deep in thought. "That's where it happened." He pointed to the center of the inlet. "I never realized we were so close to the shore. I could have swum back." They looked at the still surface of the great salt marsh. "You can just reach out and scoop up the clams."

"Active sea life?" Elliot asked.

"You name it—fish like Atlantic cod and mackerel, flounder, ducks, shellfish. You could spend a lifetime eating from here."

"So why does it need to feed on land?" Elliot asked. "The creature?" he clarified impatiently at Logan's blank look.

Logan wasn't listening. His narrowed eyes scanned the horizon intently.

"Logan?" Elliot asked, glancing at his friend.

They heard a large splash startling them both. The water rippled in concentric circles, the lazy current disturbed. Logan pushed forward.

"Did you hear that?" Logan whispered; his voice awed.

Elliot's hand stayed him. The inlet stilled once again,

and the only thing Logan heard was the chorus of frogs and the slap of Elliot's hand when he killed a mosquito.

There was a cry of a bird behind them where the trees lined the beach. The insistent barking of a dog intruded. For a second, Logan wondered about the witness. Well, there's one person in town confident about letting their pet out.

He heard something move in the water. The frogs stopped their serenade. The dog's barking became frantic.

"Shhh," Logan said. He moved forward again. Night fell like a curtain, instantly blotting out all the light. Above them stars stretched over the inky blackness. The moon, waning gibbous, dusted the rippling water silver.

"It's not a full moon, dude." Elliot kept his voice low. "All the documented attacks were on full moons."

A mist moved over the water like a layer of spider webs cocooning their bodies and muting the sounds around them.

"That's the point, the documented attacks. I doubt any of them are recorded anywhere. Who knows when this thing feeds?" Logan's voice was barely a whisper.

Logan strained his eyes in the gathering gloom but could see nothing. He inched closer, the water lapping against his shins.

"What are you going to do, swim? We need a boat," Elliot said, reaching over to pull him from moving any further. Logan shook off his friend's arm, intent on listening. He heard the sound of something treading water, the surface of the inlet was gently disturbed. "Besides, it's too dark, Logan."

There was a splash. The sound of a giant paddle or whale fluke slapped the water, as if someone had done a bellyflop.

"That's a mighty big fish," Elliot added in a nervous whisper.

"What were the tide tables for tonight?" Logan asked, his eyes never leaving the water.

"Low tide. I thought everything's happened on high tides too. Could it be a turtle?" Elliot stepped next to him, his feet sloshing beneath them loudly.

Logan turned his face to snap at him for his clumsy movements when a change in the shadows caught his attention. Barely breathing, they watched a shape stand in the darkness, heard the drips of water running off its massive humanoid figure. Logan gasped. It was taller than either of them, and as they both topped six feet, this thing was big. Even from twenty yards away, Logan could see it dwarfed them.

"Oh em gee." Elliot's voice came out as a strangled croak. "It's freakin' huge." He fumbled for his cell phone. Elliot tried to focus on the shadow, but his shaking hands made it impossible.

The creature was indistinct in the dark night. A howl split the air, the noise somewhere between the lolling of a cow and with the shrillness of a siren. It traveled through Logan, making the fillings in his teeth hurt. *If an elephant and a Tasmanian devil had a baby, it would have sounded like this,* Logan thought inanely.

It began to move purposely toward them, its arms outstretched. Its eyes shone like blazing yellow neon, mesmerizing them. There was no place to hide in the tidal pool. Logan spun, pushing Elliot toward the parking lot.

"That was no turtle," Elliot gasped.

Logan ran, his heart pumping feeling like it would jump from his chest. "Run!" he yelled.

They splashed heavily in the shallows; their feet weighted with water. Clamoring through the tide, Logan slipped, Elliot pulled him under the armpit propelling him forward. Their clothes were drenched, glued to their perspiring bodies, their feet heavy with trapped fronds and weeds. They made it onto the beach.

Logan was afraid to look behind them. "Move this way!" Logan pointed to a perimeter of shrubs lining the sand.

They took off, their arms slashed by the tall grasses. Elliot clutched his phone. He turned for a second, but Logan grabbed the back of his shirt to drag him through the reeds. "Not now, you idiot!" Logan screamed.

They could hear the heavy splashes of the creature following them. They burst out of the grasses, running at full speed onto the sandy area toward the car. The reassuring outline of the jeep greeted them at the same time a club grazed Logan's shoulder.

Logan heard Elliot grunt with pain, the distinct sound of a fist meeting flesh echoing in the still night. Ham-sized hands gripped Logan's shoulder, spinning him to plant a fist that landed under his right eye. The night went silent but for the sound of the roaring of the blood in his head. He felt the trickle of blood leak onto his lips after his nose connected with what felt like a brick wall. He was on his knees, looking down at two sets of biker boots, silver skulls dangling over the insteps right in front of him.

Logan caught sight of another pair of footwear, polished traditional lace-ups. He pushed himself up on all fours, reaching out and grabbing the legs connected to those shoes. He clutched a handful of beige trousers, the gabardine material slipping in his hand. He recognized the uniform. He felt rock-hard muscles underneath the pants leg. His assaulter kicked, Logan's head snapping back to see a field of spinning stars. Their attackers were laughing. Logan was outraged.

They wouldn't be laughing when the mermaid from hell pounced on them, he thought groggily. He opened his mouth to let them know they were about to be surprised by the alleged wild dog or imaginary alligator but decided he'd have more satisfaction watching them wrestle with whatever was following them from the marsh.

A strong hand picked him up by the hair and another pounded his ribcage. He winced, his vision blurred, trying to see when the creature from the Black Lagoon would arrive like the cavalry.

Except *that* pursuer never arrived. It appeared that the monster had more brains than he and Elliot put together.

Logan listened vainly for whatever was following them to break through the marsh, but it must have been scared off. He chose that time to swing wildly, his fist finding a face that must have been hewn of stone. The impact stunned him more than the beating his ribs were taking. His arm went numb from knuckles to elbow.

His cheek landed in the dirt while Elliot was thrown against the car wheel. A baseball bat made contact with the windshield, showering them with shards of glass. The bat sailed through the air to smash the side mirror. More glass rained down on them.

Logan lay on his face, every bone in his body aching, his

head heavy. He heard new footfalls, lighter one, followed by the sound of a plank of wood connecting with a body.

"Ow!" one of his attackers howled.

Next, he heard several grunts, and the hard slam of bodies falling.

Logan picked up his head, his vision fuzzy to see two figures in wetsuits beating the crap out of his assailants. Tilting his head, he squeezed his eyes, discerning one was decidedly curvy and feminine. "Penny?" he asked, the word garbled by his swelling lips.

Running feet penetrated the fog that was swallowing his brain. Everything sounded muffled, as if he could barely hear it. There was a loud ringing in his ears.

"Done," a woman's voice came to him from far away. "Cowards," she spat.

"What do you want to do with these too?" a male voice asked.

"Leave them. They're harmless."

"The boss isn't going to be happy."

"I said leave them," the voice commanded.

Logan tried to rise, groaned and fell down into the wet sand. "Elliot?" his voice a thread.

"He's coming around. We have to go!" a man's barked.

The cold touch of a wetsuit made his skin goosebump as a person knelt next to him. He tried to roll over. Logan felt a soft hand brush back his hair. "Stop tilting at windmills, you silly man. Go back to school." He caught sight of a smile with a mole on the upper lip.

Logan felt the blood drain from his head as it fell onto a cushion of grass.

"Did you see them?" Logan spit out a mouthful of dirt. He was sprawled on a small mound and couldn't move.

"My eye is swollen shut," Elliot's voice was gravelly. "I feel like I got hit by a train. Am I imagining it, or were we rescued by the creature?"

"It wasn't the creature." Logan was breathless with the effort, wondering if he should share what he thought. "I think it was Aimee."

"Aimee!" Elliot coughed. "What's she doing here?"

Logan ignored the question; he was wondering the same thing.

Rising painfully to his knees he crawled over to where Elliot was propped against the wheel of the jeep. "Anything broken?"

"Only my pride. I feel like I'm trapped in an eighties crime drama. What are you doing?" he asked Logan, who was pulling his phone from his pocket with a battered hand.

"I'm calling the police."

"I think that was the police," Elliot retorted weakly. "What happened to your mermaid?"

Logan growled, "She's not *my* mermaid."

"Did you get any pictures?" Logan asked.

"Let me see with my good eye." Elliot squinted as he looked at his screen. "Nothing good. Maybe it was one of those goons setting us up."

Logan shrugged. "I couldn't see much, but I know it was that monster, Mitch and his playmates," he paused and continued, "And Aimee and some other guy."

"You think she was working with them?"

Logan shook his head. "No, they beat the crap out of them. Mitch practically crawled out of here."

"Are you sure it was Aimee? This is a major complication."

Logan didn't answer. He spoke into his phone. "Pen? Can you swing by the marsh, and Penny... don't say anything to anyone."

CHAPTER 15

P ENNY ARRIVED WITHIN a half hour, clucking and fussing, helping them into their car, then followed them home. She left them only to purchase a bag of ice at the gas station.

Logan reclined across the sofa; Elliot lay in a fetal position on the love seat.

"How come you get the bigger couch," he grumbled.

"My house." Logan placed his forearm over his eyes.

Penny returned lugging the bag of ice. "Are you sure you don't want to go to the hospital? I don't like the way your ribs-"

"No," both men answered in unison.

"I've had worse," Logan said after a short silence. "Ice and sleep. That's all we need."

"Well, alright, then," Penny said with a sigh. "Your diving equipment arrived today. I'll bring it in," she informed

Logan after she wrapped two dish towels with ice for them to put on their faces.

"Leave it. We have to get out of here to go back to the estuary." He squinted at his watch. "In an hour and a half," Logan told her.

"No way. You're not going anywhere tonight," Penny responded.

"We're leaving tonight at midnight." Logan's voice was firm. "In fact." He groaned as he rose. "I have to go out and get the trailer ready."

"Leave it. We'll do it later, together," Elliot said from his spot on the loveseat.

Logan let his head drop back onto the couch.

"I don't know why you can't wait a day," Penny called from the bedroom where she pulled out a few blankets.

"Because we can't," Logan said.

"Elliot?" She turned to the other man, her arms filled with quilts. "Talk some reason with him."

Elliot gave a half-hearted chuckle. "I thought you said you knew him. Really, Penny, time is imperative."

"Aside from Rory's disappearance, what changed to make time so important? Do you think he's alive?" she asked, her voice filled with hope.

Logan gave an almost imperceptible shake, hoping Elliot understood his message. He must have because his friend didn't respond to Penny.

Penny waited through the long stretch of silence until her shoulders slumped with dismay. "Either way," she said, sadly, "with the explosion of crime in the area, I'm afraid to leave the tanks out," Penny went on, oblivious to their silent communication, bringing another blanket out of the bedroom. "Besides, after what happened, I'm afraid someone might tamper with it."

She wrapped it around Logan's legs efficiently, disappeared and brought a patched quilt out for Elliot's long torso.

Logan grunted a response. She had a point.

"Any idea who did this?" she asked as she dabbed at Logan's split lip with a damp cloth. She shimmied next to him to sit on the couch.

Logan chuckled without humor, then pressed his ribs with a grunt. "I heard bikes, I think the voice was Mitch's," he replied.

"I heard a car, too," Elliot added thickly, his lip swollen.

A warning glance from Logan was enough for Elliot to close his mouth. For a reason Logan couldn't explain he didn't want to share that he suspected Aimee was in town.

"Mitch is not a nice guy, but this is ridiculous. He's an officer. I can't believe he'd resort to violence. Intimidation, bullying, yes, but actual violence?" Penny shook her head, watching Logan, her eyes filled with concern.

He tugged her braid playfully, his hand falling heavily onto his belly. "Don't worry, Henny Penny."

She pulled away. "I'm not the little girl who followed you and Rory around anymore, Logan." Her brows lowered with consternation. She opened her mouth to say something else, then closed it abruptly.

Elliot got up and staggered to the bathroom, his eye a rainbow of purple and blue.

"I'll see you later," Logan called to Elliot. "We'll meet up at midnight?"

Elliot paused; his eyebrow raised in question.

"Please put it off for a day," Penny implored. "What did you see that's making you… "

"Making me what? I want to find out what happened to Rory." Logan lay flat on the sofa. "I don't want to move."

"That's what I mean, it's going to be impossible to swim with your injuries."

"It's not as bad as it looks," Elliot said.

Logan threw him a grateful glance.

"Why would the town do this?" Elliot called out from his doorway.

"I told you, money is a powerful motivator," said Penny. "If anything hits the papers in the city, people might avoid the area. Bertha, the waitress at the diner, she called the station today. I talked her out of writing a report. Hold on a minute, Elliot you forgot your quilt." She gathered up the comforter, following Elliot into his room.

Logan heard the low murmur of their voices and hoped she wasn't pressing Elliot for more information. "What were you talking about?" he asked when she came back. She sat down next to him on the couch, her hip pressing into his.

"This and that, nothing really. I'll stay here-" Penny stated.

"No," Logan said firmly. "Just Elliot and me." Logan took in her wounded face and explained, "We work well, and we have to be quick. Trust me, it's better this way. We need an ally on the ground. Who's going to rescue us if the shit hits the fan?"

Penny gave a watery smile. "Are you sure it was Mitch?"

Logan shrugged, then winced. "I couldn't see their faces. It was too dark," He decided not to mention the sighting of the alleged creature, or his ex-girlfriend, until he had something more concrete to share. "It was his voice," Logan continued as he got up. Penny moved her shoulder under his arm. "I can manage, it's not that bad," he said dismissing his aches.

"Yeah, sure. For once in your life, let someone help," she said.

He walked toward his bedroom; her body pressed closely to his.

"I'll call Doc Leeds. He'll do a house call for me."

"No," Logan said simply.

"But he's handled—"

"I said no."

She helped Logan to his father's bed, turning on the light on the night table. He lay down, sighing with relief. He hadn't realized the extent of his exhaustion. Penny stroked his hair from his sweaty head reviving the memories of another hand running through his hair. Her fingers drifted through his matted curls; the touch cool on his scalp. Logan shivered.

"I'm sorry. I never meant for this to happen to you." She pressed her cheek against his. Logan's eyes met hers for a long moment. Their foreheads touched. Logan could feel her light breath caressing his face. "I would die if something happened to you." Penny kissed him softly on the lips.

Logan held her face, his expression tender. "Pen… I love you. I've known you my whole life," he whispered. "It can't be like that between us."

"You aren't with Aimee anymore." Her voice broke with a sob.

"No, no I'm not. But I can't be with you like that." He

kissed her cheek, his hands on her shoulders. He felt her hot tears christen his face and closed his eyes with regret. When he reopened them, he realized he was once again alone.

Logan wasn't sure what had awakened him, but when he heard the muffled curse, he rolled painfully out of bed and entered the hallway. He picked up his phone that someone thoughtfully plugged into the charger, noting he'd slept for over four hours. Cursing at the time, he stumbled into the kitchen.

He didn't remember closing his eyes last night. Exhaustion pulled at his every fiber, but he pushed himself to move, groaning as if he'd lost a bout with Mike Tyson.

He pressed both palms into his eyes. Crickets sang a symphony from the kitchen window, and if he felt better, he might have enjoyed it. He was cold, the skin on his naked back dimpling from the cool night air.

Elliot greeted him with two mugs of coffee in his hands. He gave Logan one, then walked out of the room and returned with an armload of equipment. Logan took a satisfying sip.

"It's almost two-thirty in the morning. You were supposed to wake me hours ago." Logan stretched. His ribs protested a bit. "I see you've dressed for the occasion."

Elliot was already wearing his wetsuit and weight belt. He tossed a black rubber suit to Logan, who caught it with one hand. He held up two lethal looking knives, handing one to Logan. "You're gonna need this." Elliot proceeded to strap the knife to his thigh. "Before she left, Penny said if I woke you, she'd arrest me." He shrugged. "I didn't think an extra hour or two would make a difference. Probably the later the better."

"Elliot." Logan was annoyed.

"She cares about you. She made me promise. Besides, I checked, you were dead to the world. You needed the sleep." Elliot checked his watch. "We'll get there and back before dawn. I'm not worried."

Logan perched his hip on a stool. "I'm glad you're not worried."

Elliot grinned. "I dunno. The cops in this town dance to their own drum."

"I think everybody dances to their own drum around here," Logan mumbled under his breath.

"You're thinking about Aimee?"

"If it was her, and I think it was, we better get moving on this thing, before she finds it first."

"How do you know she hasn't?" Elliot asked, blowing on the steaming coffee.

"We'd be hearing about it, don't you think?"

Elliot shrugged. "Something's not right about all this. What I want to know, if nothing was leaked to the papers, how did she know about it?"

"Maybe someone else contacted Obsidian, or her. She is a celebrated cryptozoologist. Since her Ted talk, she's been in a few magazines." Logan put his unfinished cup in the sink.

"I think you have a warped sense of her importance." Elliot followed him as he left the room.

Logan felt himself bristling in her defense and forced himself to school his expression.

"You still got it for her." Elliot's voice was gentle.

"Enough." Logan felt his back stiffen in defense.

"It's okay, Logan. I don't know how I would manage if I broke up with James."

"Drop it." Logan stalked from the room.

"Time to go fishing anyway. Go get in your trunks," Elliot said, scratching his two-day-old beard. "I'm not shaving until I see my fiancé." His white teeth flashed through his dark stubble.

"I think you just like saying the word *fiancé*." Logan laughed as he slipped into his bathing suit. "It's going to take time loading the boat. Let's get out of here."

Carrying fins, BCD vest, and tanks, along with a slew of Cyalume light sticks and camera equipment, they walked silently to the shed in the backyard. There was soon a messy pile on the sandy grass. The sound of the surf filled the night air. Logan unlocked the padlock with a small key he found in the kitchen drawer.

Reaching up, he pulled a chain on a naked bulb that swung on a frayed wire, illuminating the tiny space. The skiff was upside down on cinder blocks. The rusty engine lay on its side in the corner. Elliot looked longingly at it. Logan shook his head. "It's been lying here for too long. I doubt the engine will turn over. There's a pump on the floor. Get started on the tires." The wheels on the trailer were flat. Logan sighed; he forgot about the tires. They were going to lose some time.

"Let's hope this works. Otherwise, we're not going anywhere tonight. We should have done this earlier."

"We were supposed to, if not for being jumped by the town goons."

Elliot looked at Logan as if he didn't believe him.

"Alright, I actually didn't think about logistics."

"Aimee always has that effect on you," Elliot said as he grabbed an old, rusted air pump while Logan ignored the comment and plugged it into the wall socket.

"It'll work," Logan responded. "We'll be on our way in no time."

Elliot made a face and said, "Your overconfidence is sometimes annoying. We should have bought a new one."

Elliot put the nozzle on the tire of the trailer while Logan observed over his shoulder. The tire expanded, raising the trailer above the ground.

"Don't say it," Elliot grumbled.

"I have to. *Told you so,*" Logan replied with a smile.

Together they lifted the boat onto the trailer, then pulled it toward the jeep. Logan hooked it up. They heaved their equipment and two oars into the vehicle and set out for the estuary.

A fog had rolled in over the water, covering the moon. Logan was glad it was pitch at the beach. With Elliot on one end and Logan on the other, they made their way down to the sandy coast, lugging the boat to where the water frothed on the sand. Logan smothered his groans, knowing Elliot was doing the same. His arms shook with the effort and his legs felt none too steady. They pushed the boat into the water, climbing aboard once they were deep enough. Each of them holding an oar, they rowed in the direction Logan pointed.

The buttery face of the three-quarter moon hung low in the sky, hiding behind the mist. It stained the sky yellow where the fog curtained it.

Every so often, Logan stopped to get his bearings. They were quiet, working in tandem, their movements precise. They had been together on many expeditions and had the ability to anticipate each other's needs without having to talk. The more he moved he less his muscles burned, and soon, they were rowing with gusto.

They approached the center of the inlet. Logan felt the cold weight of dread settle in his stomach. His body trembled, he fought the urge to turn the boat and head for the safety of home. Taking a deep breath, he pulled harder on his oar, moving closer, knowing he was doing this for Penny, Rory, and his father. Another push with the oar made him admit he was doing this for science.

His arms circled around, his sore muscles protesting once again, the oar rhythmically dipping in the black water, drops dribbling down. *Who was he kidding?* Aimee was right about him. He was doing this for his father. He wanted to know what he had seen that night. Did a mermaid or whatever the creature was change his life that fateful evening? Could finding the creature give purpose to his future and exonerate his father from his alleged suicide, or did his unhappy father take his own life, sending Logan on a lifelong quest to find the impossible?

"Do you see the irony here?" Elliot's voice broke the silence.

"Irony?" Logan asked.

"Yes," Elliot started. "Last night we were running from the creature and tonight we're running to it."

"Yeah, well," Logan said. "Yesterday it surprised us. Tonight, the surprise is on her."

"Her? That thing was mighty tall and muscular."

Logan was thoughtful. "I've never once referred to it as a merman. Always a mermaid."

"Maid, it is, then. Still either way, we have to be careful. The water is *her* territory."

The reeds grew denser as he rowed deeper into the estuary. They moved as soundlessly as they could.

From the boat, Logan could make out faint pinpricks of light on the shore. The lights flickered, then went out. The fog made the water appear thicker with a swampy feel, the foul odor of a low tide replacing the clean air of the sea.

They stopped, letting the ripples and eddies push them in the small tidal pool. Logan watched Elliot set up the camera. They had two on loan that Elliot had borrowed from a colleague in Boston, one an underwater camera with a light. With hand motions, Logan let Elliot know he was going to dive, and he should stay in the boat.

"Wait, you're not thinking of going in alone?" Elliot asked his voice low but laced with outrage.

Logan shook his head. "You stay here and keep watch. If those punks come back, they'll kill us for sure."

"You can't go down there without me." Elliot sounded harsh. "Besides, you need me to take pictures."

"I'm not going to sit and argue. We don't have time, because *you* decided to let me sleep late. I only have about an hour's worth of air underneath and then we'll have to get out of here before dawn."

"The sun will come up-" Elliot checked his watch. "In a little under two hours. You better get moving."

"I want to have a look around, that's all. I won't be long."
Logan gripped Elliot's arm.

"It'd be better if I was there, too," Elliot said.

"You have to trust me with this, El. I have to do this."

They exchanged a look and Elliot said, "You're afraid
Aimee might come here and muscle her way in and steal
the creature."

Logan responded, "Obsidian will try to claim it first
and we know they'll bury the story somewhere." Logan's face
shuttered. "You'll have to stop her."

Elliot laughed and said, "You make it sound like she's
with the KGB. They're only a corporation. Ultimately, it's
only about money to them."

Logan bit his lip. "I don't know about that. I'm beginning to suspect something else is going on with Obsidian."

Elliot nodded. "I'll beat her with one of the oars. Take
the camera."

"I'll be back soon. She… the creature may not even be
here tonight," Logan said scanning the empty shoreline.

He spit into his mask, placed it on his face, and tumbled backwards, the heavy tanks giving him buoyancy. He
turned on his flashlight, watching the artificial rays of light
cut through the murky water. Logan swam in concentric
circles, using the bottom of the boat as a reference, widening
his search with each revolution.

He knew Elliot was watching the glow from the light
attached to his regulator yoke. It was boring work. There was
not much to see, the thick growth making visibility poor.
An octopus darted past him like a speeding ghost, its legs
propelling the creature like a flower opening and closing.

Lobsters and crab crawled over the detritus—broken bottles, crushed cans, refuse of Logan's world polluting their underworld home. Schools of porgies moved in unison, their silvery bodies making a curtain dividing the gloom.

Logan saw the pale underbelly of a shark, a small one, perhaps three feet long, its sinuous movements unmistakable, its snout roving like a dog on the scent. A slithery black eel moved diagonally before the predator, ignorant of the fact its minutes were numbered. The shark followed it discreetly, slowly and patiently pursuing, the intent clear.

Something white gleamed when Logan's flashlight landed on the ocean floor. He dove deeper. The depth was barely ten or twelve feet here. He brushed silt from the floor's mottled surface. Treading water, he reached out to touch it. The sandy bottom shifted suddenly as a ray the size of a manhole cover rose, its velvety skin rippling with the currents. Logan watched its graceful ascent as it swam toward the surface, its barbed tail waving behind it.

He turned his attention to the seabed again. Pushing shells out of the way, he picked up the white object and realized it was a bone, a human bone. He hefted it in his hand, looking at the knobs on either end. This was no fish bone; it was a femur. He examined it, wondering whose thigh bone he held. He took several shots of it with the camera, knowing Chief Red Kain would say it was a cow's bone and get away with another lie.

Logan's hands grazed the ocean bed, sifting through the debris, the sand falling through his fingers. His light shined on metal objects. Floating over, he picked up a crushed beer can, a bent fork. There were Styrofoam cups lying next to starfish. The garbage of humanity cluttered the seafloor, squeezed between clams and other shells, changing nature's landscape.

People say it's silent underwater. For Logan, the sound was magnified. He could hear the sway of the boat above him as it rocked in the water. There was a fullness in the ocean. The sea teemed with life, making his senses alert, sensitive to the gentle shifts in the current, the feel of something disturbing the area next to him. Whatever swam beside him felt nonthreatening. He could sense the slow, undulating movement. He shifted, seeing the profile of a shark moving with lazy grace past him. He raised his hand to pat its rough skin, thought better of it, and resumed his search.

Logan aimed his light in small concise areas, hoping to find something. He wasn't sure exactly what, but as he'd told Elliot earlier, he'd know it when he'd see it.

He glided along the bottom like that shark he'd just seen, his eyes catching the reflection of a something glowing on the bottom. He moved quickly, knowing time was running out and Elliot would be getting nervous. He reached forward to grab the object when he felt a new shift in the current, different, heavier. His reflexes made him spin. His skin prickled and sweat broke out under his wetsuit. Nerves jangled along his spine like it was a three-alarm fire, and he didn't even know why. His movements were clumsy, sluggish.

He glimpsed a huge figure swimming almost on top of him. It brushed against him, pushing him so hard that he dropped both the bone and his flashlight. He gripped the camera, afraid to lose it. He tried to turn but felt trapped, as though something was holding his tank, preventing him from moving.

His ears registered a noise, a distorted sound, like a siren with a battery gone bad. Bubbles erupted around him, obscuring his vision. His lungs constricted, his throat convulsing as he realized his flow of oxygen was cut off.

He fought the panic that swelled in his chest, making his eyes go wide. Flailing, he reached wildly for his hose but saw the end of it floating to the right of his mask. He took a mouthful of water, choked, then sealed his lips. He was surrounded by a mass of bubbles, blinding him for a minute.

Hands pushed him face down into the sandy bottom acerbating his already bruised body. He was being crushed by the oppressive weight of this thing. Black dots darkened his vision. Clutching at anything, he grabbed a rock while he attempted to spin and hit his attacker. He realized from its smooth surface it was not a stone but something metal, smooth and man-made. Holding onto it for dear life, he smacked at the creature, but the blows bounced off without effect.

Kicking wildly, he waved his hands and feet, losing one of his fins. He watched it float upwards. He fought the spread of terror in his limbs, firming his mouth shut so he wouldn't swallow more water or allow it to fill his lungs. Logan's hands were fisted and wouldn't let go of whatever he'd picked up from the seafloor or the camera.

Pressure filled his chest. His eyes bulged. He swung his arms, but they moved as if he were in gelatin, his blows doing no damage. His mouth salivated with the oncoming feeling of nausea. His skull grew heavy. He had to get to the surface soon or he'd drown. The camera slipped out of his grasp.

His one hand free, he reached behind him, his fingers grabbing something slimy but solid on the creature. It was a fin. He could tell from the texture. It was slippery in his fingers, but he held on with both anger and determination. A hard blow hit his head; the impact cushioned by water.

He lost his hold on the creature. A thread of blood floated like a ribbon from a gash on his head. It stung, the cold seawater like needles on his exposed flesh. He was bleeding. The memory of the shark nearby made him thrash wildly. Trying to turn, he was held immobile as if he were hanging on a hook.

Logan hung suspended until his feet touched the bottom, creating a cloud of dust. He pushed upward, his head butting the underbelly of the humanoid figure. The thing grabbed him under his armpits, squeezing him like a vice. Angry eyes glowed in the gloom, narrowing as it locked its gaze on his.

It was pitch black. His flashlight lay on the floor where it had fallen. Logan could barely make out his attacker, the only illumination from the dull glow of the light attached to his mask. Freeing his arms from the tight hold, he slashed wildly, managing to separate a piece of skin from the creature's body. He heard a long, muffled roar as it smashed hard against his rib cage. His lips parted in shock, and he sucked in a mouthful of water.

Bringing his knee in as though crouching, Logan grabbed the knife attached to his calf, then sliced backward. He tore a strip of flesh from the creature's scaly hide. A loud roar filled his head. Whether it was from the creature or himself, he couldn't tell. The knife slipped from his numb fingers, and he was released so quickly, he started to descend to the seafloor.

The creature bent over, its face inches from Logan's, the light on his mask illuminating the inhuman features staring at him. Their eyes locked, and Logan jerked when he saw the intense yellow stare studying him. He felt the shock of recognition and could have sworn he saw surprise register on the creature's face. Its glare pinned him for a minute.

Logan was sinking, black shadows filling his vision from lack of air. He struggled to free himself, heaving backward, colliding with what he thought was a brick wall. The creature had moved behind him. Logan swung his tank and impacted with a softer surface. He floated upwards for a second and knew he had been released.

With his free hand, he fumbled with his weight belt. He dropped it, then frantically moved his fingers to find the lifesaving string to his buoyancy control device. He pulled it, forcing the CO_2 cartridges to send him shooting toward the boat like a rocket, his lungs bursting.

He broke the surface with great gulping sobs. Elliot was leaning over, his hands outstretched to haul him into the bottom of the boat.

Logan lay gasping, a cut over his brow bleeding into his eye. Logan dashed the blood from his face.

"What happened down there?"

"Let's get out of here." Logan coughed up a mouthful of seawater. He retched a few times. Elliot pounded him on the back. Logan halted him by holding up one of his closed fists. "I'm okay."

"Did you see something?" Elliot's voice was loud with excitement. "Hey, where's the camera?"

Logan opened and closed his hand. "I dropped it. I dropped it," he repeated. He looked up at Elliot and whispered, "I made contact."

Elliot sank to his knees, his mouth open. The boat rocked. "Oh em gee. What happened? What did she look like? What's in your other hand?"

Logan didn't realize he was clutching a hard object he'd found on the seabed and used as a weapon. He opened his frozen fist slowly.

"It's a watch," Logan said, his eyes glazed with both fatigue and shock. He was nine years old again. He stared at it numbly. He knew that watch.

"It's a Breitling." Elliot peered at it with his flashlight.

"Yes, and it belongs to Sly Shaw."

CHAPTER 16

LOGAN DROPPED THE watch onto the boat's floor, then grabbed an oar. "Let's get out of here!" he said, plunging the oar into the water and rowing as if his life depended on it.

They moved eastward for some time, paddling toward the pinkening sky where the sun peeked through the darkness, turning the black waters a gunmetal gray.

Elliot put his back into the rowing. Words tumbled from his mouth. "What did you see? What happened? How big is it? Tail or feet?"

"It's big, close to eight feet tall," Logan recounted as they heaved the oars; his arms shaking with effort, his muscles burned from the fight last night and the beating he took today. "Friggin' yellow eyes. I forgot about that." He coughed a few times to clear his lungs. "The irises are huge, like they fill the whole socket, and I think the pupil is vertical like a cat." He spoke breathlessly as they rowed. Elliot kept turning around, his face lit up like it was Christmas morning. "Did you see anything up here?" Logan asked.

"Nada."

They beached the skiff, then rushed to the car as fast as they could, the boat between them. Logan stripped out of his wetsuit, wearing only his swim trunks. They attached the boat to the trailer, Logan's arms quivered with fatigue, but he was pumped with adrenaline.

They trudged into the darkened house; Logan jumped back when someone moved from the shadows.

"Aimee," he breathed.

The region around his heart fizzled and popped, his lungs emptied as if he was starved for air.

Elliot stepped in front of him and demanded, "What are you doing here?"

Aimee tilted her chin, something she did when she was challenged, responding, "I could ask the same thing of you."

"We're on spring break," Elliot sneered.

Aimee ignored him and turned to Logan. "You're bleeding."

Logan left the room, returning with a towel.

"You don't have an exclusive on any of this," she added in her husky voice with a faint French accent Logan loved.

Taking a breath, Logan steeled his heart. "Neither do you." He brushed past her to go to his room. "I have to change."

"Please." She halted him. "I don't have much time."

Logan walked toward the living room, Elliot following them. "How did you know?" he asked.

Aimee grabbed his arm. "We need to talk- alone."

Logan looked at Elliot who shrugged and stalked to his bedroom.

Gesturing to the ratty-looking couches, they sat down. Aimee reached for the towel and said, "Let me." She took it from his hands and continued to blot the gash over his eye.

Logan said, "What you do want?"

"Did you see it?" she asked.

"It doesn't matter if we did. We are not sharing our information with anyone, especially you."

"Obsidian knows about the creature. You are swimming in dangerous waters."

"What does that have to do with anything?" He tried not to be distracted by her nearness. Aimee reached out to caress his hand. "I came back, you know."

Logan pulled away as if her hand scorched him. "What are you talking about?" He asked, not understanding her.

"The apartment. You left so quickly. The day after our fight, you went to your uncle. Why didn't you wait for me? Did you get to Russia that summer?"

Logan went silent, the words thick in his throat.

"Did you? Did you find the Chuchona?" she asked, her husky voice soft and intimate.

Logan shook his head. "No." He sat back putting a safer distance between them. "Why did you leave?"

"Why didn't you text?" Aimee demanded.

"Why didn't you?" Logan asked as though they were in a chess match.

"We can play these games all day, Logan. Listen to me.

You're in danger. This is bigger than you realize. I can get in serious trouble if they find out I've spoken to you."

"So, the town is working with Obsidian. Did you send Mitch to beat us up?"

Aimee stood and walked to the window. She used the drapes to camouflage her as she looked through the blinds. "Hardly. They are baboons. Country bumpkins, but they will respond to Obsidian's demands."

"What does that mean?" Logan rose, his breath catching in this throat.

She looked back at Elliot's closed door. "Can he hear?"

"Probably not, but it doesn't matter. I tell him everything."

"Everything?"

Logan grabbed the towel from her hands and threw it on the coffee table.

"Aimee, get to the point. I'm tired, and cold, and I don't want to play your games."

Aimee walked toward him, coming so close their breaths intermingled. She wet her lips and leaned in. Logan pulled away, but she cupped the back of his head and pulled him toward her.

When their lips met, Logan watched her eyes slide shut. He steeled his heart from reacting, fighting the familiar rhythm of hers. Her tongue met his as their kiss deepened, and he felt her body press against his.

The kiss ended, and they stared at each other breathing heavily. "We managed that rather nicely," she told him, triumph in her eyes.

He moved away, knowing something was different.

"We work well together," she continued, as if she was trying to convince him nothing has changed.

"What is your point, Aimee?"

"Let's find this creature together. Obsidian will pay you more than you can imagine. It can be the start-" Aimee moved back to the window; her eyes luminous. She looked delicate, and vulnerable. "I've missed you. It's not as much fun."

Logan sat on the couch. "I noticed you haven't had any worthwhile discoveries. Maybe it's your methods?" His voice held a hint of sarcasm.

Aimee sat down on the couch again. "That's where you're wrong. We have made discoveries. Obsidian is very successful. It's beyond your imagination."

Logan's patience was wearing thin. "They've nothing to show. No new cryptids have been released." He rose from the couch. "I don't like Obsidian, and I don't understand their agenda. If you're done, you can leave the way you got in. I'm tired and I'd like to change." He turned to leave the room.

"I can't tell you anything more, Logan. But you are in, way above your head. I don't want to see anything happen to you." She moved in front of him, stopping him, placing her palms intimately on his chest. Logan felt his skin recoil from her touch. She traced the image of the Thunderbird tattoo on the front of his shoulder, then kissed it. He pulled his shoulder away from her. "You got the colors wrong; you know." Logan knew she had the power to leave his skin tingling when she caressed him, yet for the first time, he felt himself draw away. The attraction that consumed him felt different.

Logan looked down at the glossy hair on her head, a thought occurred to him. "You saw it?"

"I captured it," she said with a smug smile.

"I doubt that." He laughed. "Even if you were in Arizona, it took off."

"Don't be so sure of that. You think I couldn't do it without a man? It's killing you to know the truth, isn't it? I did get it."

"Where is it?" He gripped both her shoulders.

"I can't tell you that," she paused, her lips coming close to his as if she were telling an intimate secret. "It could be so good between us, again."

The screen door slammed. Penny stomped into the room, stopping abruptly when she saw Logan and Aimee, their heads bowed together.

They jumped apart; Penny's eyes went wide with recognition.

"Aimee." It came out as an accusation

Aimee inclined her head like visiting royalty. "Penny."

There was a charged tension in the room, as if they were at a rumble.

Aimee pulled a card from her pocket; Logan blew a breath through his mouth. For a minute, he thought they were going to draw guns.

"Think about it." She pressed it into his hand, then stalked from the room without giving Penny a second look.

"What was she doing here?" Penny demanded, her voice cool.

Logan shook his head. "I'm not sure." He looked down at the card in his hand. "I think she was here to give us a warning."

Penny's lips firmed. "I'm not afraid of her."

"Good." He crumbled the card in his hand and tossed it into a dirty ashtray. "That makes two of us," he told her.

Penny was in her uniform. Logan looked up, a question in his eyes, his face reddening when she averted her gaze. He wanted to assure her that nothing happened between him and Aimee, but the words couldn't come out of his mouth.

He saw her take in the new abrasions on his forehead. "What happened to you? I mean other than Aimee's visit." Her voice sounded hurt.

He ducked his head. "I'm fine. It's nothing. I'll be right out." He disappeared into his room, returning a minute later in faded jeans, a shirt dangling in his hand. He threw the shirt on the back of the sofa.

She came close to him, her fingers lightly touching his face. He waved her off.

Elliot entered the room. "Is she gone?" he asked, his eyes going wide when he noticed Penny. He looked at the two of them, standing close together, then raised his eyebrows at Logan, his smirk indicating *I told you so.*

Penny's face was troubled, her color drained.

"What's the matter? Did something happen in town?" Logan asked, putting on his shirt.

She went to stand by the window, her face closed up. They heard the sounds of a vehicle starting. Penny watched as the SUV pulled away. "I never liked her. Neither did Rory. She tried so hard to ruin our friendship."

Logan didn't answer. Penny lips turned down, then turned to the them.

Pulling her badge from her pocket, she threw it onto the

scarred surface of the coffee table, where it skidded to the end and fell off. "I'm done. I quit."

Penny's eye caught the watch that lay on the coffee table. She reached over to pick it up and examine it, Aimee forgotten. She turned it over, peering at the inscription on the back.

"This is Sly's? Where'd you get it?"

Logan held out his hand palm up for Penny to give it to him. He put it on his wrist, snapping it closed. "The bottom of the estuary, next to a human thigh bone."

Penny's mouth opened in a circle of surprise that turned to horror. "Not Sly."

Logan sat gingerly on the edge of the couch. Tossing the shirt over his shoulder, he caught Penny's stare when she noticed the giant Thunderbird tattoo.

Elliot looked up, catching her studying the design. "A little too dramatic for my taste."

"What?" she asked Elliot.

"His ink. At this rate, he'll be covered with tats if he keeps memorializing his expeditions."

Penny wouldn't look at Logan, as though she were uncomfortable. "Is that what it is?" she asked. Her eyes narrowed at the large bruise covering his abdomen and the abraded skin down his flank.

He put on his tee shirt, covering his body art, feeling oddly shy in front of her. "It's a Thunderbird I saw in Arizona."

"The one that got away?" She looked at Logan. He wondered if she was talking about birds, Aimee, or herself.

He motioned to the badge. "What's going on?"

Penny reached into her back pocket and pulled out a rolled-up newspaper. It was the local rag, the one she usually sent him. "I give up. I can't do this job anymore." She unrolled the paper carefully, then spread it on the table. It was from last night. Logan leaned over to read it. Elliot whistled from over his shoulder.

"'Homeless man arrested in brutal slaying of couple on beach,'" Elliot read. "They're blaming this guy?"

Penny picked up the paper. "'Chief Kain once again has cracked the case,'" she read cynically. "'Raymond Putnam, a vagrant frequenting the beaches, was charged yesterday with multiple homicides as well as the ritual killing of several dogs and one cat in the area. Doc Leeds confirmed the evidence…'" Penny continued to read, her voice choking. Logan leaned forward and took the paper from her hands. "I wasn't finished," she said.

"Look." He turned it around for them to see the headline: "One cow and three sheep go missing from Henson farm." He read the article aloud. "'One cow and three sheep were stolen right out of the barn on the Henson farm last night. Police suspect mischief, but the Henson's claim they don't have a *beef* with anyone.'"

"Ha," Elliot laughed. "They don't have a beef with anyone." Elliot moved to the sofa, putting his feet on the coffee table and opened his laptop.

"It's gravitating from humans and domestic animals. What's it up to?" Logan said, more to himself than to anyone else.

"It doesn't matter anymore. They've closed the case. I quit," Penny said. "Rory's disappearance will be forgotten."

She looked at him, her eyes deep wells of sadness. "Like your father. Is that why you didn't want me to call Doc Leeds? Is he involved?"

"Up to his stethoscope. Besides, you can't quit," Logan said, shaking his head.

"Too late." Penny sounded disgusted. "I can't put up with the hypocrisy. A man will go to jail for a crime he never committed." She paused as if she just realized something. "What do you mean, it graduated from humans? Did you see something?" She looked miserable.

Elliot lowered his feet, sitting up abruptly. "Whoa. I got a note from Vadim. Took him long enough. Wait." He scanned the email. "Weird," he said absently.

"What?" Penny asked.

"A guy at the school lab. He's running some DNA samples. But there's like a bunch of emails here."

Elliot read the first email out loud. "'Hi. Tests started coming back. Your *Branta canadensis* is a standard Canadian goose.' No surprises there. Wait a minute. Here's where it starts getting strange. Another email ten minutes later. 'What are you two doing? I've been trying to get in touch with you. Haversham says for you to call in now.'" Elliot looked at Logan. "Check your phone."

"Five missed calls, two from Haversham," Logan confirmed. "When did all this happen?"

"They must have been calling while we were out." He looked at Elliot. "What else did he write?"

"'Preliminary results in. What the hell have you two stumbled into?'" Elliot's voice trailed off as he looked up at Logan.

"That's it?" Logan asked.

Elliot scrolled down his messages. "Nothing else." He glanced at his watch. "Do you think it's too early to call them?"

Logan shrugged. "Vadim's usually at the lab before dawn. Haversham was leaving for a conference in New Zealand last night. He won't be reachable until he lands."

Elliot pulled out his phone. "I'll try Vadim."

He scrolled the contacts, found the number, called, then laid his head wearily on the back of the sofa, waiting for Vadim to answer.

Logan took Penny's hand within his own. She pulled away, uncomfortable and not meeting his eyes. He leaned forward. "Pen, you can't leave," he said softly. "You've had a horrible week, but they need people like you here."

"What's the use?" She stood up, facing the large window bringing in the morning sunlight. She played with the frayed ends of the cheap curtains. "He threatened me."

"Who?" Logan demanded, his hackles rising like an angry dog. Balling his hands into fists, he ground out. "If Mitch touches-"

"The chief, that's who!" she said angrily. "I am nothing, a cog in a wheel. I don't make a difference. My brother—"

"Holy crap!" Elliot's voice rose. He sat up.

Logan and Penny both turned to him, their argument interrupted.

"The lab's phones have been turned off."

"Impossible," Logan said in disbelief.

"Listen." Elliot put the phone on speaker after he pressed the number. Logan could see the word *LAB* in caps on the face of the screen. Nothing happened. A strange beep emitted from the speaker, followed by a recorded message indicating the line had been disconnected.

"It's out of order." Logan shook his head. "Call the main number and transfer over."

"You don't think I tried that? Watch." Elliot called the switchboard and asked for the lab. The nasal voice of the operator paused, then ordered, "Hold on."

There was a series of clicks, and the unfamiliar voice of a man answered. "Yes?" he said simply.

"Vadim?" Elliot asked.

There was another noise, a tapping followed by a burst of static. They could hear the sound of distant voices as though the room was filled with people.

"Who is this?" the voice asked with quiet authority.

Penny's jaw dropped, her hand motioning a slicing movement by her neck. "Cut the call," she mouthed. "They're tracking the phone."

Elliot ended the conversation. "How did you know?"

Penny picked up the badge on the floor, her fingers running over the raised lettering. "The sounds. The FBI was here once on a mobster case. I heard the same noise."

Logan got up to pace the room. "What do you think is going on? I'll call Vadim's cell." He punched in the call, listened for a second, then hung up. "It went straight to voicemail."

They sat in silent misery, horror beginning to fill every crevice of the room. "Let me see what happens when I call Haversham," Elliot said.

He scrolled and found the number, his face going white

while the tinny sound of a programmed voice filled the room. "Haversham's phone's been disconnected."

"You don't think it's because of us?" Penny's eyes were huge in her pale face.

Elliot scratched his head. "I have no idea. Wait, I might have Vadim's girlfriend's number."

"Hallo?" A female answered with a foreign accent.

"Svetlana? This is El—"

She disconnected the call. Elliot cursed.

Logan's phone buzzed thirty seconds later, making them all jump. The caller was an unknown number. Logan put the phone on speaker so they could all hear. "Yes?" he said evenly.

"I can't talk long." It was Vadim. "I'm at friend. Svetlana called. Where you two been? It's big mess. They closed lab down. Haversham said… he said keep doing what you are doing. Don't let them stop you," his Russian accent was thick and nervous. "I don't know what you got, but you make lot of trouble."

"Where is Haversham?" Logan demanded.

"He's out of picture for now," Vadim responded.

"*Out of the picture*…. What does that mean? I need to talk to him now!"

"I don't have time for all your stupid questions." Vadim was curt. "I have to go."

"Wait, Vadim! Tell me what happened."

"I put in sample to national database to compare the base pairs of new DNA to animal already present. I run a comparison test. You understand? I swear, it only five minutes, not even. Report come back, then poof. My computer shut down, phone lines down. Nothing work. I have friend, you know. Someone in Washington. He call me right then. He tell me leave Dodge; you know? I don't know what he talking about. 'Get out!' he say. 'Take nothing. Lay low for couple weeks.'"

"Where did Haversham go?" Logan demanded, the hair on his neck sticking up.

"He safe. That's all you need to know. I'm only talking to you because he make sure I speak to you. He say you must stick with it. You have something. Oh, and Logan, don't call Svetlana again."

Logan felt his scalp tighten with fear. He had a flashback to conversations when his father died. Pressing his hands into his eyes, he asked, "What did the report say?"

"Don't you hear me?" Vadim was screaming. "They shut my lab. They take everything. They don't get what I read already. I read it and destroy it. You all crazy! Haversham is insane. They call themselves the U.N.I.T. You know what that means?" Vadim was shrieking. "I left Russia because of those people. What you find?"

"What did it say!" Logan shouted back. "The report… what did it say!"

"I going to leave country for a while, Logan. That DNA you sent. That DNA belong not to no animal or vegetable."

"OK…" Logan said. "But bacteria are being discovered all the time Vadim, and new DNA is being uploaded every day as well."

"You hear me?" Vadim yelled. "Nothing from this earth!" The line went dead.

"What does that mean?" Penny asked.

Elliot sat up with an excited look on his face, fear forgotten. "It means we might have found an entirely new species." He jumped off the couch. "It means the money will start rolling in!"

"Is that what this is for?" Penny stood in fury, her back rigid. "I thought you didn't care about money."

"Not for us," Logan said, looking at them both. "Although the idea that I'll be taken seriously for once has a certain appeal."

"That thing might have murdered my brother!"

"My father as well, Pen. I'm here to—"

"Study it, learn from it," Elliot told her.

"Stop it from killing," Logan interrupted him. "I won't say I'm not interested in examining it, but make no mistake, I'm here to stop it from killing more people."

Penny walked away, her back stiff, to stare out the window bleakly. "It's no better than a serial killer."

"It's a living being doing what it does naturally, that's all." Logan said. "It has no malice."

"I think it's pretty malicious." Penny burst out.

"It is doing what it must for survival. It works on instinct," Logan told her slowly.

"You don't know that." Her voice was forlorn.

"It needs to be studied," Elliot added.

She looked out the window, gasping when a pair of black SUVs abruptly pulled into the front drive. She watched the doors open, and two teams of black-suited people filed out. "Logan," she said urgently, "we have to leave." She turned to them. "Now!"

Logan rose to see people who scared him more than any other creature walking purposefully up his drive. There were at least ten of them, all in dark suits. Another car pulled up. Aimee slid out of the passenger seat, her face blank. He didn't see any weapons, but he didn't want to hang out long enough to see if they had them concealed. They made the motorcycle gang look like preschoolers.

"Who are they… Men in Black?" Elliot said. "This can't be real."

"Believe me," Logan stated. "This is real. Let's get out of here."

They sprinted to the back door, flying down the stoop and over the sand in the backyard. They came to the end of the property, breathing heavily. "Any ideas?" Logan asked. They saw two men walking around each side of the house.

The sun had risen, burning off the night's haze. It was promising to be hot and humid. A fine sheen of sweat coated their bodies. Seagulls screamed an alarm as if they had intruded upon their territory. Logan grabbed Penny's arm and said, "We gotta go."

Penny looked both ways. Logan realized she knew every house in the entire town and the families inside them. "The Prestons." She pointed down the beach to the minimansion next door. "They have a new boat." They heard the back-screen door slam and the shouts of their pursuers. "Their kid always leaves the key in the ignition."

"How do you know that?" All Logan could manage was a gasp as they ran over the dunes.

"The water patrol caught him twice last night." She was already running toward the other house. "The oldest sneaks out after his parents are sleeping."

"Faster," Logan said, running after her.

They followed her through the brush, ducking between a red-slatted fence that listed toward the deep drifts of sand surrounding it. A gray-shingled house loomed ahead with a moored craft at the end of the floating dock. Its blue canvas wakeboard tower stood out like a beacon. Four jet skis bobbed in the water behind it. Logan remembered them from the other day when he'd met his neighbor.

Stealthily, they scrambled down the weathered boards to the Sea Ray. The three of them jumped onto the boat's deck. Penny crawled toward the captain's chair.

The keys swung from the ignition. Penny smirked as she pointed to them, needing no more urging. She gunned the engine while both Logan and Elliot unmoored the boat from the pier pilings. The sputtering of the motor drowned out the pounding of the multiple feet of their pursuers.

"Who are those guys?" Elliot shouted as they stared after them. "Where are we going?" he asked no one in particular. "And why is Aimee with them? Isn't she with Obsidian?"

"I'm not sure, but I don't want to stick around to find out," Logan said grimly.

Penny turned the boat and let it race toward the inlet.

CHAPTER 17

THE BOAT'S ENGINE roared to life, startling the agents crowding the dock. Logan watched them freeze at the sound. A tall, bald-headed man who appeared to be in charge pointed to the four jet skis. Logan squinted, trying to identify the commander. There was something familiar about him. Logan cursed softly when he saw them leap onto the watercraft and take off after them.

"What is it?" Penny shouted, her white blond hair flying around her face.

"They're following us."

"What?" She was incredulous.

It looked like something out of a movie, black-suited agents on pursuing jet skis, the water plastering the clothes to their bodies.

"Punch it, Penny!" Elliot screamed, pointing to them.

Logan nodded, hoping they didn't have guns.

Elliot was rooting around, lifting seats, pulling out supplies, and throwing them on the deck of the boat. Soon two
wetsuits, a couple of tanks, one of them half filled, even a
harpoon were piled in the center of the craft.

The boat swerved. Penny made a fast right, trying to
evade their pursuers. The wake of the water spiraled behind
them like a giant fan. One of the jet skis rose half-way out
of the water attempting the same sharp turn. It toppled,
sending the rider flying into the bay. He went down and
then bobbed to the surface, his jacket ballooning around
him, his sunglasses askew on his face.

Elliot's hands were resting possessively on a filthy cooler
with a few forgotten bottles of beer and water. The roar of
another jet ski filled their ears. It was fast approaching them,
looking to come alongside. Elliot took a brown-tinted beer
bottle and lobbed it at the pursuer. Using a lifesaver like a frisbee, Logan tossed it at the rider of the jet ski. She twisted the
throttle ducking sideways as it sailed harmlessly over her head.

She was gaining on them. Logan watched in horror as
she moved alongside of their craft, reaching out to attempt
a leap onto the boat. Elliot ran over, trying to dislodge her.
Her legs locked around the base of the jet ski, the attacker
used her upper body to grip Elliot, half pulling him from
the deck. Logan saw Elliot's feet lift off the floor. Grabbing
the harpoon, he swung it like a baseball bat, catching the
agent in the midsection. It was as if she was made of iron.
Her hands wrapped around the harpoon, and she tugged,
drawing Logan closer. They wrestled with the weapon.

Logan heard Penny yell, "Hold on!"

He turned his face to see her fly into a wave. The spray

drenched him, and for a minute he couldn't see. The harpoon had gone slack. He opened his eyes to see the female unseated, her arms waving from her spot in the water.

Penny raced toward open water and once she was out of the harbor, she moved the boat in a tight circle, creating turbulent ripples of water. Logan fought nausea, the world sliding past him in a jumble of colors. He heard Elliot retching and hoped whatever came up managed to land outside the boat. A third jet ski picked up speed behind them, the craft got caught in the swirling wake of the boat. It flipped out from under the rider and flew toward them like a javelin. It smashed against the aft with a jarring thud, then flew backward landing on top of its former occupant. The jet ski floated riderless on the waves; a hand clawed at the base trying to get back on.

"Ouch," Elliot said with a wince.

"Three down, one to go," Penny called, her teeth bared, as if she were fighting with the wheel. Logan couldn't help the chuckle that escaped his lips. She looked like she was possessed by a pirate. Toned muscles he never noticed twisted the steering taking them out into the open water, escaping the shore.

Penny had them going so fast, the boat's nose appeared to be several feet above the water. The last jet ski sputtered, the engine grinding to a halt plainly out of gas.

Both Logan and Elliot looked up to see a motorboat bearing down on them. Logan counted four people in the bow, one of them a familiar female silhouette. In fact, he realized he recognized most of the group. He stared hard at the bald-headed man, trying to place him in his memory.

"Well, that ain't the cavalry!" Elliot shouted, squinting his eyes in an attempt to make out the newcomers.

"It's Chief Kain!" Penny yelled back. "Hold tight! We can outrun him with this lighter craft." Penny gunned the engine forcing the boat to rise out of the water again. Logan came to stand next to her, his hand on the chair behind her back. Penny did a U-turn, slipping past the larger boat, narrowly missing its bow.

The cumbersome craft attempted to turn, but Penny's choppy wake made circling slower. Logan could count the hairs on Mitch's head as they whizzed past. He turned around to see Mitch holding a gun trained on his back. Positioning himself behind Penny, Logan protected her.

Logan held onto the chair and console, making his body the larger target. He stood rigidly, his breath caught in his chest, expecting to hear the sound of the gun's report. An unmistakable female figure in a dark suit placed a hand over Mitch's extended one, stopping him from taking aim. Logan's eyes met Aimee's. He could see her shout something at Mitch, who reluctantly lowered the gun.

Chief Kain stalked over, and as they took off, he could see Aimee rest her hands on her hips, her face sober as the chief argued with her.

"What's Aimee doing with Kain?" Elliot asked.

"Could the Chief be working with Obsidian?" he shouted to Penny.

"Anything's possible, but I've never seen these people or their scary black suits before." She looked backwards. "Dump your cell phones. They won't be able to trace us."

Elliot glanced regretfully at his smartphone before he

chucked in the waves. Logan tossed his and Penny's as far as he could watching them sink into the ocean.

Penny plowed through the water, the bigger boat vainly trying to pull back and turn around. She zipped into the ocean, flying further from the jagged shoreline until all they saw were little specks behind them. Penny soon slowed. Logan didn't ask her where they were going. They hugged the shoreline for close to an hour, slowing as they pulled into tall reeds. She did this when the sound of rotors confirmed air support, the swampy grasslands serving as a convenient hideaway. She cut the engines to conserve fuel, and make sure they weren't heard. When she spoke, her voice was hushed.

"When did the town buy a helicopter?" Logan asked.

"They didn't." Penny frowned. "That's high tech. Military, by the looks of it."

"Do you think it's Obsidian?" Elliot ducked his head as the chopper swung by.

"Maybe, it's definitely private. No markings or insignias. We can't stay this close to shore, or hide in the grass forever," Logan said, his eyes looking for a place to escape. "We could get off and take that road to the old Sullivan place and stay there." He pointed to a dirt path that led from a rotten dock, half of the planks gone from the pilings.

Penny shook her head. "It's gone. It burned down a year ago." She squinted at the sun. "If we leave the boat, they'll track us down easily enough. They'll expect us to try that. Waves don't leave trails."

"That's profound," Elliot said. "If we go too far out to

the open sea, we'll get stuck." He glanced at the fuel gauge. "We won't make New Jersey, let alone any other state."

"True," Logan agreed. "We don't have food or supplies, either. We need to find a place to hide. Somewhere they'll never think to look for us."

"I don't like staying here. I feel like a sitting duck," Elliot complained.

Logan stared out into the horizon. "No, it's a good idea. She's letting them exhaust their resources looking for us while she conserves ours."

Penny smiled. "We used to do this when we were kids. Then we'd explore some of the small islands along the coast."

"Let's get out of here," Logan said.

Penny shouted "Not yet. Down!" They all crouched low.

The patrol boat slid past them. Logan peered over the bow. Aimee was there, her hands resting on the rails, her face searching the grasslands. He made out Mitch, the Chief and another man with a bald head. He was older, in his late fifties. Something stirred in Logan's memory and try as he might he could place it. The man had a thick orbital ridge, with dark brows. There were no soft angles to his face, and Logan couldn't help the shiver that ran down his spine.

"You okay?" Penny examined him with her sharp eyes.

"Yeah," he whispered. But he wasn't and he knew it.

"The weather's turning?" Elliot looked upward and pointed to the sky where a huge front was moving in. "I smell rain."

"Always a Debbie Downer," Logan said, his voice hushed. "Sly had a good fishing spot off Reed's Island."

Penny thought for a bit. "Let me think."

"Don't spend too much time thinking because it's going to pour," Elliot warned.

"That will make the hunt for us harder. The helicopter will have to be brought in."

As if nature were working with them, the sky opened up, sheets of rain obscured them from their pursuers. The helicopter was forced to return to its base. When it cleared, they became invisible by sliding into the tall grasses. Satisfied that their pursuers were gone and couldn't find them, Penny said. "I have an idea.".

They barely spoke, and as the day waned, Penny eased out of their hiding spot. The air had become thick with fog. "It's perfect," Penny said. "Perfect cover to protect us."

Dusk had them shivering, their clothes stuck to their backs, soaked from the drenching they received earlier.

Night fell, making the water look like black glass. Penny moved down an inlet leading to a narrow beach. Logan looked around, seeing the hulking shapes of rusted boats lying on the shore as in a war zone. Their faces were numb from the wind, and the silence was heavy in their ears. Overgrown bushes crowded the stretch of land. Logan could hear the rustle of lush vegetation.

"Where is this place?" Elliot asked. No one answered him.

The large shape of a broken-down building loomed before them. The words were out of Logan's mouth before he could help it. "Cedar Haven? You're taking us to *Cedar Haven*?"

"Well, I always said you were crazy," said Penny.

Logan heard the smile in her words. He could see the ghost of a grin on her face.

"That's where… that's the place where… ?" Elliot asked.

"It's the place where nightmares were invented," Logan finished.

He put his hand on Penny's back and squeezed her shoulder. He looked around, trying to get his bearings.

"How much do you know about Cedar Haven?" Penny asked Elliot.

"Just what Logan told me. It's a closed-up nuthouse."

"It was actually a private sanatorium built after the Civil War. Wealthy people put embarrassing family members here who they needed to hide. It was closed a little over a decade ago when its history of barbaric shock treatments was revealed to the world. It's where Chief Kain threatened to put Logan if he spoke about what happened to his father."

They both looked at Logan, who stared at the dark outline of the building.

Penny slid into a broken jetty and leapt out of the boat. She fumbled with the ropes as she hooked it to the pilings. "Come on. We have to find something to hide the boat." She took off running toward the yawning front door of a garage to the left of the building, using the moonlight to guide her steps.

The garage yielded nothing but the scattering of frightened rodents.

"There's nothing in here." Elliot rummaged through the garbage.

"Let's check the main building," Logan said.

The cobbled path was slick with rainwater. It looked like a mercury-covered snake. Logan stumbled after Penny, followed by Elliot, their feet echoing on the paving stones.

The hospital was centered in a huge courtyard, with a

portico held up by Doric columns. Penny, Logan, and Elliot raced up the concrete steps into a vast cavern of a hall. They burst into the building, disturbing the nesting bats, which took off, squeaking their complaints.

Penny entered first, pausing to catch her breath. Logan was right behind her. Their eyes found each other in the darkness, and they each smiled, laughter escaping when they caught Elliot instinctively ducking from the flock of bats loudly protesting their invasion.

"Are you thinking…?"

"Remember, Rory climbed to the roof…"

Logan and Penny spoke in unison. Logan jerked with a jolt as if he'd noticed Penny for the first time. Sweat shined on her coffee-colored skin. Her white hair gleamed; the braid was a tangled mess. She had a smudge of dirt on her cheek. Logan reached out to wipe it, pulling away when a frisson ran from his fingers to his midsection as if he'd been touched by lightning.

Logan shook himself unsure of his feelings. He made himself turn to survey the room, getting his racing heart under control. The moment had passed.

"This place is a dump." Elliot's voice echoed against the empty walls. "I wonder what kind of monsters we'll find in here."

Piles of trash were strewn across the tiled floor.

"Here!" Penny raced to a mountain of old furniture covered by a filthy tarp. "Help me!"

Logan trotted over. Together, they pulled the tarp free, then dragged it back to the boat, the canvas like a giant parachute between them.

Penny jumped back on the boat and took stock of their provisions. She pulled out two fishing rods and matches, and she grabbed what was left of the beer.

They threw the canvas over the craft. Logan brushed his hands together, satisfied the boat was not as obvious as it was before.

"What's the plan? We don't even have our laptops," Elliot rubbed his hands together. "Man, it's getting chilly."

"We'll lay low here for now, head out to the estuary later tonight. I've got to bring back proof once and for all," Logan stated.

"Proof of what?" Penny asked. "That thing? Is it a mermaid?"

"I don't know what it is, but I mean to find out."

CHAPTER 18

ELLIOT SAT IN the shadows watching Logan and Penny cast out lines, their feet dangling from the pier. Nobody spoke, they had exhausted all their conversation. A small campfire to the left of the pier illuminated their faces, the heat warming their bodies.

Logan glanced at Elliot's blank stare and said, "Go find a place and lay down. You look like you're about to drop."

Elliot yawned, then said, "I'm okay." He patted his pockets and cursed. "I forgot we threw our phones overboard. I'm lost without it. I'll miss my goodnight call to James." He got up. "I'll see you later. Let me know when you score some dinner."

He turned and wandered off toward their small camp.

Penny moved closer, their arms, hips, and thighs touching, their clothes still clammy from the drenching earlier. They were all cold and uncomfortable, Logan saw Penny shiver.

"Hold this," he said as he rose, his knees cracking.

"Ow." Penny looked up concerned.

"Old war injury," Logan said as he jumped over a two-foot concrete retaining wall and ran toward the wharf. He lifted the end of the tarp and pulled out an extra hoodie Elliot had retrieved from the storage bin. He draped it around Penny's shoulders.

"Thanks," she said, her voice soft. "War injury?"

"War to find cryptids," he said. "I took a spill in Arizona. My left knee is still recovering."

"For a guy that's been bashed around quite a bit, you seem to take it well."

Logan shrugged. "It comes with the territory. We, meaning cryptozoologists work in rough terrain, and very often in hostile circumstances, sometimes the locals are protective, other times they just are aggressive."

"Sounds dangerous." Penny watched him fiddle with the hook, then cast his line out again. "Why do you do this, put yourself at risk, that kind of thing?'

Logan looked up to watch the night sky. Jupiter shone bright against the velvet blackness of the heavens. His experienced eyes sought the constellations, each star a road map for the other.

"I guess you could say I went into the family business."

They both laughed.

Logan went on, "My interest shouldn't be surprising. Some would call it an obsession," he said, in an undertone. "I've known about many of the creatures my entire life. When you were reading about giants and fairies in grade school, my dad was out there searching for real ones."

"He never found one, though," she asked, the gentle arc of her eyebrow raised.

Logan shook his head. "No, but it was fun. Going to all those exotic places, camping out, I won't deny that I enjoyed most of it. It got harder after my mom left. I didn't want to do it."

"So, what changed your mind," Penny asked, her eyes bright.

Logan stared out to the rippling sea; he licked his lips tasting the salt on his skin. He opened his mouth to give his patented answer, the one that describes his dedication to finding new species, his love for adventure, shocking the establishment revealing new animals, but he didn't. "I want to prove she's real. I want my father not to have died in vain. He was murdered."

"Revenge?"

"No, validation."

Penny snuggled up closer to him when he took his seat.

Logan was intensely aware of everywhere their skin made contact. Glued together by their past, they supported each other's weight, knowing if one tilted to the side, the other would be there to prop them up. There was comfort between them, whatever differences melted away with the dying light. Logan was back at being nine years old again, unaware of the coming storm of adulthood that would have the ability to make strangers out of friends.

"I can't believe this is happening. When did we really lose him?"

Penny's response was immediate. She knew he was talking about Rory. There was no artificialness between them. "It was those stupid drugs." She rested her head on his shoulder. "He changed. I think he was taking more than he was supposed to."

"Do you think drugs were involved?"

"Only that his relationships were fueled by them."

Logan felt the air leave his lungs. "If I knew, I would have tried to get him into rehab."

"I tried. My parents tried. He was disappointed with his life, his writing career, started keeping more to himself." She looked up at him. "Like someone else I know."

"Me?"

"Uh-huh. After Aimee moved in. We knew she didn't like us. She made that abundantly clear."

Logan stiffened his spine. "That wouldn't have mattered, to me."

"I know that. The calls work both ways."

"When she made things tough about us all vacationing together, I stopped trying, and I admit, we kind of fell away. Rory was struggling."

"I wish I had known."

"We were pretty sure we had it under control. We all knew he had an issue with depression. I just don't think we all realized how serious it was."

"Pen? Do you think he killed himself?"

"It entered my mind, it did." Penny gulped; a tear rolled down her cheek. "But then we found his sneaker, and the woman was gone."

"And then there was David Wagner, the pets that have been missing, not to mention Sly." Logan glanced at the Breitling on his wrist. "Too many incidents," he added under his breath.

"I don't think he would have committed suicide. I just don't, he would have reached out. He'd done it in the past."

"Is that when he was away?"

"Yes, he was writing again, living in your place. No, he was definitely on the way back, if you know what I mean."

They sat in companionable silence, neither talking, but both enjoying a moment of quiet.

With Penny, his friend and companion, Logan was safe, he could talk about everything without judgement, say what he felt without worry of the overreactions of Aimee.

Penny cleared her throat. "Can we address the elephant in the room?" she asked after a long minute.

Logan looked at her, her gaze was downward, where the water swirled beneath their feet.

"I think we have a whole zoo to discuss."

"Don't play games. We know each other too long for that."

Logan hung his head, his chin resting on his chest. "Aimee," he whispered.

Penny took a deep breath, as if she were inhaling all the air around them. "Yeah. Like what's up with that?"

He felt Penny squirm a bit. "I thought you were done with her."

Logan looked down at her, but before he could answer she blurted, "I'm not asking because of what happened last night." She twisted, her eyes imploring. "I hope it's not going to affect-"

Logan wrapped his arm around her shoulders. "Don't be an idiot. You… and Rory mean everything to me." He laced his fingers with hers and gave her hand a reassuring squeeze. "You are going through the worst possible time in your life. You reached out."

Penny looked away.

Logan nudged her shoulder playfully. She stiffened. He did it again, this time staying closer, smiling when she leaned against him, their calves touching as they hung suspended from the wooden planks.

His line pulled. The moment was broken. Logan reeled in his catch. The fish wiggled on the line. Penny grabbed it with capable hands and gutted it as she did when they were kids and fished for their lunch.

Elliot built up the small fire where they roasted their catch. He sat in a nest of filthy blankets, only his head and hands poking out.

"Where'd you get those?" Logan asked.

"Do you have any idea who might have used them?" Penny was horrified.

Elliot shrugged. "Doesn't matter. I'm cold, and hungry." He eyed their catch. "Porgies, ugh."

"Beggars can't be choosers," Penny said, spitting the fish on a couple of branches. Oily and strong tasting, their meal made for unappetizing fare, but no one complained. Logan, Penny, and Elliot were dirty and exhausted, the adrenaline rush of the chase subsiding.

Logan disappeared into the building and found a soft pile of discarded cushions and a piece of broken plexiglass. Outside near their campfire, he created a makeshift bed using the cushions, shielding them from the wind with a row of plastic drums. He placed the plexiglass over the top of the drums to act as a protecting against any rain. He glanced over to see Elliot on his side, snoring gustily.

Penny yawned loudly. Logan pulled her next to him, his back against a plastic yellow barrel. They were facing away from the sea. Penny rested her head on his shoulder.

"You might as well go to sleep," she said. "We won't have much time."

Logan felt her head move against his chest. "I'm wired. I can't sleep." Another yawn belied that statement.

Logan grinned, his cheek resting against her head. She seemed to fit right in there as though she were made for the spot. Aimee had a way of competing for territory. He enjoyed the challenge, the tug of war whether they were arguing about some hominid roaming the Caucasus mountains or trying to best each other spinning invented facts on dragons, the passion spilled over to every aspect of their lives. He looked down at Penny's blonde head, which moved with the rise and fall of his chest. Strong emotions, those giant swings from ecstasy to extreme pain was exhausting. The highs and lows of caring for someone who had the power to suck the energy from your soul, took other things as well.

Logan felt a sense of peace steal over him. The same feeling of joyous belonging that came when he stayed with his aunt and uncle stole through him, made the coiled tenseness ease, and he felt himself relax.

Penny asked him something, but her voice was so low, he barely heard her. "What?" he asked

"Aimee." Her voice was soft. "Did you love her?"

Logan thought for a minute. "I guess. I mean, I… I did," he admitted.

He heard Penny chuckle.

"What's so funny?" he asked, bending his head to see her face.

The flames lit the soft curve of her cheek and danced in the reflection of her eyes. She had a sweetness, tempered with a mischievous grin he imagined on the Huldufólk, elves said to be found in Iceland. Logan studied her for a minute. "Life, her ambition. She wanted different things than I did."

"Like what?"

"Like… I don't know, Pen." He shifted uncomfortably.

Penny sat up to look at him, "I know you. There's more."

Logan straightened putting some distance between them. He crossed his legs and explained. "When it was good, it was amazing, you know what I mean? She had this passion that made even the mundane seem fascinating."

Penny nodded. "So, what was the matter?"

"I never put my finger on it, but after a while, it got… tiresome."

"Logan." Penny stroked his hand. "Life can't be a constant rollercoaster. Sometimes it has to be tranquil. If you live in a continual state of flux, it will destroy you. Passion is great, but sometimes it just burns too hot, too fast. Promise me, something."

"Anything."

"Promise you won't let what happened back at the house to come between us."

His response was automatic. He grabbed her face between his hands.

"Don't be silly. Nothing could ever come between us."

"Do you still love her?" she whispered.

He stared at her face, a strange tingling in his chest.

Logan leaned into her, his lips brushing hers softly. Penny sighed, her arms wrapping around his neck. He pulled her up against him, deepening his kiss, feeling for the first time that he was home.

They looked at each other, seeing things with different eyes. Penny settled back, melting against him. He felt her go boneless, the tension seeping from her body. Her soft snuffle made him realize she'd dozed off before he'd responded to her last question. Truthfully, he wasn't sure of the answer.

Logan didn't rest. He watched the dark horizon, his thoughts roiling in his head. When had his feelings changed, he wondered, and why had it hit him like a tsunami?

Logan let them sleep for an hour or so, then with a whisper woke Penny.

The sky had cleared, and the rain had ceased its endless pattering. Elliot was already pulling the tarp off the boat. His keen eyes caught Logan's face. Elliot cocked his head as if asking a question. Logan avoided looking at him. Elliot smiled.

"You fall in love too easily," Elliot said when they were alone on the deck.

Logan pointedly ignored him. Elliot repeated his statement.

"I heard you the first time," Logan replied crankily. He stripped down, pulled on the wetsuit, then checked the tanks and diving equipment they'd discovered on the boat.

"I'm going with you this time," Elliot stated. His face was set as if he'd brook no argument.

Logan shook his head. "Not enough air in the tanks."

He motioned his head at Penny. "Someone has to stay with Penny while I dive."

"I can hear you. I'm neither deaf nor incapable of taking care of myself," Penny said crossly. "I am the one who's technically here to protect both of you."

Both Elliot and Logan's heads snapped up, and they wondered just how much she'd heard.

Elliot pointed to the holster strapped to her waist. "She is better armed than me."

"Good. Then she can protect you," Logan said.

A half-moon floated above them. It looked like a balloon held captive by a string. Penny hugged the coastline, prepared to duck in the tall reeds if they were spotted.

They set off determinedly to the inlet, each doing his or her job as if they had worked in tandem for years. They pulled into the estuary, using the constellations to navigate to the exact position. Logan looked up in time to catch a shooting star propelling itself overhead. He closed his eyes, dread and unease filling him. He felt so close. He knew tonight would bring him what he yearned for, what Penny needed to know, or perhaps he would die trying.

"Cut the engine," he ordered.

Penny turned off the engine allowing the thick silence to engulf them. Grabbing a flashlight and putting on his mask, Logan nodded to them both, then flipped backwards, slicing into the dark waters of the bay.

The inky blackness surrounded him. Fronds and seagrass undulated like ghosts in the currents. Logan shined a flashlight through the murky depths. His skin prickled with the awareness he was not alone.

Searching the darkness, he discerned assorted shapes, identifying them as harmless. Still, he had a strange feeling of being watched. He wished he could have prepared better, but their flight and the circumstances made it impossible. He felt uneasy with anticipation.

Sea turtles and schools of fish crowded around him, swirling with the current, making him feel cocooned. Logan rotated slowly, his breath quickening, his eyes darting around, looking for the shadowy figure.

He glanced up to see the outline of the bottom of the boat bobbing gently above him. It was deceptively serene, the intense silence deafening, the darkness closing around him like velvet, smothering him.

Sound intruded, eerily magnified in the water. Logan followed the noise, realizing another boat had stealthily approached their craft, then pulled next to it. The two boats nearly met; the second one so close the bows were side by side.

He watched the craft he knew held Penny and Elliot dip as though someone had jumped onto its deck. Cursing softly, Logan darted upwards and reached noiselessly for the ladder. Slipping off his fins, he pulled himself out of the water and hid behind the bulkhead. The tanks were heavy on his back, but he dared not remove them. He ripped off his mask, making breathing easier.

Penny and Elliot were frozen in the spotlight of the intruder. Chief Kain's voice echoed over the water. "...three counts of theft, evading arrest, destruction of property..." He was listing the charges against them.

Both Penny and Elliot had their hands pulled behind them. Mitch the Gorgon was cuffing them, not with metal ones but with white plastic, the type they used to tag specimens in the lab. Nobody had noticed Logan sneak onto the boat. He stood behind them on the deck, crouching in the darkness.

Mitch pushed Elliot onto the floor, where he sat cross-legged.

Chief Kain droned on. "I told you, Penny, to keep your nose out of the estuary business."

Penny lashed out with her foot. Mitch pulled her backward, yanking her arm. "You knew it was a mermaid all this time," Penny said.

"It's no mermaid." Chief Kain laughed. "It's a sea monster. You leave it alone, and it will go back for another few years and disappear. It always has. It's Minatuck's dirty little secret. Why did you have to stir the whole business up with Loco Logan over here and bring back outsiders to nose around? We had it all under control."

"Outsiders?" Penny asked.

"The psychos in the suits, the nuts from U.N.I.T.," he clarified. "Now they'll want to close the beaches. It's bad business, Penny. You think you're a hero?" He smiled like a wolf. "Nobody wants this investigation. Restaurants will shut down. There will be no rentals. Our regulars will move to beaches in Jersey, and believe me with the casino there, it is hard to bring them back. Wineries will dry up. Why'd you have to be such a busybody?" He kicked Elliot angrily on the leg.

"What are you talking about?" Penny demanded; her face sweaty. Mitch pushed her down so that she was sitting on the deck next to Elliot.

"Now they are going to start interfering. They already have someone sitting in my office going through all the files. It's not like it will make a difference to anybody. They don't care about the creature. They've known about it for years. It did a bunch of stuff twenty years ago, but we buried it nice and deep. The records, I mean. With their blessing too," he added at her look of horror. "They knew all about it. The government or whomever they work for, doesn't want anyone to know either, you know. They are going to burn the files just like we did the last time. Osbourne and his mermaid." He was leaning casually against the railing of the boat, chuckling. "I told Doc we got lucky this time again. It was just your stupid brother and that rock star's ex-wife. The husband was only too happy to say she cut out of town with Rory. Why you had to poke the hornet's nest, I'll never understand."

"It was my brother!" Penny cried out. "You know he didn't leave or kill himself."

Mitch answered. "He was a loser anyway."

"Oh, he killed himself, alright. That thing doesn't walk into houses and drag its victim out. He put himself and that girl in harm's way. He was probably hyped up on something."

"How would you know?" Penny demanded; her face shiny with tears. "How would you know he was drugged."

"I make it my business to know." He walked toward her. "Damn Rory for stirring the shit up. It's summer season." Chief Kain was angry. "If word got out, it would affect tourists."

"You're an animal!"

"Girl, you are so naive." Chief Kain went on conversationally. "The incidences were all reported in the beginning, we did the right thing. Forty-five years ago it happened. The suits came down. They were called something else then and helped us destroy all the paperwork." He walked over to her and leaned down as if to make a point. "Said there'd be a problem if we let the truth get out. I wasn't going to mess with them. Every so often the creature feeds or whatever. So, it's like the olden days," he said with a laugh. "We allow the thing it's sacrifices, and then it disappears for a while, leaving us alone. It's no different from throwing someone down a volcano to appease the gods." He laughed.

"You're insane," Elliot accused.

Mitch swung his gun, ready to whip it against Elliot's face, when the sound of another engine broke the silence. Chief Kain halted him with a wave.

Logan looked around for something to use as a weapon. He spied the empty harpoon gun leaning against the back of the boat. He'd have to plow through Mitch in order to reach it.

"You're nothing but a murderer," Penny spat. "You allowed this creature to feed on the people of this town."

"Penny, Penny, Penny. I had no choice. This is bigger than you could imagine. Periodically the U.N.I.T. sends their divers down there. They never find anything. They can't. She doesn't want to be found. She knows when it's safe for her. You can't fight a monster like that. Usually, it's just dogs and the occasional vagrant. What's the big deal?"

Penny pulled herself to her knees, her face mottled with rage. With a roar, she jumped up and ran like a linebacker at Chief Kain. Her head connected with his soft midsection.

He made a sound like a *whoosh*, then doubled over. Mitch leaped forward; his fist raised. He was going to smash Penny. Logan put out his foot and tripped him. Mitch landed with a thud.

Logan raced for the harpoon gun, realizing it wasn't loaded. Chief Kain spotted him roaring a ferocious growl. He had recovered enough from Penny's head butt to come at him, his hands raised, his face snarling. Logan used the harpoon as a club, swinging it. He heard Penny screaming his name. Something hard connected with his skull, and for a second, he was counting birds flying around his head. He fell hard, his body sore and heavy from the accumulation of blows.

Penny turned and kneed Mitch in the groin. Logan was still too stunned to care. Mitch socked her in the jaw.

Elliot rose unsteadily to his feet, then used them to kick Mitch. Chief Kain reached for the tackle box and hit Elliot on the forehead. He went down like a marionette with its strings cut.

The other boat was closer. Logan could make out a line of impossibly imposing people in those dark suits on its deck. He wasn't sure if he was seeing double or if there were ten of them. He weaved to Chief Kain and grabbed him by the lapels.

"You knew all along my father didn't kill himself," he ground out between gritted teeth.

"What difference did it make?" Chief Kain said, his voice harsh.

Logan shook with hatred. He launched himself at the chief. The diving equipment made him slow and clumsy. Locked together, they grappled along the railing. Kain's beefy hands made quick work of him and shoved him against the deck, the heavy tanks clanking on the floor.

Mitch ran toward them, his legs unsteady. His ham-shaped hands fell on both of the men heavily. Logan felt himself being dragged up by Mitch. His feet left the deck as he teetered over the side of the boat. With a grunt, Mitch shoved him overboard. Logan locked his hands around Kain's shoulders, dragging the older man in with him.

They fell into the water with a noisy splash. Kain bobbed a few times, cursing each time his face broke water. He called for Mitch to throw him a float.

"I'm going to tear you limb from limb!" Kain yelled to Logan. The chief began swimming toward him, his face a mask of evil.

Logan turned in horrified fascination as the creature broke water behind the police chief. Its pitch-black hair was plastered to its egg-shaped head. Yellow eyes glared from a green-tinted face that glistened as if it were dusted with diamonds. Its mouth opened in a parody of a grin, and Logan heard the snuffles of its flat nose across the water. The chief slowed his swim. He huffed as he treaded water, his face turning red from the effort.

"Throw me a damn lifesaver, you moron," Kain called to Mitch impatiently. "I should be up there, and you should be doing this," he grumbled.

Mitch pointed, his mouth moving soundlessly, his eyes popping from his head.

"What?" Kain demanded. He made a rude noise, then began to swim toward the boat. "Once I get up there, you are diving in to get Osbourne, and we are finishing this thing once and for all," he complained.

The creature arced, splashing. Kain turned cursing loudly. Logan could see him squinting as he tried to make out the shape in the water.

Kain's head dipped as if he were being tugged. The older man swallowed a mouthful of water, his arms windmilling frantically. Garbled shouts rent the air, turning into a panicked scream for help.

Logan began to move while Mitch stood rooted to the deck, his face a frozen rictus of horror.

Kain splashed noisily as he struggled with the creature. He wheezed when his head came up for air but was pulled under again. Kain broke the surface of the water again, screaming. His shout was cut off when long green fingers reached up and over the chief's head, pulled his face around, with a quick snap separated his head from his body. The headless torso rolled sideways, the water turning oily with blood. Logan watched helplessly as the blood fountained from the bobbing corpse.

"Chief!" Mitch wailed.

"Put your hands in the air!" blared from the oncoming boat from the opposite direction.

Logan looked from his captive friends to Mitch's stupefied face. He made eye contact with Penny, who hung over the edge of the boat, her face bleached of color. She screamed, "Go!"

Logan turned and dove deep after the creature. He put his mouthpiece in, allowing the oxygen from the tanks to flow into his lungs. He saw the creature's sleek body move ahead of him, her long legs kicking furiously, her speed hampered by the head she had tucked under her arm.

They moved away from the bay, the distance from the surface deepening. Logan followed her speeding form, a trail of blood in her wake. Fish closed in around him. The cold dread that Kain's severed head might interest a shark made his blood run cold. Still, he swam after her.

Logan sucked the air from his mouthpiece, praying for the reserve to last until he reached the creature. He felt the pressure change but persisted, his lungs burning from the effort. He moved his arms as fast as he could, his legs kicking to push him further.

The creature zigzagged. Once he caught it facing him, pausing, watching him eat up the distance between them. He reached forward with each stroke, determined to catch up. He wanted to examine its distorted face, the yellow eyes, acknowledge it was real and not a figment of his imagination.

It was dark. He could barely see, but he followed the iridescent flashes of the creature's feet, like sparks in the water.

The sea floor dropped away. The water grew colder. One-minute Logan was looking at the creature, and in an instant, it was gone, leaving only a thread of blood floating in the water.

Logan blinked, feeling as though he'd lost a minute or two and couldn't figure out what happened. The creature was there and then gone. Logan drifted on the current, sprinting across the murky depths, making the fish scurry away when he waved his arms in the water. He swam in a tight circle, searching to see where it had vanished to in the darkness.

Holding his hands out he examined his surroundings.

There was a wall of rock with a bulge in front of him. It rose straight up as if planted in the seafloor and had a type of smooth symmetry contrary to nature. The outcropping of rock appeared to be shaped like a tower and seemed oddly out of place. Moving closer, he hugged the surface of the boulders, his fingers feeling for an opening.

An alarm sounded, the beeping loud in his ears. He looked at the blinking light of the gauge and cursed the dwindling oxygen. Forcing himself to take shallow breaths, he tried to conserve his air supply.

He was so close. The answers he needed to the questions that had plagued him his entire life were right here. He couldn't go back to the surface.

He hit the overhanging ledge with his palms in frustration. A bubble erupted from underneath, noisy gears breaking the underwater silence. Two stones separated like Ali Baba's rock wall.

Logan peered into a polished tube-like entrance with tiny pinpricks of light illuminating his path. He pushed himself down and through the narrow opening. It was tight, the walls smooth but close to his body.

He swam in, noticing the water level moved down as though it was an air lock. He pushed himself forward until he had no choice but to travel the rest of the way on his hands and knees. The water was soon nothing more than a puddle at his feet. The floor was smooth and black, with a metallic quality. Logan couldn't even guess what it was made of.

He spat out his mouthpiece and took great gulps of fresh air. He pushed his mask onto his head. Unhooking his equipment, he put it aside. His feet were silent on the cold surface.

It was freezing. His breath was clouded with condensation, and goose bumps traveled up his body, making him shiver. He padded through the rest of the tunnel on his hands and knees on the smooth rock, his eyes alert.

The tunnel opened into a huge chamber. Logan hung back in the corridor. The room was brightly lit with a reddish glow. He squinted, the glare making him wince.

Shading his eyes, he peered in. There was shelving made from a metal he had never seen before. Electric blue, it took up one wall, its surface filled with blocks not unlike the glass squares people used for privacy windows on houses. These squares were different somehow, the glass more delicate, each one lit from underneath, an illuminated series of symbols neatly along the bottom. There were thousands of them.

Logan didn't need to question what he saw. He was a scientist. He recognized a lab anywhere. His stomach rose and his jaw dropped when he slowly identified the objects stored in perfect condition through the glass. Eyeballs, heads, and body parts floated in neon blue solution. Here was a human tongue next to a dogs. Chicken, cow, and countless other species—hands, feet, hooves, claws, all colors and sizes. Knees, knuckles, hair samples, skin, all displayed in a macabre museum. Clothing, shoes, and glasses next to fingers and toes.

Logan walked past the racks; his face frozen with horror. He placed his palm on a glass block as if he could touch the human hand bobbing inside.

He walked to the next row, realizing the specimens represented different time periods. He moved faster, his face close to the cubes, frantically searching.

His eyes were drawn to a cube with a pair of glasses resting against its side. They were a wire-rimmed pair, the earpiece half-chewed. He reached out a finger to touch the pulsing glass, his eyes stinging. His father's glasses were as familiar to him as his own hand. Next to them floated a blue eyeball, the optic nerve dangling from the orb like a string on a balloon. Logan closed his own eyes, his chest constricting with grief.

He heard a noise, distinctly feminine, the contralto wobbly but clear, making sounds in an organized fashion. He cocked his ear, listening. It was singing. The creature's feet slapped on the floor as she came into the room, holding a new glass block in her hands.

The creature stopped short and dropped the jar. It smashed onto the hard floor. The head of Chief Kain landed with a loud thud, then skittered across the ground, leaving a slimy smear. It came to a halt inches from Logan, the blank eyes staring up at him.

The creature hissed, her perfectly round mouth revealing rows of sharp needle- like teeth, her eyes widening with interest.

Logan stared at her, shocked when he realized she was wearing clothes. She was not naked as he'd originally thought. The material moved as though it were a second skin. The creature was female, of that he was now sure from her distinctly feminine shape. Logan and the creature warily circled the perimeter of the room, locked in a dance of death.

"What are you?" he asked, keeping his voice level as they continued studying each other. Logan's knees were slightly bent, his arms ready to strike. His eyes darted around the room, looking for a weapon. He spied the branch of an apple tree, fruit dangling in rotted glory from the withering limbs.

He feinted left but dove and rolled for the weapon, snatching it in time to hit the oncoming monster as she attacked him.

She screamed furiously, slamming his shoulder, nearly dislocating it. Logan swung the branch mightily, ramming her square on the back of her head with a resounding *thunk*. The thing reared up, smacking him the face, leaving him seeing all the stars in the galaxy. He wobbled aimlessly for a few seconds.

She grabbed his shoulder and with a perfect right, punched him in the face. He was sure he heard his nose crack. He lashed out, his fist connecting with her eye. Her howl of pain turned into a furious hiss. She picked him up and threw him against the wall. He bounced off and landed at her feet.

Logan was bleeding onto the floor, leaving it slippery. He got up wobbling onto all fours, shaking his head to clear it. The creature launched herself at him. He rose to a crouch only to have the creature do a credible tackle, sending him to the opposite wall, where he slammed into one of the rows of shelves.

Body parts rained down on him. The chamber filled with the tinkling of breaking glass or whatever substance held the specimens.

His mermaid, he thought woozily, was picking him up. She then spun him over her head, finally throwing him against the wall, which seemed to absorb him into total blackness.

CHAPTER 19

LOGAN BECAME AWARE of a blinding orange light first. His body ached. His bones felt broken. He attempted to move, first by trying to raise his arm. He was attached to a table, with no mobility. He was bound by bands not only constricting him but also making it hard to breath. His wetsuit squeaked as he squirmed.

A trickle of blood made its way from his hairline pooling on the hard surface of the slab where he lay. Strange sounds filled his ears, beeps and buzzes. He could smell her, the creature, and he was sure of only two things, she was no mermaid, and her intent was not to feed, but to study and collect.

The strange musty odor of her body filled the room, making him gag. He knew she was nearby, he could hear metal touching metal, and glass clinking.

Logan cracked open his eyes to see her leaning close.

Reared as far as his bound body allowed, a gasp escaping his mouth. Her round maw open in amusement, her yellow eyes gleamed with mischief.

She snorted, the small stilts of her nose narrowed and widened with each sound. She touched his hair, with almost a caress, making him shiver in revulsion. It must have shown in his eyes, because her webbed hand fisted around a hank of his hair, and she slammed his head on the hard slab.

Logan lost consciousness for a second. When he opened his eyes, she was waiting, watching for a reaction. Her slimy fingers jabbed his cut, followed by a snuffle of callous disdain. He fought against the restraints to no avail. He was trapped. Above him, a u-shaped light source blinded him. He squinted, trying to make out the room around him.

The creature caught his chin in her strong hands, razor nails scoring his cheeks leaving a dripping trail of blood.

She made a few clicks, her tongue moving noisily, a thick mucus gathering near the corner of her mouth leaking from her flat blue lips to land on the table and mix with his blood. He smelled something caustic and realized the muddled puddle of his blood and her saliva was sizzling.

She reached for his hand, releasing it from its bonds to study his palm. She stared at his strange childhood scar, her mouth opening in a wide grin. She made a different chuffing noise. Still holding his hand, she banged on the table with glee. Logan realized with a start that she was laughing.

"I'm glad you find this amusing," he said weakly.

She placed her nails against the indentation of the scar, her eyes widening to take up almost all of her face. He could swear he saw her nod. Her eyes narrowed, impaling him with their intensity. She dropped his hand, imprisoning it in the binding and walked away for a minute.

He heard the whine of a motor and the sound of her moving things around the laboratory. It was a lab, or at the very least a morgue where she autopsied and catalogued her specimens. Her big flat feet made weird suction noises as she walked across the floor. She returned, staying out of his line of sight, the sound of her chuckles turning into a hysterical wheeze.

Logan craned his neck to get a look at her, but movement was impossible. He kicked his trussed legs, but he was tied up tighter than a swaddled baby. There was no escape.

Wrinkled paper appeared in his line of sight. She rattled it, bringing it to his attention. Logan looked up, and his eyes opened wide with recognition.

His father's naive illustration of a mermaid was before his face. The creature was mocking him with it. She waved it, her nasal voice making whiny sounds. A long, green-tinted finger pointed to the picture, then gestured to herself. Logan turned his face away. Strong fingers grabbed his chin in a merciless grip forcing him to look at the notebook. She held the notebook inches from his eyes.

"Yeah, ain't that ironic?" he told her. Fury boiled in his chest, replacing any sense of fear that he had.

Carelessly, she tossed his father's precious notebook behind her. Logan heard it smash against the wall, then fall to the floor.

He strained against the bindings holding him again. The creature exchanged a look that was cold, reptilian. She patted his stomach, crooning as if to calm him. He relaxed for a minute, and she took that opportunity to bring a sharp black object down swiftly on his leg. It sliced fast and deep. Logan arched upwards, sucking in a quick breath as the scalpel-like weapon tore into his wetsuit and flayed his skin.

He broke out in a cold sweat, adrenaline coursed through his body making him shake with shock. He took great heaving breaths, fighting the burning pain on his leg.

His hands balled impotently into fists as the creature parted the black rubber from his leg, revealing his bloody skin. She ran her hands up and down his limb, making him shudder with revulsion.

Looking up, she peered at him, her yellow eyes glowing with triumph. She released his leg from its bindings then held it up under the knee to admire it. A loud sound chirped over a sound-system making her angry. She dropped his limb hard on the table, sending a voltage of pure agony to his spine.

He thought briefly about the egg he had held so carelessly in his hands on an Arizona mountain, the baby Thunderbird. He regretted ever touching it. Had he hurt it in any way? *What was I thinking?* he wondered. *How could I have done that?* He sent a silent apology to the raptor's mother.

Science, if he got out alive, was never going to be the same.

The chirp sound again. The creature walked to an intercom, passed a hand over a light and started her clicking noises. She was answered by another voice making the same sounds. She sounded heated and slapped the light with the palm of her hand cutting off the conversation. She stomped back, and efficiently as a surgeon shredded the middle of his wetsuit exposing his abdomen. His chest and arms remained covered.

Here it comes, Logan swallowed. This was no gall bladder surgery.

Walked her fingers up and down his stomach, she prodded deeply, feeling his toned muscles, her long nails hurting his exposed skin. He felt blood fill the gash on his leg, then heard the steady plop of it onto the icy table.

She picked up a long silver cloth that had several knots in its length, then pressed one of the knots against the bloody flesh of his leg. The material absorbed his blood instantly. She cleaned the area around his thigh, her face deep in thought.

The chirping started again, this time more insistent, and louder. The creature threw down the cloth, making an impatient sound.

She frowned, her face becoming dark, inscrutable while she continued to apply the absorbent cloth to his leg again. Logan tried to focus through the pain to observe her face.

The strident note blared from another speaker in the room attached to the lab. A third alarm sounded, and Logan said, "I think it's for you."

She stopped to look at him, her mouth opened to reveal rows of tiny sharp teeth in a macabre grin. *She understood him!*

"You're a scientist. Like me," he told her. He needed to stop his dissection. He needed a way to negotiate. He blurted, "Perhaps we can work together."

The alarm went off again with an ear-splitting siren.

The creature warbled a sound, threw the cloth impatiently, and walked away in irritation stomping to the next chamber.

He heard her screaming. It was loud and angry. Something slammed, and there was the clatter of metal hitting the floor. Her clicks and groans came faster together. He heard a burst of static and a new voice, a deeper one, responding to her howls. This one sounded commanding, there was a loud crash against a wall, followed by a frustrated scream.

She duck-walked back into the room, her face thunderous, the yellow eyes slivered. Her greenish skin had a rusty stain on each side of her round face. She picked up her scalpel, slashing down toward his chest quickly and effectively.

He wasn't prepared for her quicksilver change. He opened his mouth to say something, but only a groan escaped his lips as the knife cut into the top layer of his skin.

Logan closed his eyes in resignation, hoping his vivisection wasn't going to hurt. Sucking in a deep breath, he let it out slowly, shuddering from the pain.

She peeled off his wetsuit from his arm, frustrated when it refused to separate from his skin. His sweat had glued it to his body.

She pulled impatiently at the rubber on his shoulder, then stopped, the scalpel clattering onto the floor. She said something to him, but Logan heard her only through a haze of agony.

The creature peered closely, rubbing his skin with a caress. Her fingers lightly grazed him, and she leaned so close he could feel her wet breath chilling him. Logan realized she was holding his arm reverently, her fingers stroking with a delicacy alien to her former treatment. Several furrows on her forehead appeared, giving her an almost human appearance. It startled him for a minute. A bubble of laughter escaped his mouth.

She gasped, the surprise in her eyes softening to sympathy. She kissed his shoulder, her lips stained red by his blood. Twin blue tears leaked from her eyes, as she wiped with the iridescent cloth.

The creature dropped the rag on the floor, her expression changing to horror. Logan raised his head to look down. His suit was peeled away like an onion. His shoulder was exposed, the tattoo of the Thunderbird was weeping blood. She fell to her knees, her mouth exploding in an ear-splitting cry that reverberated in the chamber, shattering glass. Hands fisted, she hit the floor, and with each pound, a string of sounds came from the monster's lips.

Logan painfully stretched his neck. He caught the horrified gaze peering up at his tattoo. He stared back at her through eye slits, and then he noticed it, a patch on the side of her arm, a badge on the material he had originally thought was her skin. It was almost the same image as his Thunderbird, its red feathers faint against the silvery material, the only difference was some of the plumage. He opened his mouth and cawed loudly in a credible imitation of the monster bird that had almost killed him a few weeks ago.

The creature lay prostrate on the floor, her arms outstretched, her chest rising and falling, the unmistakable sounds of weeping filling the chamber. Logan screamed at her, the veins protruding on his neck. She whimpered, scurrying across the floor on her knees, afraid to make eye contact. He yelled, looking at his shackles, his meaning clear.

The effort caused blood to well and cascade from the cut on his leg.

She raised her hands, shielding her face, her eyes downcast. He chirped and whistled watching her reaction. She inched forward on her hands and knees. Holding up the rag, her face averted, she was asking permission to address his wounds. Logan nodded, keeping his face angry, indignant. The creature rose, approaching him slowly to wrap the strange cloth around his cuts. She stroked his arm, her voice now a litany of soft moans and whispered, apologetic clicks. The bleeding, along with the pain, ceased.

Logan struggled against the bonds; his teeth clenched. He shouted at her, raising his fisted hand. She sliced through his straps, releasing him.

Logan stood unsteadily, his wetsuit hanging in shreds from one arm and both legs. The creature shielded her eyes from him as she curled into a cowering ball on the floor.

Logan staggered toward the wall, knocking the jar holding his father's glasses down, where it shattered across the stone floor. He bent over and picked them up, his fist closing around them.

"You had no right!" he screamed.

The creature lay prone on the floor, her body trembling.

Lights blinked. The room filled with the shrieking siren again. Logan covered his ears, immobilized by the loud sound. Blood loss made him sway and he weakly fell to his knees. The room heaved as if there was an earthquake.

The shelves holding the specimens shook, one by one the glass jars tumbled to the floor to shatter, releasing foul smelling body parts and offal.

The suspended lights above them moved in a gentle arc from the wires holding them aloft.

Rising onto all fours, Logan glanced up, realizing it wasn't him. The room was shaking. The entire chamber was vibrating. Dust filtered from the rocks, coating his sweating body.

The creature was sobbing, scrambling on the floor sweeping up her collection of body parts in a manic frenzy. She screamed in frustration; her hands loaded slippery organs that were falling apart.

The thing stopped her moaning slowly rising to her webbed feet. Her ugly face turned skyward as her obscene eyes closed in resignation, her shoulders slumped. She looked at Logan and pointed to the tunnel.

"Go." The word was torn from her throat.

A sob escaped her. She picked up a broken piece of glass throwing it in his direction. Logan ducked, but he didn't have to, she missed him on purpose.

He looked down the dark tunnel and then back at her face. She fisted her hand touching the image of the Thunderbird on her shoulder and raised her clenched fingers to him. With a nod, he realized it was a salute. He returned the gesture.

A great hum filled the room, causing stones on the wall to crack and crumble. The rocks appeared to be trilling from the energy. An orange light pulsed with a vibrancy that heated the chamber.

Logan blinked; the air was shimmering as if dusted with stars. He rubbed his eyes, to see, but it didn't help.

He backed up to a wall watching as the creature spread

her legs and reached for the ceiling. An opalesque aura surrounded her as well as every object in the room. She gave him one last look, defiantly raising her chin toward the exit.

Logan's skin crawled as if a thousand ants covered his body. He glanced at his hand. It was encased in the strange glow.

The creature was transparent, covering in a sparkling net of tiny points of bright lights.

Pushing himself away from the wall, he dashed on weak legs looking for the entrance to the tunnel, his chest and thigh burning from the effort.

The monster opened her mouth, a deep, mournful cry erupting, then her body broke into a dazzling haze.

Logan stood transfixed by the shimmering sight. His body erupted into a mass of tingling electricity. The entire room was shaking now, rocks tumbling, but all the objects in the room grew fainter as though they were translucent.

He felt as if he were on fire. Shaking himself like a dog, he forced one foot in front of the other weaving as far from the forcefield as he could.

He saw an archway, the pillars holding it open were shaking from the stress of whatever was attacking the room. His feet slid on fluids from the broken jars. He went down, landing hard on his side. Grunting, he forced himself up, his eyes rested on his father's discarded notebook lying like a broken bird against the wall. He scrambled up, his hand scooped up the spiral notebook, and he tucked it into the waistband of his wetsuit.

The rock walls were collapsing. Pivoting, he ran towards the trembling opening, going down on his hip to slide through the wet floor making it possible. He heard the crash of its destruction sealing the chamber behind him.

Logan ran through the corridor, the strange sensation covering his skin easing the further he got from the main area. His tanks lay on the floor where he'd abandoned them. He buckled them on and pushed hard against the rock.

Behind him, he heard an explosion. The wind barreled through the tunnel, hitting him so that he collided against the exit and smashed his head against metal. He pushed at it. The roar of flames raced through the space toward him.

Sweat mixed with blood trickled into his eyes blinding him. He strained against the portal. The area was heating with flames that crackled and spit behind him. The door didn't budge. He banged it with his fists, bruising his flesh, turning his hands into a bloody mess. Breathing hard, he leaned against the jagged wall and pounded desperately at the solid face of the entry. Using all his might, he shoved his shoulder against the door.

The craggy surface gave way, groaning loudly as it slid open. He didn't wait a second longer and burst through the opening as if he were ejected. He closed his eyes instinctively as he speared through the water.

Behind him the cave exploded.

Logan choked. His air was almost gone, but the force of the impact sent him surging toward the surface. Eyes closed; he sliced through the water. His mouthpiece long gone, he sealed his lips, holding in his last breath of air. Just when he thought his lungs would burst, his head broke the surface of the water, and he sputtered and coughed then gasped a lungful of blessed oxygen.

Above him, the entire sky was blotted by the giant shape of a disc. The choppy water rocked both him and three boats in the estuary like toys in a tub. The saucer in the sky hovered over them for a minute, then zoomed straight up, leaving them staring open-mouthed at its retreating underside. The image of the Thunderbird covered the entire bottom of the saucer.

Logan heard Elliot screaming, "I…I…I…! Oh! Em! Gee! Did you see that? Did you see the illustration of the thunderbird on the bottom?"

Rough hands reached out to grab Logan by the shoulders to haul him into the boat, where he then lay panting on the deck. Within minutes Aimee was dabbing his sore chest and leg with a towel.

Penny stormed over, grabbing the cloth from Aimee and hissed, "I'll do that!"

Logan fell back on the floor, too winded to care. A trio of faces stared down at him.

Elliot was on his knees. "What happened down there? What happened to the mermaid?"

Logan registered that both Penny and Elliot had their hands free. He looked over at Aimee, and then her dark-suited companions on the deck.

"Care to tell me what's going on?" he said between coughs.

Elliot was pulled up by an older man, his face grim. "Nothing. He saw nothing, and nothing's going on."

"But that bird, that crazy bird was on the bottom of that spaceship. We all saw it." Penny pointed to the tattoo on Logan's shoulder.

Logan studied the bald-headed man. "I know you. You had more hair, then, but I know you."

The man ignored him, turning away to speak with another person. Penny sat on the floor, stemming the blood from his cuts. He took hold of her hand and whispered, "I'm good. I need a minute."

Penny looked from him to Aimee, her lips turned down. She stood, her face sad, and walked to the side of the boat peering over the bow.

"You're not about discovery," he said to Aimee. "Or even science."

"Not anymore." Aimee shook her head. She rested her hand on his knee, possessively. "It's not what you think. They are protecting the public."

"Who are *they*?" He removed her hand.

"You don't need to know unless you want to join us?" She cocked her head, a smile on her face. "Sam's been at it a long time. You remember him from when you were in the hospital, when you father was taken."

Logan looked at her with distrust. "How do you know?"

She explained, "I saw your file, Logan. He was there to protect you."

A thought occurred to him and his jaw dropped. He glanced from the man she called Sam to her face. Aimee lowered her gaze, not meeting his eyes. "How long?" he asked.

She didn't answer and he repeated the question more forcefully.

"A while," she said with a shrug. The silence was thick, and she admitted in a small voice. "Since before I met you."

"Was it all an act? The desire for money, the television shows? Us?"

Aimee shook her head, her face wistful. "No, not everything."

Logan looked away and cursed, damning his eyes for smarting. He swallowed hard. "I don't believe it."

"What we had…" she paused and looked for her superior. "You meant something to me."

Logan laughed mirthlessly. "Yeah, I'll bet."

"They still want you," she added softly. "I want you."

Logan shook his head wearily. "Not a chance."

The boat's rocking had slowly gentled from the wake of the engine's propulsion blasting the water. Logan was exhausted. He wanted nothing more than to get away from Aimee and her people. He had to think, but Elliot's loud conversation burrowed through his confusion and pain.

"Are you kidding me?" Elliot was screaming at the man called Sam. "This is what we've worked for, this is an abomination, Outrageous! You can't hide this from the public!"

The older man pulled out his phone, punched a number, then turned on the speaker. A man's voice answered the call. "Hello."

"James Farrell?" Sam said, his voice low and ominous.

"No," Elliot whispered as he reached to snatch the phone from his hand. "Stop!"

"Hello? … Who's there? Listen, whoever you are, you'd better stop these calls, or I'm contacting the—" The man on the receiver sounded nervous.

A thick finger clicked off the phone, terminating the call.

"It's almost too easy," Sam said with deadly calm to Elliot. "Do we pick him up?"

"You can't do this," Elliot whispered. "You have nothing on him. He's law abiding-"

"We can think of something," Sam interrupted him, his eyes steely.

"You can't just go around and charge people with non-existing crimes," Elliot pleaded.

"We can and we will. Listen," Sam said in a calm tone. "Someday science will catch up, but for now it has to remain a secret." He stepped toward his boat. "I don't have to spell this out for you, do I?"

"But the chief?" Penny said, walking toward them from the rail. Her eyes flashed with anger. She gave Aimee a filthy look.

"Met with an accident, a fishing accident," Sam said with finality.

"Who are you people?" Logan demanded. He rose shakily.

Sam looked at Aimee, who shook her head. "No?" He glanced back to Logan. "Then you don't need to know." They all stood staring at each other as if it were a standoff.

Mitch moaned breaking the silence. He sat huddled in the corner, his face blank. Someone had thrown a blanket over his shoulders.

"Have they known all along?" Penny looked at Aimee, her eyes accusing.

Aimee didn't answer and Sam moved forward, his dark eyes held no warmth. "We've suspected. We had Osbourne's descriptions from when he was a child. It matches a... well, let's just say it's not an isolated case. This area has always been a hotbed for UFO sightings." He took a long look at Logan.

"Why hasn't the press reported it?" Penny shouted.

Logan responded to her. "They control the press. What does U.N.I.T. stand for?"

"Does it matter? We are dispatched to keep the country from panicking."

"What about Obsidian?" Elliot sneered at Aimee.

"It's a front for them," Logan said. "They are afraid of mass hysteria."

"Absolutely correct, Osbourne," Sam replied. "Some-day, they'll be allowed full disclosure. Can you imagine what it would do if people realized have been landing here and using the earth as a research laboratory?"

"People have a right to know!" Penny cried hotly, her face a mess of tears. Her ivory hair was snarled and tangled, and her skin was mottled.

"Sure, and who is going to keep the peace, stop the economy from collapsing, or the government from top-pling?" Sam asked. "We will release information in man-ageable pieces and allowing the public to digest the truth in small amounts."

Penny folded her arms over her chest stubbornly.

Sam rounded on them. "You think we like this?" he demanded. He pointed to the sky. "You think we can push around beings like that?"

"What about Vadim and Haversham?" Logan inter-rupted, his gaze on the older man.

Sam walked toward him and smiled. It was not friendly

but triumphant. Logan knew Sam was aware he had won. "Are you bargaining with me?"

Logan didn't answer. He glanced at Penny, then nodded his head. "Yes."

"They are back at work, no harm, no foul. A glitch. He understands, Haversham. It may work out with an additional grant. Your Russian colleague, he's no stranger to these types of things. He knows the routine." Sam sighed deeply. "Osbourne, we are not the enemy."

Logan stared at the water moodily.

"What did it want?" Penny asked.

"Specimens," Logan answered. "They were exploring."

"Logan you should really identify with them," Aimee said, walking toward him. "It was only doing what you do every day."

"I don't harm living things." Logan ground out.

"Don't you? When you find them, you think it will end there? Your discoveries will bring the curious, the opportunists. Their habitats will be destroyed."

"Are you saying that all crypto creatures are aliens?" Penny asked in a shocked whisper

"It's over, Deputy. Go back to work. Forget what happened," Sam didn't answer her question as he walked away, his black coat flapping in the breeze. "Consider yourself debriefed. I don't want to meet you or your families again."

Sam stopped, then turned to Logan. "I'm sorry about your father, but we had to follow our protocol."

Logan stared at him coldly. "You ruined my life."

The older man considered him for a minute, took a long

look at Aimee, Penny, and then at Elliot. "I have a hard time believing that."

"Believe what you want," Logan said angrily. "You manipulate the truth to suit your needs."

"You know, Osbourne, I have a funny feeling this is not going to be the last we see of each other." He might have been smiling, but Logan swore it never reached those cold eyes. He turned to Aimee. "Are you coming, Dupres?"

Aimee nodded curtly and followed him to their boat. Before she boarded the other ship, she looked back at Logan. He wouldn't meet her eyes.

"Was that a threat?" Penny asked after they had left them alone on the craft.

Logan laughed without humor. "For me it was a promise."

They sat on the floor of the boat, the steady sea rocking them like babies. The sun burned through the clouds, creating a mist off the water.

Penny turned to them, her face stark. "Rory is gone. I have nothing to lose," she said, issuing a challenge.

Elliot shook his head. "Yeah, but I have something to lose."

"So do I." Logan looked up at her, his blue eyes caressing her face.

"James?" she asked.

Elliot smiled brightly. "My fiancé. That was him on the phone. I can't."

"They were making it clear that they were threatening you," Logan said.

"Well, it worked. I'll risk myself, but I won't let anyone hurt James. I have some explaining to do when I get home."

Penny grinned back. "What do you have to lose?" she asked, looking at Logan.

Logan nodded. "You. I don't want to lose you," he said simply.

He held out a hand to her, pulling her down next to him. She rested her head against his shoulder.

"There is more to this universe than just us," she said.

Logan took her hand and kissed her palm. "Yeah, but according to those guys, no one needs to know that yet."

CHAPTER 20

LOGAN LAY IN an exhausted stupor on the bed, a bulky bandage around his thigh, a matching one on his chest just under his tattoo. His facial cuts had been cleaned and deemed not serious. He had dozed for a bit but felt no respite. He heard Elliot on a new phone talking softly to James. Logan couldn't move. His eyes were gritty.

Penny had left to write reports, ones that would satisfy the authorities but would leave her feeling bitter and betrayed.

He knew that Mitch was going to spend a few days resting in the local hospital. He had been traumatized. Experience told him the bully would come out of it a changed individual. Mitch seemed to remember very little about the previous night. Experience told him; Mitch would never have that cocky self-assuredness again.

Logan reached for his father's notebook on the bed next to him. He had been reading it earlier before he fell asleep.

The pages were stiff from being in the saltwater. Some of the text was illegible. It didn't matter. He knew it all by heart and could fill in the blanks.

He rubbed his eyes, his arm aching. Aimee's conversation kept running through his mind like a hamster on a wheel. *How had he missed it all?* For someone who spent his life observing and studying other lifeforms, he was oblivious to anything in his own existence.

He wondered, feeling like a fool questioning what else did he miss in his life? His ego stung. Logan rolled over to look at the journal. The curled pages were filled with the study of life. Little snippets of details, things his father had recorded to memorialize, everything from plants, animals, fish, the taste of fresh fruit, the smell of the ocean, even his broken heart kicked to the curb by his wife. The one thread that appeared on every page, lovingly written, sometimes funny, mostly poignant, were observations about him, Logan, his only child. Pages were dedicated to the minutiae of everyday life, things that popped out of Logan's mouth, the way he held his pencil, the shape of his determined chin, his open hand lying full of trust on the pillow at night like a starfish. His father had been overwhelmed with his child's every breath, his life dependent on seeing Logan each day, his sole source of happiness being next to him.

Logan realized he had been noticed all that time and, more than that, truly loved. A great hole Logan didn't know existed filled with deep satisfaction as though he'd eaten a comforting meal or awakened after a refreshing night's sleep. He lost something in Aimee's revelation but gained everything with his father's.

He now understood his dad better. George had lived through his writing. His stubby pencil did what his mouth could not. It voiced his love for all living things, most of all his son.

Logan went through the notebook four or five times, smiling at the notations, feeling his father's presence in the room. Logan wished that just once he could look up from his spot on the bed and see his father hunched over his desk writing furiously, saving for posterity what he couldn't express verbally.

The sun slanted through the venetian blinds, the humid air making the sheet stick to Logan's clammy skin. He threw a wrist over his hot head. He needed to drink. The antibiotics had to be taken with plenty of water.

He glanced at the Breitling watch lying on the bedside table. He picked it up, wondering if Sly's remains were on their way to an alien planet to be studied. He put the watch on his arm. It would travel with him everywhere from now on.

He rolled onto his side, glancing down to consider the Thunderbird on his shoulder. Elliot was right; he did get the colors wrong. Life had changed his perspective.

Logan smiled. Sometimes things were not what you imagined. The merest shift could change how everything appears. He raised his arm, knowing he could finally finish his mermaid. His piscine amphibian humanoid would be inked with its distinct webbed feet, not the tail he'd always imagined belonged on her. He'd have to go to Israel to see a mermaid, he thought with a smile.

The glare from the sun hit his eyes. He turned to face the

desk, his lips twitching when he saw his father's last surprise for him. A small compartment was opened, a twist of waxy paper sticking out. A Tootsie Roll lay where George had left it, abandoned in its hiding place, waiting twenty years for his son to discover. Logan's eyes narrowed for a second as he looked at the compartment. He pushed himself painfully onto his elbows, his dark hair falling messily over his forehead. He craned his neck seeing the outline of another surprise. There was something else in there.

He got up, padded to the desk. Bending down, he placed the candy on the surface of the desk. It was hard, like petrified wood. He stuck his hand deeply into the compartment, his sore knuckles ripped anew by the unfinished wood in the tight space. A paper was stuck. It was stiff, curved, as if it had been carefully placed in there, tucked away not to be seen but never forgotten. He peeled it away from where it was jammed tightly against the wood. He heard a faint ripping sound and cursed. It was thick paper, like a postcard. His thumb told him one side was smooth like a photo. It came free.

The ink was faded, written a long time ago. It was in handwriting he never thought he'd see again. It was a tourist postcard from somewhere in South America. There was a dated photo of a mountainside, villagers pulling a cart with a donkey, straw hats and all, the colors hot and bright.

Taking a deep breath, he looked at the note. His heart skipped a beat, and he shuddered in shock. It was his mother's strong handwriting, all angles and harshly crossed-out letters. The date made his eyes smart. It was twenty years ago, a few months after she'd left. It was addressed to his father.

George, I can't repair the damage of the past. What can I say? I'm sorry. I love you. I've always loved you. I miss Logan. Don't do this to me, to us. I can't stay there anymore. Your obsession with that thing in the water—it's overtaking everything. I need more. The affair meant nothing, a passing thing. I could say the same about you, but I won't. I accept my part in this farce. But George, don't you remember what it was like in school?

Logan felt like a voyeur and wanted to stop reading. He tapped the missive against the bandage on his thigh. Curiosity got to him, and he continued with the rest of the message.

We can have that again here in Chile. It's perfect here. Logan will have other children to play with. We always said we wanted to travel with him, don't you remember? They are lovely people. He'll learn Spanish in no time. The light is just right for me. I am doing a series on the locals, their history, their myths. They have such strength. There is something for you too, George. The villagers talk about a monster. A strange doglike thing. There's real proof. You could do something with that, couldn't you? It will be a damn sight easier to chase a monster on dry land rather than in the water, don't you think? Come, please. I miss you. You can find the Chupacabra. It's all waiting for you here.

Logan looked at the picture of the town on the postcard, his heart quickening in his chest.

"Elliot," he called, walking into the living room. Elliot stopped talking and looked up, a question in his eyes. "Elliot, book us a flight to Chile."

AUTHOR'S NOTE

I hope you enjoyed the first adventure of Logan Osbourne and his friends. I certainly had a great time creating them.

Special thanks to several important people in my life who give me support and encouragement.

My wife, Sharon, who never tires of hearing my ideas or taking over with the everyday stuff of life, giving me the freedom to do this.

My brother, Eric, who lobs the tennis balls of thought right back at me, challenging my imagination, and who comes up with the best titles.

Alexander, Cayla, Hallie, Zachary, Jennifer, and Kevin, who push me to press the boundaries of my imagination.

Jon Levin, my patient Sherpa.

Lastly my dad, who always pushed me to follow my dreams, and my mom, who nurtured my imagination, gave it the sustenance it needed, and helped it blossom.

The town of Minatuck in the Hamptons doesn't actually exist. It's a description of a combination of small towns that dot the North Fork. The police precinct and the chief who rules it like a personal kingdom are my invention. Reports of mermaids and UFOs for the area also derive from my imagination. There is some speculation about Plum Island and some weird rumors associated with it, but that's in some other guy's novel.

Cryptozoology is indeed a real but not really recognized field in science. Technically it is the study of creatures that are on the borderline of fact and legend. Do I believe in their existence? I must refer to William Shakespeare on that one when he said so aptly in *Hamlet*, "There are more things in heaven and earth, Horatio, than are dreamt of in your philosophy."

Just because we haven't found something doesn't mean it isn't there.

Michael Okon
Long Island, NY
11-11-24